THE LAST

DAY

A NOVEL

By

Robert L. Bryan

The Last Day

By Robert L. Bryan

Copyright 2017 by Robert L. Bryan

This is a work of fiction. Any resemblance to the living or dead is entirely coincidental.

From the Author

Thank you for downloading THE LAST DAY. This is my first work of fiction and I hope you enjoy it. I have spent my entire adult life in law enforcement and security, retiring from the NYPD at the rank of Captain. I began writing about two years ago and published several non-fiction titles dealing mainly with my law enforcement career.

C-CASE: is the story of the two years I was drafted as a lieutenant into the NYPD Internal Affairs Bureau.

https://www.amazon.com/Unlikely-Journey-Transit-Internal-Commander/dp/1684096863

DARK KNIGHTS: chronicles the timeline of my twenty-year career to show the inside world of a police officer through stories that are sometimes tragic, dark, inappropriate, but still funny.

https://www.amazon.com/dp/B0711CB8K2

WHY ME?: is a research based work inspired by my interactions with crime victims. Many people do not realize that there are specific things that they may do or not do that can make them and their homes attractive targets for criminals.

https://www.amazon.com/Why-Me-Enforcement-Officer-Becoming-ebook/dp/B01N19KF2E

CONDUCTOR: is a change of pace from my law enforcement themed books. In 2013 my son was hired as a conductor with the Long Island Railroad. I was amazed at the amount of training required to become a federally qualified conductor. The book traces the history of this fabled profession, and provides insights for aspiring conductors.

https://www.amazon.com/Conductor-Railroad-Robert-L-Bryan-ebook/dp/B01N5QNT6Q

You can check out all my books on my Amazon Author Page and website. Again, thanks, and I hope you enjoy The Last Day. I would greatly appreciate a brief review when you have completed the book.

Bob

https://www.amazon.com/Robert-L.-Bryan/e/B01LXUSALG/ref=dp_byline_cont_ebooks_1

http://www.authorsexpresspromotion.net/robert-l-bryan

Dedicated to Marilyn, Bryan, and Meghan, who will always be the angel on my shoulder

CONTENTS

PROLOGUE:	There is no Perfect Security	8
CHAPTER 1:	Little Nagasaki	18
CHAPTER 2:	The Last Day – The Beginning	42
CHAPTER 3:	The Cell	51
CHAPTER 4:	The Cop	56
CHAPTER 5:	The Lieutenant	84
CHAPTER 6:	The Undercover	111
CHAPTER 7:	The Inspector	159
CHAPTER 8:	The Last Day – The End	194
CHAPTER 9:	The Aftermath	214
EPILOGUE:		219

PROLOGUE: THERE IS NO PERFECT SECURITY

October 8, 2003 – New York City – Undisclosed Location

Kristin Bermudez was well past the initial stages of panic, barely looking both ways before accelerating through the red light. Traffic was light in this remote section of a New York City outer borough, so congestion would not be a viable excuse for her lateness. It had only been five months since she was hired by the NYPD – not as a cop, but as an analyst, and she did not want to draw negative attention to herself. Her efforts were failing due in large part to three prior occasions where she could not arrive by the start of her 7 AM shift. Kristin's four years in army intelligence along with her freshly minted master's degree made her a prime candidate to be scooped up by the newly opened Counterterrorism Bureau, but her tardiness was beginning to put her on her boss's radar, and not in a positive way.

With five minutes until the start of her tour Kristin's Toyota sped through a maze of streets lined with junkyards and auto-body shops before finally coming to a stop in a parking lot adjacent to an unmarked red brick building. Here, miles from Manhattan, was the headquarters of the NYPD's new Counterterrorism Bureau. Kristin trotted through the parking lot and through the plain metal door at the side of the building. Entering through that door had the same effect as falling down the rabbit hole, as Kristin was instantly transported from the mostly desolate, semi-industrial area in the shadow of an elevated highway into the new, high-tech, post-9/11 world of the New York City Police Department. The interior was gleaming and futuristic – so unlike the average police precinct with furniture and equipment circa 1960. Headlines raced across LED news tickers. There were electronic maps and international-time walls with digital readouts for cities such as Moscow, London, Tel Aviv, Riyadh, Islamabad, Manila, Sydney, Baghdad, and Tokyo. In the Global Intelligence Room, twelve large flat-screen TVs hung from ceiling mounts broadcasting Al-Jazeera and a variety of other foreign programming received via satellite. The police department's newly identified language specialists—who spoke, among other tongues, Arabic, Pashto, and Urdu—sat with headphones on, monitoring the broadcasts. There were racks of high-end audio equipment for listening, taping, and dubbing; computer access to a host of super databases; stacks of intelligence reports and briefing books on all the world's known terrorist organizations; and a big bulletin board featuring a grid with the names and phone numbers of key people in other police departments in the United States and around the world. The security area just inside the door was encased not only in bulletproof glass but in ballistic sheetrock as well.

Kristin had not lost her sense of urgency as she stopped at her cubicle and rummaged through the clutter on her desktop. She grabbed a folder labeled DAILY BRIEFING and was again moving at a near trot. Kristin hesitated momentarily and took a deep breath before attempting to covertly slide into the crowded conference room. She was relieved upon observing Inspector Morgan at the head of the table, fully engrossed in buttering a bagel. Kristin claimed an empty chair next to Sean McGinn and tried to appear as if she had been present for fifteen minutes. The inspector appeared satisfied with his buttering job as evidenced by the huge bite. With his mouth full of bagel, he addressed the staff gathered around the table.

"OK, who has something?"

Sean McGinn, an analyst hired two weeks after Kristin, cautiously raised his hand. Inspector Morgan wiped his mouth with a napkin.

"Yeah, what is it Steve?"

"Sean sir."

The next big bite was fully underway

"Yeah, yeah, Sean – what do you have?"

"Well, sir, I have a report from British Intelligence. It seems the Brits intercepted a communication from Zawahiri."

"Who's Zorro Hero?" Inspector Morgan inquired as he worked the buttered knife across the remaining portion of his bagel. Sean shot a quick glance at Kristin and rolled his eyes.

From the chair next to Morgan, Lieutenant Joey Galeno interjected,

"Dr. Ayman al-Zawahiri is Al Qaeda's number 2."

The inspector shot back with bagel in hand.

"Of course – all those names sound alike to me." He took the first bite of a new bagel.

"So, what was Zorro Hero talking about?"

Sean realized there was no point trying to correct the pronunciation, so he sighed deeply and continued.

"Zawahiri was talking about a plot to unleash poison gas in the New York City subway system."

Inspector Morgan cut Sean off.

"Yeah, yeah – that's old news. They've been talking about this subway chemical attack for months." Morgan returned to his bagel while Sean again raised his right hand.

"Excuse me inspector, but this intercept does contain new information."

Between chews, Morgan mouthed, "Continue."

Sean opened his folder to make sure he relayed the information correctly.

"In this intercept, Zawahiri is calling off the chemical attack."

"Why would he do that?" asked Morgan.

Sean put the folder down on the table.

"The intercept says that Zawahari was dropping the chemical attack for something better."

Inspector Morgan had the last big piece of the bagel in his mouth when it hit him. He grabbed some napkins to spit out the bagel remnants as best he could, but the majority of the bits found their way to Lt. Galeno's uniform shirt.

"Jesus Christ – what if they have a nuke."

March 12, 2017: New York City

Dr. John Hickey had lost interest in the current speech. He was the next scheduled speaker and was desperately attempting to get a waiter's attention to bring water to the dais. His wave finally caught the eye of a fast-moving young server, and a minute later he was clearing his throat with a much-needed cold drink. The symposium on subway crime was his first public event as NYPD Deputy Commissioner for Counterterrorism, and he found himself unexpectedly nervous while waiting to speak.

Just one month earlier, Dr. Hickey was the youngest chairman of the Department of Terrorism Studies at John Jay College of Criminal Justice. One long conversation at a dinner party with the progressive mayor regarding strategies for fighting terrorism in the city was all it took for the 36-year old Hickey to be appointed the youngest NYPD deputy commissioner. Over the last month, however, reality was setting in for the doctor. His background was purely academic, and he was quickly finding a huge divide between the theoretical world of academia and the real world of counter terrorism operations. The symposium was his first opportunity to establish himself as the NYPDs counterterrorism czar.

The five hundred guests mostly represented management from transportation systems throughout the United States and Canada. As Dr. Hickey drained his water glass and scanned the ball room, he noted the elegant décor. The grand ballroom in Manhattan's luxurious Four Seasons Hotel was truly awe inspiring, with finely adorned tables, 35-foot ceilings, turn-of-the-century teardrop chandeliers, blonde hardwood floors, a horseshoe-shaped balcony, and a built-in stage. The scene reminded Dr. Hickey of an upscale wedding reception, rather than a subway crime conference.

The polite applause signaled that the chief of the NYPD Transit Bureau was done with his remarks. Dr. Hickey fidgeted in his chair as the master of ceremonies read a very complementary introduction. As the applause resonated, Dr. Hickey collected his notes and moved behind the ornate wooden podium. Despite drinking so much water, he still had to clear his throat several times before commencing his speech.

"Good morning. It is imperative to understand that the open nature of the subway system will always leave it vulnerable. How is this potential target defended, when some experts assert that the environment is indefensible? Herein lies the dilemma of a free society. We simply cannot protect every person against every risk at every moment in every place. There is no perfect security. If we tried to attain total security the cost would be exorbitant -- in financial terms and in lost freedom and prosperity. Balancing risk necessarily means applying resources against the highest risks -- and not against all risk."

Dr. Hickey then switched to another set of notes to highlight the tactics utilized by the NYPD. He mentioned rapid deployment of assets like the heavily armed Hercules teams; the public awareness "see something – say something" campaign; and the random bag check program on subway stations.

Dr. Hickey placed his notes on the podium and removed his reading glasses.

"Any questions?"

A hand shot up from one of the rear tables.

"Go ahead sir," Dr. Hickey acknowledged as a conference worker sprinted to the table with a microphone.

The bald, heavyset male at the SEPTA table rose from his chair.

"What would be the result of a nuclear bomb detonating in the New York City subway system?"

Lacking the expertise to respond to the query, Dr. Hickey quickly scanned the dais, focusing his attention to the man at the last chair to his right.

"Perhaps Dr. Cummings would like to handle the question?"

Preston Cummings was not on the agenda to speak at the symposium, but Hickey was aware of the physicist's scholarly research regarding the effects of a nuclear attack on New York City. The 68-year-old, silver haired Cummings shifted in his seat and shrugged, indicating "Why not" to Dr. Hickey's offer. Showing no sign of vacating his seat on the dais, the MC hurried to Dr. Cummings and handed him a wireless microphone. Cummings then commenced speaking in an emotionless, monotone manner that would have been well suited for a routine weather forecast as opposed to a description of a nuclear holocaust.

"My study identifies Manhattan as a target – not specifically the subway. Detonating a nuclear device in Midtown positions the bomb where the largest number of people would be located. Assume the device is detonated near the Empire State Building at 11:45 AM. Assume that the weapon is a 150-kiloton HEU gun-type bomb. Damage estimates can be scaled down to approximate damage and casualties should the bomb be a lower-yield weapon. Assume the day is the beautiful day that 9/11 was – clear and cool, few clouds in the sky, with a light wind from the east. Assume the population density is uniform, with an average of 125,000 people per square mile. Assume the bomb's shock wave spreads out evenly, not affected by the structures. Within the first second, a shock wave with an overpressure of 20 psi extends four-tenths of a mile from ground zero. This destroys the Empire State Building and all other buildings within that radius, including Madison Square Garden, Penn Station and the New York Public Library. The reinforced steel in the skyscrapers does nothing to support them. Everything within the first four-tenths of a mile from ground zero is reduced to a pile of debris hundreds of feet deep in places. No one in this area survives or even knows what happened to them. The blast kills somewhere between 75,000 and 100,000 people instantly. Those outside in direct line with the blast are vaporized from the heat. Those inside the buildings who survive the blast are killed as the buildings collapse. A mushroom cloud and fireball expand upward. Instantly, all communications that depend on this area for broadcast stop. National television stations and hundreds of radio channels are instantly off the air. Cell phones throughout the region malfunction. New York City drops off the world communication map. It is not like 9-11, where the rest of the world could switch on their televisions and watch live what was happening.

Four seconds after detonation, the shock wave extends for at least a mile with an overpressure of 10 psi at the periphery of this radius. Out to the edge of this ring, all concrete and steel-reinforced commercial buildings are destroyed or so severely damaged that they begin to collapse. The few buildings at the edge of this ring that remain standing have their interiors destroyed. Many of those within still-standing buildings are protected enough to survive the initial blast but are killed by flying debris. As the shock wave spreads out, an additional 300,000 people are killed and 100,000 more are injured. Almost no one in this ring escapes injury. Those below ground in the subways will escape this first blast with few injuries, though the loss of electricity may shock the cars to a stop. Blocked exits may trap all subway passengers underground indefinitely. All power in New York City goes out or experiences difficulty. Telephone service stops. There is no radio or television from New York City and no information passing to the outside world about the damage or casualties. Six seconds after detonation,
the shock wave expands to 1.5 miles from ground zero. The pressure at the edge of this ring has dropped to an overpressure of 5 psi, enough force to severely damage steel-reinforced commercial buildings. The damage spreads to Carnegie Hall, the Lincoln Center and the Queensboro Bridge. Gone are Grand Central Station and the

Met Life Building. The Chrysler Building is gone, as are virtually all the name-recognized buildings along Park Avenue and Fifth Avenue. The thermal pulse kills another 30,000 people who were in direct sight of the blast, including virtually everyone on the street at the time of the blast. Some 500,000 people in this ring are dead. Another 190,000 within buildings are killed by flying debris or are crushed when the buildings collapse. Of those buildings left standing, about 5 percent burst into flames instantly .Within 24 hours virtually all buildings that remain standing catch fire."

Dr. Cummings removed his glasses and placed them on the table. A slight smirk appeared on his face as he continued in his emotionless tone.

"Now that I've scared the heck out of you, let me say that it is extremely unlikely that an entity other than a very few nation states would have the capability to build and deploy a 150-kiloton nuclear weapon. The much greater risk comes from the possibility of a much smaller weapon being smuggled into the country. It is well documented that during the cold war, both the United States and Soviet Union produced miniature, suitcase nuclear weapons. Supposedly, they weighed anywhere from 35-50 pounds and were in the 3-5 kiloton range. The lightest nuclear warhead ever acknowledged to have been manufactured by the U.S. is the W54, which was used in both the Davy Crockett 120 mm recoilless rifle–launched warhead, and the backpack-carried version called the Mk-54 SADM, or Special Atomic Demolition Munition. The bare warhead package was an 11 inches by 16 inches cylinder that weighed 51 pounds. It was, however, small enough to fit in a footlocker-sized container. While the explosive power of the W54—up to an equivalent of 6 kiloton—is not much by the normal standards of a nuclear weapon, their value lies in their ability to be easily smuggled across borders, transported by means widely available, and placed as close to the target as possible. Even a 1 kiloton nuclear weapon would be many times more powerful than even the largest truck bombs for purposes of destroying a single building or target."

Dr. Cummings wiped his brow with a napkin and put his glasses back on.

"Let's face reality. If an organization was committed to acquiring nuclear materials they could do so. Finding the scientists to build such a weapon, whether dirty or actual, wouldn't be all that difficult."

Cummings paused for a quick sip of water.
"Let me throw a hypothetical operation onto the table. The Islamic State has billions of dollars in the bank, so they call on their friendly province in Pakistan to purchase a nuclear device through weapons dealers with links to corrupt officials in the region. The weapon is then transported overland until it makes it to Libya, where the mujahidin move it south to Nigeria. Drug shipments from Columbia bound for Europe pass through West Africa, so moving other types of contraband from East to West is just as possible. The nuke and accompanying mujahidin arrive on the shorelines of South America and are transported through the porous borders of Central America before arriving in Mexico and up to the border with the United States. From there it's just a quick hop through a smuggling tunnel and hey, presto, they're mingling with another 12 million "illegal" aliens in America with a nuclear bomb in the trunk of their car."

Dr. Cummings sat back in his chair, looked at Hickey and shrugged his shoulders again, "That's all I have."

There was complete silence in the room. Only the distant sound of clanging silverware in the kitchen could be heard.

Dr. Hickey broke the silence. "Any other questions?"

A middle age woman sitting at the Baltimore Area Rapid Transit table raised her hand.
"Yes, ma'am."

"New York City has such a huge subway system. What would stop a terrorist from entering the subway in one of the outer boroughs with one of these suitcase devices and simply riding the train into midtown Manhattan?"

Dr. Hickey took one last sip of water and cleared his throat. He leaned in closer to the microphone.

"Nothing."

CHAPTER 1: LITTLE NAGASAKI

March 15, 2017: Paris

Dr. Khaled Fadel squirmed in his chair and glanced impatiently at his watch. The French president seemed to be droning on forever at the podium, but his gold Rolex revealed a truth reflecting only five minutes. At least he could marvel at the elegance of the main ballroom of the La Clef Lourve Hotel while waiting for the key note speaker to finish. He realized that the conference was the reason for his presence, but the parade of speakers was boring him, and he still had his own business to take care of before tasting the night life in the City of Lights.

Dr. Fadel mockingly referred to the conference on fighting ISIS as a "Coalition of Repenters" who after providing support to ISIS in one form or another, were only now seeing that they had created a monster. Along with the Europeans and Americans, delegations from ten Gulf States were among the countries attending the summit.

Dr. Fadel was a member of the delegation from Qatar. He was not a government official or a member of the royal family, but the Qatari government wanted to include a prominent private businessman in their delegation, and Dr. Fadel fit that bill perfectly. His family's oil business had made him fabulously wealthy, allowing him to sit back and reap the benefits of a luxurious, pampered lifestyle. His business card read *Chief Operating Officer, Gulf State Energy,* but there was a much darker side to this well-polished, educated man of privilege, with a PHD in international economics.

Dr. Fadel considered himself a holy warrior. In fact, he was the most dangerous kind of jihadist – a financier. Fadel was one of the many rich "angel investors" in the region providing seed money to the most violent militants that helped to launch ISIS and other jihadi groups. The Qatari government was famous for talking a good game regarding the war on terror, while turning their backs to the activities of these rich Arabs who did for terrorist groups what "angel investors" did for tech start-ups. Dr. Fadel and many others would provide early seed money until a group could get on its feet and become capable of raising money on its own through means like kidnapping, oil smuggling, and selling women into slavery. Most of the Arab states had laws prohibiting such fundraising, but the Qataris never seemed to be too concerned with enforcing their laws.

The polite applause served notice that the French president had finally concluded his speech bringing closure to the conference. The attendees circulated in the grand ballroom shaking hands and congratulating themselves at being masters of the world. Dr. Fadel shook several hands before breaking free from the Qatari delegation and heading for the exit of the hotel.

The cab ride to Rue du Pont Neuf took fifteen minutes. Diners leisurely sipped wine and conversed under red umbrellas at sidewalk tables in front of the le Pont 9 Café. As he exited the cab Dr. Fadel noticed a waving arm from a man seated alone at one of the sidewalk tables. The umbrella provided protection from the sun, as he took the seat directly across from Waheed Mosaab. Over the past year Dr. Fadel had become bored with financing the jihad and decided to assume a more active operational role. This meeting with Mosaab was not about financing. They both sipped red wine and enjoyed the passing feminine scenery.

Mosaab finally broke off from the girl watching.

"Why did you call me all the way to Paris, and why did we have to meet here? Why couldn't we just go to the hotel and meet with all the other brothers?"

Dr. Fadel drained his wine glass, placed the empty glass on the table, and sat back in his chair contemplating the man questioning him. In almost every respect they were different. Fadel was a privileged, polished, educated 55-year-old, while Mosaab was an uneducated 30-year-old raised on the streets of Doha. While Dr. Fadel reaped the benefits of an oil rich nation, Mosaab's reality was much different. In Waheed Mosaab's Qatar, the streets in the capital city of Doha were not paved with gold. To the contrary, they were covered with dust and rocks.

Dr. Fadel responded,

"I'm sure you recall the invasion of Europe during WWII. Do you know why the Normandy invasion was successful?"

Dr. Fadel did not really believe Mosaab knew anything about WWII and did not wait for an answer to his rhetorical question.

"Deception was the key to success. The Allies knew the Germans believed the American general Patton would lead the invasion of Europe, so the Allies made it appear to the Germans that Patton was going to spearhead the invasion at Caen. They brought Patton to England and put him in command of a completely phantom army, causing the Germans to prepare for his invasion at Caen."

Mosaab still had no idea what the doctor was talking about as Fadel continued,

"We will do the same thing to the Americans. We will tell them about a strike on America via a cargo ship. Meanwhile, we will strike at them from a completely different route."

The seedy Hotel Du Parc was a stark contrast to the luxurious La Clef Lourve. Dr. Fadel and Mosaab were both breathing heavily when they emerged from the stairwell onto the dimly lit fourth floor. The walls were cracked and dirty with threadbare carpeting running the length of the hall. The dim illumination from a series of red bulbs made the setting very brothel-like. Halfway down the hall Dr. Fadel abruptly stopped and knocked lightly on the door of room 414.

There were eight Arab men inside the room and Mosaab knew none of them. Before addressing the gathered contingent, Dr. Fadel could not help but gaze disgustingly at the terrible décor, with every wall containing cracked plaster and ridiculous looking enormous flowers on wallpaper.

Dr. Fadel snapped out of his trance and addressed a tall stocky, dangerous looking man with a large jagged scar on his right cheek.

"Has the room been swept?"

"Done" was the one word reply.

"Sit brothers." Dr. Fadel waved his right hand in a sweeping manner to encourage the men to find seats on the three chairs and twin beds in the small room.

"I'll make this fast because we are all busy men, and the less we are seen together, the better."

Dr. Fadel took a deep breath, nodded his head and smiled.

"God is truly great, brothers. Through his goodness we will soon have the power and ability to strike a devastating blow at the infidels. We will make the Americans forget about the World Trade Center with the magnitude of our attack."

A short, thin man with a long nose interjected from one of the beds.
"How will we strike such a blow Doctor?"

"With a nuclear bomb brothers."

There was silence in the room as Dr. Fadel continued.
"Through God's graces we have acquired the ability to produce a small nuclear device the size of a suitcase. When the time is right a holy martyr will bring the bomb in a cargo ship to a port on America's east coast and detonate it."

Throughout the room rose the chant of "God is great."

Dr. Fadel raised both his hands.
"You will all be contacted with specific instructions in the near future. Now, my brothers I must take my leave of you and spend some time with some beautiful French ladies."

Laughter filled the room as Dr. Fadel and Mosaab made their exit. Once on the street Mosaab expressed his confusion.

"Forgive me Doctor, but I don't understand. Everything you told me earlier about deception and the invasion of Normandy - I don't ……"

Dr. Fadel stopped and turned to face Mosaab, cutting him off in mid-sentence.
"The Americans will think that we are going to bring the nuke in on a ship. While they focus all their efforts on their east coast ports, we will bring the device across their southern border."

The look on Mosaab's face indicated that he was no less confused.

"But how will the Americans find out about the plan to bring the bomb in by ship?"

Dr. Fadel turned and began to walk again.
"They'll know because we just told them."

Mosaab was momentarily stunned, and then broke into a trot to catch up.
"What do you mean?"

Dr. Fadel kept walking at a brisk pace as he spoke.
"I know there is a traitor in our group, and he will be dealt with in due time. I'm not certain who the snake is, so I had to bring all of our brothers here.

Waheed was again confused, but now also concerned.
"Surely, you don't suspect me doctor."

Dr. Fadel patted Mosaab's shoulder.
"Rest easy brother. I know you and your brother are loyal to me, and I only need you and Rashid to carry out the operation."

Dr. Fadel took a deep breath and continued,
"But for now, the traitor will serve our cause by telling the Americans of our plan and validating our deception."

Mosaab fell a few steps behind and stared straight ahead. He understood perfectly.
"God truly is great."

The brisk pace of their walk soon brought them to Rue St Denis which is a red-light district. The street was a garment district, but Dr. Fadel did not go there to shop for fabric. He stopped at the corner and marveled at the wide variety of women lining the street. The sun was just starting to go down, so he had plenty of time to finish with Mosaab before turning his attention exclusively to the women.

"Waheed, my brother, you have been loyal to me for many years. Even before you joined the caliphate you were loyal to my family business. Now, I need your loyalty again to strike a death blow at the belly of the beast."

Mosaab wasted no time in responding.
"Just tell me what you need me to do Doctor."

"Good." Dr. Fadel placed his right hand on Mosaab's left shoulder. "Let's walk a little more, brother."

The women on all sides tried to gain their attention, but Fadel and Mosaab strode by them without acknowledgement.

"I have a physicist – a Saudi – putting the final touches on the bomb. He and his team assure me that the device is the size of a large suitcase, but will produce a nuclear explosion."

Mosaab listened silently as Dr. Fadel continued.
"This Saudi, however, is not in Saudi Arabia, or Qatar, or anywhere in the Middle East. He is in Guatemala."

Fadel realized that he could not take for granted Mosaab's knowledge of geography. "Guatemala is in South America."

Mosaab was already overloaded with information to process, and he could only think of one question.

"How can a bomb as small as a suitcase cause such a large explosion?"

Dr. Fadel was very proud of his endeavor, so he readily provided an explanation.
"The bomb we have is called a Mark 3. It is a prototype of the obsolete bomb the Americans dropped on Nagasaki, only much smaller. Modern nuclear weapons utilize Insensitive High Explosives."

Dr. Fadel realized that Mosaab had no idea what he was talking about, but he enjoyed going over his own plan.
"IHEs are much more difficult to detonate accidentally, making the bombs much safer, even in an aircraft crash. We, however, will use the obsolete nature of our bomb to our advantage. The final phase of the bomb development is creating the nuclear trigger, which, unfortunately, is beyond the capabilities of our team. But by using the obsolete Mark 3 prototype, a conventional explosion will cause our nuke to detonate."

Dr. Fadel stopped and again faced Mosaab with his hand on his shoulder. Now, it was important for Mosaab to understand.

"Our heroic martyr will carry both our nuclear bomb and a conventional explosive. God willing, when you trigger the conventional bomb, the explosion will detonate the nuclear bomb."

Mosaab understood perfectly, but he was hung up on one word – you.
"Doctor, you mean you want me to…….."

Dr. Fadel cut Mosaab off with an annoyed tone.
"Of course, I expect you to carry out your responsibilities, brother. Why else did I arrange for you and your brother to go to America? Why else did I finance your business? It was certainly not for you to live the American dream my brother."

Mosaab said "I understand Doctor," but he did not sound very enthusiastic.

In any event, Dr. Fadel was done, and it was time to enjoy the pleasures of the night on Rue St. Denis.

"Go back to your hotel Waleed. Return to America and your store. I'll be in touch."

Fadel embraced Mosaab but seemed to have an afterthought before completely releasing him.

"By the way brother, how is your store?"

Mosaab immediately perked up.

"Business is great. We were just able to enlarge the store so we now have a food counter to go along with the newspapers and magazines."

"That's great Waheed. Just remember where your priorities lie."

Mosaab's voice took a somber tone again, "I will Doctor."

August 1, 2017: Qatar:

The vibration and buzz of the phone had no effect on his deep, blissful sleep. The phone took a short break and tried again. This time it broke through the barrier as his hand pawed across the bed until it found the device. Before placing phone to ear Doctor Fadel took note of both the time and the caller. As much as he wanted to hear from Abadi, he groaned at noting the 3 AM time.

"I don't hear from you for weeks, and when you decide to call, it is 3 AM."

"Sorry doctor, but it is only 6 PM here. Sometimes I lose track of the time difference."

"Well, what do you want to tell me?"

"I want to tell you that I am homesick doctor."

"Well then, the sooner you finish working on my car, the sooner you can come home."

"Your car is finished doctor."

Dr. Fadel paused a moment before responding

"Repeat what you just said please"

"Your car is finished."

"It is running well?"

"It runs perfectly. You just need to send someone to pick it up."

"I'll get back to you when I know when it will be picked up."

"Make it soon, doctor. I want to get back to Riyadh. Eighteen months in Guatemala is more than enough."

August 6, 2017: Qatar

Despite the roomy nature of the limo, Waheed Mosaab's legs still ached. He could not help but feel bitter at the accommodations for the thirteen-hour flight from New York City to Qatar. Someone as rich as Dr. Fadel should have provided a first-class ticket, yet now, as with his March flight to Paris, basic coach accommodations were provided. Mosaab was still attempting to stretch his legs as he waited in the huge entrance hall of Dr. Fadel's posh waterside villa in the West Bay section of Doha. A servant led Mosaab into Dr. Fadel's private study, and he continued his leg stretching as he turned 360 degrees admiring the expensive looking paintings and walls lined with books.

"Pleasant flight, brother?" Dr. Fadel entered the room.

Mosaab could have gone on for an hour about the flight, but instead responded meekly, "The flight was fine, doctor."

When both were seated on opposite sides of the huge oak desk, Fadel got right down to business.

"God is truly great, brother. Our time is at hand."

Mosaab remained silent. He suspected why Dr. Fadel had summoned him, and the doctor's opening statement was reinforcing his suspicions.

"The bomb is ready."

They stared silently at each other.

Finally, Mosaab gulped. "What must I do?"

Dr. Fadel responded incredulously, "You will pick up the bomb and carry out your mission, of course."

Mosaab sighed, "How will I do this doctor?"

Dr. Fadel pointed to a fifty-inch monitor on the wall. A map of Guatemala appeared on the screen as Dr. Fadel began to detail the plan. Mosaab would board the container ship Al Bidda at the Al Rayyan Marine Terminal. Fadel had paid off the ship's captain and obtained credentials reflecting that Mosaab was an oiler on the vessel. The ship was sailing to Puerto Quetzal, Guatemala's largest port. With his seaman credentials Mosaab would have no problem leaving the ship. He would travel to 46 Calle La Esso in Puerto San Jose, the city adjacent to Puerto Quetzal. 46 Calle La Esso was a small warehouse where he would find the Saudi scientist and the bomb. Mosaab would take possession of the bomb and begin the trek north.

Most of the Guatemalan-Mexican border was relatively easy to cross. The border was covered by either jungles in the north, or swamps and lowlands in the southwest, in addition to the highlands of Huehuetenango department in Guatemala, making this a particularly hard border to secure. Mosaab was given a piece of paper containing the names and phone numbers of coyotes, or smugglers, who would take him north. The first coyote would transport Mosaab and his package north on CA-2 highway into the Guatemalan highlands, and finally across the border into Mexico. Once in Mexico a Mexican coyote would bring Mosaab all the way through Mexico to the Tijuana / California border. The coyote would walk Mosaab across the border like any other wetback and put him in a waiting car heading north. The final hurdle would be clearing the border patrol checkpoint on Interstate 5 near San Clemente before being dropped off in Los Angeles. Once in LA, Mosaab would be on his own. He would then start the long trek cross country on a Greyhound bus.

There were a million things that could go wrong along the way, so Dr. Fadel also gave Mosaab fifty thousand dollars to pay the coyotes, cover expenses, and to provide pay offs for any exigencies that should arise.

"I am allowing one month for you to complete the entire trip."

Dr. Fadel received no response from Mosaab.

"One month, is that sufficient brother?"

Mosaab came out of his trance, "Fine – a month will be fine."

"Good. You already have the conventional bomb vest in New York, correct?"

"Yes doctor. The vest is ready."

"Excellent. You will wear the vest and carry the bomb like a suitcase. You will board a subway train in Queens and ride it into

Times Square. Once you get to Times Square you will detonate the vest, and God willing, our nuclear bomb will detonate."

Mosaab simply nodded his head affirmatively with a blank stare on his face. Dr. Fadel came around the desk and embraced him.

"You will be a hero of the jihad."

Mosaab nodded his head in agreement. His thoughts, however, had drifted. He was still definitely a warrior in the jihad, but maybe he wasn't quite as heroic as Dr. Fadel believed he was.

August 4, 2017: Qatar – Al Rayyan Marine Terminal

Mosaab stood on the deck of the Al Bidda, enjoying the sunrise and smoking a cigarette. The ship would be underway in an hour, marking the beginning of month long journey culminating in his suicide mission. The calm waters of the port produced only the slightest roll as Mosaab puffed and contemplated his future – or lack thereof. He owed a lot to Dr. Fadel. As orphans living on the streets, he and his brother Rashid were anomalies as native Qataris living in poverty in the tiny rich country. It was Dr. Fadel who took them in and gave them jobs in his oil fields. It was also the doctor who sent them to America and financed their convenience store in the Queens section of New York City. And it was Dr. Fadel who taught them about the evil of the American infidels, and the responsibility of all true Muslims to make jihad.

Mosaab stood at a crossroad. He still believed in the jihad, but for as much as Dr. Fadel had radicalized him, his experience in New York City for the past four years had also worked to westernize him. He and his brother had worked hard to build the store into a successful business and they took pride in their capitalistic accomplishment. As he stood on the deck of the cargo ship in the morning sunlight, martyrdom did not seem as appealing to him as it did four years earlier. Mosaab also realized that a man with the wealth and influence of Dr. Fadel had a long reach. He did not want to imagine how vicious his death would be if he chose to abandon the mission and return to New York City. It was a dilemma that Mosaab had contemplated continually over the past two years. The mission had to be completed, but he did not want to be the martyr. One last long puff before he flicked the cigarette over the side. He reached into his back pocket for his smartphone and dialed.

"Rashid, I'll be back in about a month. Have Marwan ready to go."

August 17, 2017: Puerto San Jose, Guatemala

46 Calle La Esso was a two-story building crammed between two motorcycle shops. In fact, except for number 46, every building on both sides of the block was a motorcycle shop. Number 46 was nondescript with no outward signs of life. At street level there was a dirty, pale green concrete wall interrupted only by a similar green roll up gate. Two large padlocks were present on the gate, which, judging from the dust buildup, appeared to have been closed for a long period of time. A very dark narrow alley on the south side of the building provided access to very flimsy looking metal stairs that led to the second-floor balcony. The balcony was protected by a three-foot-high white metal railing. On the opposite side of the five-foot-wide balcony stood a filthy yellow concrete wall equally as unattractive as the green wall at street level. The only clue to possible life was the white wooden door.

With no visible bell or buzzer, Mosaab pounded the door three times with his right fist. He then stepped back to the railing and waited. The sound of the latch was followed by the creaking of the door opening approximately 6-inches. Mosaab saw nothing in the darkness of the door crack. He called out, "Abadi?"

The door opened wide revealing the smiling face of Dr. Karim Abadi. Mosaab entered to find that the entire second floor of the building consisted of one large room. He looked around and noted the lack of people and furnishings.

"Where is everyone?"

"When we finished work I let my staff return to Riyadh; hee, hee, hee."

Mosaab wondered what Abadi found so funny, but he soon realized that the doctor laughed and giggled after just about every statement he made.

"There it is; hee, hee, hee."

Abadi pointed towards a steel table in the southwest corner of the room. Sitting on top of the table was something that resembled a cross between a large back pack and a duffel bag. The military green bag was about 30-inches by 20-inches with straps to wear as a backpack. It was also rigged with small wheels and a handle to wheel like a luggage carrier.

Mosaab stared at the bag. "Is it ready?"

"Oh, it's ready: ha, ha, ha, ha."

"Is it heavy?"

"Exactly 41.5 pounds: ho, ho, ho."

Mosaab glared at Dr. Abadi. He was already very tired of his giggling routine. But what else should he have expected. Dr. Abadi was tall and thin, with a dirty white lab coat and wildly unkempt black hair. He looked every inch the mad scientist.

Mosaab focused his attention on the bag. "Is it stable?"

"Very stable. But I wouldn't drop it if I were you: hee, ho, ha hee." Abadi nearly fell over in hilarity.

Mosaab tried to ignore the giggling idiot and continued voicing his concerns.

"What about radiation?"

Dr. Abadi had composed himself enough to respond.

"Not a problem, friend. The package has a lead lining, so radiation will not be an issue."

Mosaab was surprised that no hilarity followed the statement, but he quickly realized that Abadi hadn't come to his punch line.

"But if you begin to glow in the dark, it will be safe to say the lining didn't work."

Dr. Abadi began to crumble against the wall, unable to withstand the magnitude of his laughter.

Two hours later Mosaab sat in the passenger seat of a brown 1995 Jeep Cherokee traveling north on CA-2. He could not help but be very aware of the Jeep's cargo, and he cautioned Jorge, the Guatemalan coyote in English, their common language.

"Watch the bumps."

Jorge spoke only when he had to, but Mosaab welcomed the long periods of silence during the uneventful three-hour drive north. Without uttering a word Jorge exited the highway and continued north on a narrow dirt road bordered by forest. After fifteen minutes of slow progress north, the road ended and all that Mosaab could see was a foot path that continued into the forest.

"We walk," were the first words spoken by Jorge in hours.

As he followed Jorge through the highlands, Mosaab for the first time could test his ability to walk with the 41.5-pound weight strapped to his back. "Not too bad," he thought, if the walk was on a relatively flat surface. Thirty minutes into the walk sunlight was beginning to break through the thinning trees. Mosaab could also hear the sound of flowing water in the distance. They were about to come out of the highlands at the Suchiate River.

Mexico's southern frontier with Guatemala - 541 miles - was in a zone of dense, tropical forest. Two rivers served as the border for about a third of its length, and on the southern end, migrants were ferried across the Suchiate River on inner-tube rafts. The border area was barely guarded by Mexico's migration services and the only semblance of a fence came in the form of rusty barbed wire attached to rotting wood posts – barely able to keep cattle at bay and certainly no deterrent to human traffic.

Mexico had little interest in deterring Central Americans from crossing the country since it wasn't the final destination of most migrants. Most of the Central Americans paused briefly in southern cities like Tapachula or Tenosique, to catch "La Bestia," the infamous train that ferried people close to the U.S. border, or to meet up with the smuggler who would take them northward in a motor vehicle.

Distant figures on the Guatemalan bank of the river began to board a flotilla of wooden rafts, moored beneath a white cross tinting pink as dusk approached. The Rio Suchiate had long been one of the world's great migratory way stations, an illicit crossing point for generations of Central Americans seeking to enter Mexico on their way to the United States. Multitudes of Salvadorans, Hondurans, Guatemalans and others now settled in cities from Los Angeles to Washington, D.C., initially crossed into Mexico aboard those same inner tube rafts, fording the river that separates Mexico from the isthmus of Central America.

Mosaab watched Jorge disappear back into the forest, his only additional baggage being $2 thousand of Dr. Fadel's money. With his backpack secure, Mosaab carefully began a slow walk down to the river bank and the waiting armada of inner tubes. Soon, the wobbly fleet plunged into the murky water, the passengers perched unsteadily on planks lashed to the inner tubes. The drivers dipped long poles into the river bed for propulsion.

Mosaab's fleet consisted of approximately 60 travelers — all black, mostly young men, but also several women and children.

A thirty-year-old man seated on a plank next to Mosaab tried to make conversation in very broken English. "We are from the Congo."

Mosaab tried to ignore the male, his wife and infant son during the short trip across the river. Once on the Mexican side, they quickly disembarked and gathered up their backpacks and bags. Three Somali women donned the distinctive headdresses of their East African homeland. All made their way hastily up the slippery incline, passing trash heaps, scurrying rats and campfires warming coffee and tortillas.

Mosaab was beginning to feel the strain from his 41.5-pound load. As they navigated the muddy path beneath the majestic ceiba trees the male again tried to make contact.

"We would like to go to the USA."

"Good luck," Mosaab insincerely muttered as he tried to put some distance between himself and any further conversation.

Tapachula, a bustling, sweltering city in the shadow of the Tacaná volcano, had all the usual amenities of a border town — flop houses, cellphone shops, mini-markets and scores of bars and travel agencies. Many of the migrants from the inner tube fleet found their way to "Mama Africa's," a budget hotel formally known as The Imperial. Its manager was Concepcion Gonzalez Ramirez, whom everyone called Mama Africa. Residents paid about $2.50 a night, often for a mattress in the lobby, which was inevitably filled with migrants chatting with relatives and friends back home on their cellphones. The conditions at Mama Africa's quickly provided Mosaab the motivation to gladly carry his load another block.

Rooms at the Palofox Hotel started at $12 a night. The patio was festooned with drying laundry, and some rooms were labeled with the homelands of the residents. As Mosaab readied the key to enter his room, he noticed that the sign on the adjacent door read "Somalia."

Around 8 PM Mosaab sat in a rickety wooden chair, steadying himself on an equally unsteady wood table. The lack of lighting made it difficult to read the Spanish/English sign "Comida Economica, Cheap Food." The eatery was better known as the "Bangladeshi Restaurant." in reference to its owner, Shabbir Suhal. Three years earlier Suhal arrived in South America, intending to join the migration north to the United States, but made it only as far as Tapachula, where he abandoned his dream. Instead, Suhal became an entrepreneur in this polyglot way station, providing a crucial service to a burgeoning migrant population who, after all, must eat. For $2, Suhal offered a square meal of meat, rice and vegetables. At dinner time, a lively, multi-lingual clientele filled the house and patio, exchanging gossip in sundry tongues and watching movies on their cellphones in Punjabi, Hindi, French and English. Suhal loved to talk, and he had invited himself to sit at Mosaab's table. The only redeeming factor to this intrusion was that Mosaab could continue with his meal and ignore Suhal's English conversation.

The only trait that Felipe shared with Jorge was that they were both coyotes. Aside from that they were polar opposites. Jorge hardly said a word during the trip to the Suchiate River while Felipe had not shut up since joining him at the restaurant.

Felipe and Suhal bantered back and forth about the weather, America, and the economy of Mexico before Suhal apparently tired of Felipe and departed for gossip at other tables.

"We depart in the morning amigo. I drive a safe route at slow speed, so it will take us four days to reach Tijuana. I will meet you back here at 6 AM."

Felipe stood up, but had one more request before departing. "You pay me now amigo."

Mosaab reached into his pocket and handed over $ 4 thousand. As Felipe faded away into the darkened street still crowded with newly arrived migrants, Mosaab panicked. Now that he was paid, what if Felipe never returned. 6 AM the next morning found Mosaab sitting in the same rickety chair. His fears were allayed when Felipe's smiling face appeared approaching the restaurant from the south.

Four days, 2500 miles, and three hotels later Felipe pulled his Ford Explorer to a stop at the curb on Baja California, in Tijuana. They were directly in front of a storefront with a plywood façade painted orange. The orange paint was chipping everywhere and the word CANTINA was unprofessionally painted in black on top of the remaining orange paint. Mosaab assumed the sign read CANTINA because a huge missing piece of plywood obliterated most of the A and N. The condition of the façade combined with two locked roll up gates presented the appearance that this establishment had not been open in many months. Mosaab strapped on his backpack and was shocked when he followed Felipe through the open front door and into the crowded floor of a thriving bar.

Mosaab did not realize he was going to be passed off again, but after sitting down at a table, Felipe introduced Carlos. Carlos was short and thin, fluent in English, and appeared to be no more than eighteen years of age. Felipe explained to Mosaab that Carlos was an expert coyote, and that Carlos would take him the rest of the way across the border and to Los Angeles.

After finishing his beer, Carlos led Mosaab on a half mile walk to Calle Emiliano Zapata. They were in the middle of a residential neighborhood and they stopped at a vacant lot that showed the remnants of a recently demolished home. From the north end of the vacant lot the border fence was visible in the distance no more than a mile away. As with Jorge and Felipe, Mosaab believed that he would be Carlos's exclusive client for the trip north. As they waited in the lot, baking in Tijuana's afternoon heat, it became apparent that this smuggler was exercising some good old American style capitalism as more and more people began to join with him. Everybody's nerves were on edge as the Coyote gave final instructions in the afternoon. Carlos wanted them to be alert and awake as they crossed the border into California. He split the group into smaller teams to balance the men and the women, the weak and the strong, the younger and the elders.

They were told they would cross the border at night, and to be ready at any moment for the signal. The group gathered in their vacant lot, like an eerily quiet picnic. Apparently, there were more groups in the same area, which Mosaab could only hear. On cue, they ran across the valley, across a creek, and then into bushes. Quietly they ran and ran staying close, without looking back. Mosaab was finally feeling real pain from carrying his backpack. As they went further in the bushes, it got darker and darker. Together they moved as one, for they could not see ahead. The stars provided some light when they were in the open, but most of the time in the bushes it was pitch dark. Finally, they stopped on cue and laid down on the ground to rest. As they caught their breath, they could hear their own breathing, and some distant chatter. It got colder than Mosaab expected. In the dark, on the ground, he could see other eyeballs, if only for a second. They kept quiet as instructed. It was so dark it was not possible to tell if Carlos was standing or not. Mosaab could not even see eyeballs anymore, but could hear the breathing and feel the warmth. After a long time, they got up and continued walking towards a hill, slowly and quietly, in a single line formation. It got darker around them as they climbed, but from this new vantage point Mosaab could see at the distance behind him. It was not a tall hill. They were under trees and bushes as they climbed down, and somehow Mosaab developed the ability to see in the dark, at least to see where to step. On the bottom of the hill, a pick-up truck awaited.

Mosaab was surprised, he did not hear it nor see it until he was right next to it. Carlos directed them to enter quickly and lay flat on top of each other. No one complained. Carlos grabbed Mosaab's arm and escorted him to the truck's cab. After a half –hour ride, the truck slowed down. The truck's lights were off so Mosaab still found it very difficult to see anything. At the last moment he perceived they entered a garage. Once inside, with the garage lights on, everyone exited the truck and Carlos confirmed that everybody in his group made it to safety. Everybody smiled, but there could not be any loud celebration. Mosaab spent the night with the rest of the group at this farm.

Next morning, Carlos divided the group once more. Mosaab was still exhausted from the previous night's blind sprint, but his spirits rose when it appeared that finally, he would be Carlos's exclusive client for the trip to Los Angeles. Carlos escorted Mosaab to a green 2012 Chevy Impala parked outside the farmhouse. His hopes for exclusivity, however, were dashed when Carlos tossed the keys to him.

"You follow me, amigo."

Carlos smiled and pointed to the red pick-up truck parked in front of the Impala.

Mosaab carefully placed his backpack on the passenger seat and settled into the driver's seat. He turned the ignition key and waited for the pick-up truck to move. Mosaab squinted. Wait a minute, where was Carlos? The driver's seat of the pick–up appeared to be empty. Mosaab had his hand on the door handle, but his exit was interrupted by the sound of the Impala's trunk opening. A glance at his side view mirror solved the mystery of Carlos's whereabouts. Mosaab watched in horror as Carlos assisted two men and two women from the previous night's group into the vehicle's trunk.

Carlos bent over at the driver's window.

"If La Migra stops you, you are the smuggler amigo." Carlos let out a hearty laugh.

Carlos regained his composure and addressed Mosaab in a serious, almost fatherly tone in explaining how to handle the San Clemente Border Patrol checkpoint.

"Look La Migra right in the eye if you are stopped," was the advice offered. "They know the wets by their thousand-mile stare."

Finally, the young smuggler's laugh returned as he reiterated, "Remember, if they catch you amigo, you are the coyote, eh?" The chuckling coyote said "Sigame" before vanishing into the pick-up truck.

Off in the distance Mosaab could see flashing yellow lights. As his progress north continued at a slower speed, he could see the flashing lights were on a huge structure that read U.S. OFFICERS. Orange traffic cones reduced Interstate-5 to two lanes, and a portable stop sign was directly in the middle of the two open lanes. Behind the stop sign stood a large, imposing, figure in a dark green uniform and Smokey the Bear style hat. La Migra was taking a close look at the vehicles passing the checkpoint on either side of him. As Mosaab drove closer to the stop sign he could see that the Border Patrol Agent would give a quick wave of his right hand if he allowed a vehicle to proceed north. Suspicious vehicles were being waved to the right shoulder of the highway where two other agents were waiting to perform a closer inspection.

The nervousness Mosaab felt the previous night was transforming to sheer terror as the Impala crept closer to the checkpoint. After a cursory look, the red pick-up truck was waved north, and now Mosaab was at the stop sign. From his position in the driver's seat, the green monster appeared to be at least seven feet tall, and for a brief moment Mosaab sat frozen like a statue, staring north to a destination he would likely never see. Before La Migra could make any assessment, Mosaab's head cleared and he remembered the warning of the snickering coyote. Mosaab instantly turned his head left and up, and locked eyes with La Migra. The agent walked past the driver's window to the back of the Chevy. He pushed down hard on the trunk two times, trying to gauge the weight of the load inside. The agent then appeared at the passenger window where Mosaab was waiting with another icy stare. La Migra stood up straight and pondered the situation for what seemed like an eternity. Finally, with a quick snap of the right hand, Mosaab was moving north again.

    Mosaab followed the red pick-up into East Los Angeles, and into the driveway of a run down, one story house. For some reason there was still a sense of urgency in Carlos's voice as he told Mosaab how to get to the Los Angeles bus depot, and he gave him the bus tickets necessary to get to New York. Mosaab then turned over $216 for the bus tickets and $2 thousand for Carlos's fee.

    Carlos fanned the bills quickly. "Buenos suerte amigo," Mosaab was on his own.

    The trip had gone well thus far, and while waiting in the LA bus terminal he discreetly confirmed that he possessed $41 thousand of Dr. Fadel's money. As he waited to board the bus he tried to come up with various excuses that would allow him to keep at least some of the money.

    When the bus pulled out of the terminal, Mosaab mistakenly believed he was on the last leg of his journey. He was grossly mistaken, however, as he still had 31 unique stops and five bus transfers over the course of 75 hours.

    Over the course of the trip, Mosaab met a number of interesting infidels. The man he sat next to from LA to Las Vegas boarded the bus unsure if he had just been robbed, and he spent the duration of the trip playing a weathered PlayStation Portable he claimed to have found on the streets of LA. While waiting for a delayed bus in Salt Lake City, he met Jim, sporting a ponytail and decked out in all camo. Jim hailed from Alaska and claimed to make his living mining gold and hunting caribou passing through his land. He lived in a remote cabin with no electricity, but fortunately for Jim he was being wooed by a princess from a nearby Eskimo tribe. His seatmate from Salt Lake City to Denver was a 38-year-old homeless woman with a labret piercing. Mosaab found the trip from Denver to Kansas City particularly appalling, as he sat next to an evangelist headed home to Baton Rouge. She traveled with a copy of T.L. Osborn's "Healing the Sick" and spent large portions of the ride praying with friends on her cell phone. She was an incredibly upbeat person and repeatedly filled the bus with cheers of "2, 4, 6, 8, who do we appreciate?! The bus driver!" any time he relayed good news about the journey.

. Like Mosaab, many passengers carried all of the belongings to their name in a backpack. The only difference being that the contents in Mosaab's backpack was quite different than all the others on the bus. As he boarded the final bus that would take him into New York City, Mosaab questioned why anyone would choose these uncomfortable, endless string of buses as a mode of transportation. The answer came to him in a flash. These buses were the only mode of transportation that these foolish Americans could afford.

Three and a half days after pulling out of the terminal in LA, the bus pulled into the Port Authority Bus Terminal on the west side of Manhattan. Mosaab submerged into the subway and boarded a Queens-bound E train. He detrained at Roosevelt Avenue and went upstairs to transfer to the 7-train. Twenty minutes later he was carefully navigating down the steps of the elevated 103rd Street subway station.

The sidewalk teemed with all types of infidels as he carefully carried his backpack past the Chinese produce market, the Argentine restaurant, the Mexican bakery, and the sneaker outlet. Mosaab looked up to the familiar yellow awning that contained the simple red letters spelling out VARIETY STORE. It had been twenty days since he last set foot inside his store.

Rashid was behind the counter transacting the sale of several pornographic magazines to a greasy looking infidel. He did not greet or acknowledge his brother, but walked directly to the rear of the store and entered the store room. Once Little Nagasaki was safely placed in the corner of the store room he returned to the front of the store. The greasy infidel was gone and Mosaab embraced his brother.

"How have things been, Rashid?"

"Business has been very good Waheed. The signs in the window are bringing in a lot of food business."

"That's great, brother."

Mosaab nodded his head slightly as he looked around at the familiar sights of his store. At least for the moment, it was back to business as usual.

CHAPTER 2: THE LAST DAY – THE BEGINNING

August 24, 2017: New York City

0400 hours: Sweat flowed freely down his forehead and onto the pillow case, turning the sleeping cushion into something akin to a wet towel. Despite the cool climate in the apartment, his body lay sprawled over the rumpled sheets, legs sticking over the end of the bed. His eyes remained closed as he listened to the monotonous ticking of the clock on the night table. Slowly, his eyes opened from another night of miserable sleep. He momentarily focused on the streetlight outside his bedroom window, the sole source of illumination at 4 AM. He lifted his head and one by one he slid his legs off the bed and touched the floor. The cheap acoustic tile felt hard and cold against his feet. Light-headed, he collapsed over the bed, his legs dangling over the side. He rested, gathering his strength, and several minutes later he tried again. This time he made it completely out of the bed, but ended up on his hands and knees on the tile floor. His chest heaved as he took several deep, deliberate breaths, causing the blood vessels inside his head to throb. He rarely drank, but the three beers could not have put him in this pathetic condition, could they? Perhaps he needed to come to grips with the reality that his imminent sixty third birthday was sure to bring many similar mornings. Then again, there was the dream. The same recurring dream that had plagued him most nights over the prior twenty-two years.

He never used an alarm clock, and it was only after stepping out of the head clearing shower that he realized he had gotten up forty minutes earlier than he had to. With time to spare he decided on an additional bowl of Special K. Even with breakfast seconds, he was still ahead of schedule when his apartment door locked behind him.

There was just the slightest hint of morning light when he emerged from his weary looking one hundred-year-old three-story walk up. The still, humid air, even at the pre-dawn hour provided evidence that one of those hot, sticky, miserable New York City summer days lie ahead. The city that never sleeps had obviously forgotten about this small stretch of Brooklyn on Havemeyer Street.

The slight clicking of his shoes on the sidewalk was the only sound as he strode silently past the closed security gates on the meat market, shoe maker, nail salon, and cell phone store. A right turn on Borinquin Place and the early morning silence was replaced by the steady drone of vehicles on the elevated approach to the Williamsburg Bridge. As he neared the entrance to the bridge footpath he could see in the dim illumination of several street lights that his old friend was there to greet him, as he had for every morning for the past twenty-two years. Normally, he would just acknowledge his friend with a quick glance before continuing to the bridge, but today, he detoured into Continental Army Plaza to say a formal farewell to the striking bronze equestrian figure of George Washington at Valley Forge.

He placed his hand on the concrete pedestal and whispered "This is it, general – the last day."

He began negotiating the steep incline of the bridge, keeping focused on the path immediately ahead. 5:30 AM found him breathing heavily at the apex of the bridge where he paused momentarily to gaze north and south at the expanse of Manhattan, and to ponder the significance of the day. At 6:30 AM his northern path along Broadway brought him to 14th Street.

Since 1839 Union Square Park had served as home base for countless community events and festivals-from the first Labor Day parade in 1882 to workers' rallies in the 1930s to the first Earth Day in 1970. This former burial ground had seamlessly transitioned from a town square to a bustling city park. He continued toward the west side of the park and his usual subway entrance. The blue and white NYPD radio cars and barriers lining the curb gave evidence to some police facility nearby, but none was visible at street level. Looks can sometimes be deceiving, however, as descent to the BMT mezzanine revealed a full-service police station - NYPD Transit Bureau District 4.

He waved to the desk lieutenant as he entered the district, walked through the muster room and down a winding hallway to arrive at the police officer locker room. He opened the combination lock and grabbed a uniform shirt off a hanger. He hesitated for a moment before placing the shirt back inside the locker and collapsing on the bench. It was way too early to suit up when the alternative of sprawling out on the bench for thirty minutes was an option.

At 7:35 AM Sergeant Henry Harrison stepped behind District 4's massive desk and flipped the pages of the sergeant's clipboard. It was time to turn out the second platoon.

Looking down at the desk lieutenant, Harrison asked, "Got anything, Lou?"

The lieutenant looked up. "Tell the car I want some General Tso for lunch."

"You got it, Lou." Harrison tucked the clipboard under his arm and stepped out from behind the desk. "All right, fall in," Harrison shouted, walking into the muster room.

The sergeant's command was a huge relief to him as it served to terminate the back slapping, hand shaking, and well wishing. The relief was short lived, however, when he spied Captain Ruiz striding down the hall towards the muster room cradling a large plaque under his right arm. He wanted no part of this pomp, but he had no choice.

The captain took a position to the right of Sergeant Harrison and remained silent while he called the roll. "Moylan".

From the second row of the assembled platoon, Police Officer Bobby Moylan responded, "Here sarge," for the final time.

0535 hours: Ellen emerged from the shower and completely wrapped herself in a towel before exiting the bathroom. As she traversed the living room and arrived in the bedroom, she chuckled at her display of modesty. Who was she hiding her body from? Her entire life she had lived with other people. First, of course, there were her parents, followed by Steve and Patrick. With Steve long gone via divorce and Patrick away at school, Ellen was not adjusting well to being alone. Approximately a month after Patrick had left for Penn State, Ellen had actually toyed with the idea of moving back in with her mother. No matter how lonely she was, however, she could not fathom the thought of the Commanding Officer of NYPD Transit Borough Manhattan running home to mommy

The dawn's early light was just flickering as Inspector Ellen Tomlinson eased her Category 1 NYPD department vehicle out of her Massapequa, Long Island driveway, and began the trek into Manhattan. Ellen's plate was extremely full today. First, she had to stop at her midtown Columbus Circle office to get into uniform and review crime statistics. Ellen then had to rush down to One Police Plaza to be grilled at a Compstat meeting, and then hurry back uptown to attend a community board luncheon. Finally, the most important item on the day's agenda would occur at 4 PM at District 4, and no matter what came up during the day, Inspector Ellen Tomlinson would be there for Bobby Moylan.

0540 hours: Joey inhaled deeply as he lowered the bar to his chest. A loud grunt was an integral part of his exhale as he labored to push the bar up to arms-length. He quickly realized that fifteen bench press reps may not be a reality. At this early morning hour, the empty gym provided no potential assistance should the 185-pound barbell become too much to raise off his chest. With his arms perilously shaking after rep number eight, Joey guided the barbell into its two upright holders with a loud clang. He then sat up on the bench, took a deep breath, toweled the sweat from his head and face and resolved that it was no fun getting old.

The battle with physical conditioning and the inevitable aging process was not the only source of stress for Joey Galeno on this new day. He was on edge, and he hated this anxious feeling. It had been eight months since Joey had been placed in sole command of the New York City office of the Joint Terrorism Task Force.

The JTTF had been created in the wake of the FALN bombings of the 1970s. It was an elite and important assignment where NYPD detectives were grouped together with FBI agents. The JTTF concept had expanded from its roots in New York to 104 cities nationwide. Now approximately 4,000 members from more than 500 state and local agencies and 55 federal agencies worked together to investigate and prevent domestic and international terrorism. Since its inception in 1980, the New York JTTF had been instrumental in this fight. It had aggressively investigated criminal activity, including a 2007 plot to bomb John F. Kennedy Airport, a 2009 plot to attack New York's subway system, and a 2010 attempted bombing in Times Square. The New York JTTF also took part in investigating international events like the U.S. Embassy bombings in East Africa in 1998 and the 2000 terrorist attack on the USS Cole in Yemen.

Lethal attacks like the 1993 bombing of the World Trade Center and the tragic events of 9/11 created a need for JTTFs nationwide to increase their investigative resources and collaborative efforts to combat terrorism on a national and international scale. The New York JTTF had provided an effective framework for other task forces to follow.

New York had the largest JTTF in the country and for the first time it was being commanded by a member of the NYPD. Specifically, Joseph P. Galeno, LCDS. LCDS stood for Lieutenant Commander Detective Squad, and was for a lieutenant, the same type of appointed promotion as when a police officer was promoted to detective. For a twenty-nine year veteran who had seen pretty much everything throughout the years, this morning's nervousness was unsettling. Something was going on, but he could not put his finger on it. There was always intelligence flowing, but this recent chatter was different. Something was happening and his frustration was growing in part from the lack of information flowing from one of his undercovers.

Several months earlier a new FBI undercover agent had been assigned to the New York JTTF, but as far as Joey was concerned, an act of purely political retribution had saddled him with a ludicrous situation that was inherently dangerous. Today, his philosophy of strategic patience ended. The location the UC was working had suddenly and unexpectedly become hot, and he could no longer hide him to keep him out of trouble. Joey Galeno desperately needed information. If there was no credible intelligence received from the undercover, Joey was going to call Washington and the FBI Director himself, if necessary, to have the UC relieved from his assignment.

0545 hours: Although completely inebriated, Jimmy Boy had enough of his faculties working to set the alarm on his smart phone to "Good Morning," its loudest, most annoying tone. The title of the tone seemed benign, but this musical version of the cheeriest person known to mankind bouncing into the room with an equally zesty flash mob choir behind him was the only way to ensure that despite the massive hangover, he would have no choice but to spring from the bed, if only to silence the insidious tone.

Jimmy Boy knew he had to rise early, but he could not resist the temptation of a ticket to see his beloved Red Sox play at Yankee Stadium. These weren't just any tickets. Three childhood friends from Boston had invited him to be the fourth occupant of first row seats on the third base side of the Red Sox dugout. The fact that it was an afternoon game resulted in Jimmy Boy's instant acceptance of the invitation.

From Jimmy Boy's point of view the day had been exceptional. The Red Sox offensive explosion inspired him to stand in exultation with his Red Sox cap proudly on his head every time the "SAWKS" added to their lead. Jimmy Boy was ecstatic, but the Yankee stadium crowd did not share his delight. His companions could feel the hostility raining down on them, along with various foreign objects. Before the objects turned into bottles, one of Jimmy Boy's friends snatched the Red Sox cap from his head and handed him a less controversial replacement.

"Here, put this on before we all get killed." Patrick McKeon pled in a concerned tone. "But this was my gift to you," Jimmy Boy protested as he reluctantly placed the FBI Academy baseball cap squarely on his head.

Not only had the Red Sox beaten the Yankees, but Jimmy Boy actually caught a foul ball. To make the situation even sweeter, Jimmy Boy prevented Yankee shortstop Didi Gregorius from making an amazing catch when he snatched the ball just as it was about to fall into the shortstop's outstretched glove.

The early conclusion time of the game was supposed to ensure a good night's sleep for Jimmy Boy, but in reality, all it ensured was many more hours of drinking time. When his friends finally dragged him from the cab, and into his Corona, Queens apartment, it was 12:15 AM. When the "Good Morning" tone blasted from his phone at 5:45 AM, he had no choice but to try to pull himself together as best as he could. Lieutenant Galeno would be furious beyond comprehension if he did not provide some information later in the day. With his head pounding like a sledgehammer, Jimmy Boy stepped into the shower and turned on only the cold water. He needed something to shock his system into some type of functioning condition. FBI Special Agent James "Jimmy Boy" Craig, aka Ahmed Al-Fadhill had to make it to the mosque in time for the pre-dawn prayer.

0550 hours: A steady stream of perspiration disappeared into an unkempt beard. The filthy studio apartment was illuminated by only one forty-watt bulb as he knelt in prayer next to the only furnishing in the room, a dirty, worn mattress. One day soon, this somber young man would offer up a final prayer and then blow himself up along with as many infidels as he could reach. Marwan Abu Abbas had been prepared for months to carry out a suicide mission. He didn't know when or where his trusted older cousin Waheed Mosaab would order him to climb into a bomb-laden vehicle or strap on an explosives-filled vest, but he was eager for the moment to come. While he waited, he spent much of his time rehearsing that last prayer Mosaab had taught him.

"First I will ask Allah to bless my mission with a high rate of casualties among the Americans," he said, speaking softly in a matter-of-fact monotone, as if dictating a shopping list. "Then I will ask him to purify my soul so I am fit to see him, and I will ask to see my mujahedin brothers who are already with him." He paused to run the list through his mind again, then resumed: "The most important thing is that he should let me kill many Americans."

At 22, the slightly built Marwan was a Sunni Muslim born in Qatar, who had moved with his family to Iraq when he was three years old. In his town of Fallujah, Marwan was known mainly as a simpleton who could be easily talked into doing most anything, no matter how ridiculous it was. When Waheed Mosaab realized that a stooge would be necessary to prevent his personal rendezvous with

Allah, his cousin Marwan was the obvious choice and a crash course in radicalization began.

Marwan had spent almost two years living in the dilapidated apartment. He did not realize that these recent days of near seclusion, holed up in the safe house, was the final stage of his preparation period. Any day that he made his daily trek to the mosque could be the day of his operation.

Marwan knew that he would have no input into planning his operation. The logistics--choosing targets, checking out the site, preparing the bomb-laden vehicles or vests--were left to field commanders like Mosaab. It was not unusual for a bomber to be told about the details of a mission mere minutes before launching the attack.

Marwan seemed certain he was on a "pure" path. Unlike many other jihadists, who rejected the terrorist label and called themselves freedom fighters or holy warriors, Marwan embraced it. "Yes, I am a terrorist," he would say. "Write that down: I admit I am a terrorist. The Koran says it is the duty of Muslims to bring terror to the enemy, so being a terrorist makes me a good Muslim." If he could choose, Marwan would like his operation to be a car bombing targeting U.S. police or military personnel. But if he was ordered to strap on explosives and walk to his target on a downtown street, he would do so. Whatever the target, he hoped it would be a high-profile hit, the dramatic, headline-grabbing kind that would leave him revered as a great Islamic hero. Regardless of the target and notoriety, Marwan ultimately understood that the only person who mattered was Allah--and the only question he would ask was 'How many infidels did you kill?'"

Marwan emerged from the building's front door and into the pre-dawn heat. He walked north with only the distant sound of a dog barking to disrupt the prayers going through his head. Everything was progressing normally as he navigated his way through the darkened streets towards the mosque. He had made this walk every day for the past two years, but he would never make it again. These were not the streets of Fallujah, or any other location in Iraq or the

Middle East. Marwan was striding along 108th Street in the Corona section of Queens, New York City.

CHAPTER 3: THE CELL

Radicalization is usually seen as a process through which extremist groups or "hate preachers" groom vulnerable Muslims for jihadism by indoctrinating them with extremist ideas.
What is striking about the stories of wannabe jihadis is their diversity. There is no "typical" recruit, no single path to jihadism.

The usual clichés about jihadis – that they are poor, uneducated, badly integrated – are rarely true. In fact, most are highly educated young people from comfortable families who speak English at home. Dr. Khaled Fadel fit this profile perfectly. He was not the poor, uneducated, brainwashed zealot stereotypically associated with the jihad. To the contrary, Dr. Fadel was well educated and wealthy beyond imagination. Why then would a man of such wealth and privilege disrupt his pampered lifestyle to finance terrorism and eventually progress to the active side of terror operations?

What drew Dr. Fadel and most wannabe jihadis was neither politics nor religion. It was a search for something a lot less definable: for identity, for meaning, for "belongingness", for respect. In Dr. Fadel's case there was another applicable word – boredom. Everything in his life had been handed to him – the business, wealth, status. Life presented no challenge for Dr. Fadel and the great Satan in America provided a renewed meaning in his life.

There is, of course, nothing new in the youthful search for identity and meaning. What varies today is the social context and timing in which this search takes place. Dr. Fadel was 43 years old when he wired fifty thousand dollars to a non-profit group in Saudi Arabia, knowing full well that the money was destined for Al Qaeda. An equally salient question was how Dr. Fadel was able to recruit members for his new operational cell.

In an age in which traditional anti-imperialist movements have faded and belief in alternatives to capitalism dissolved, radical Islam provides the illusion of a struggle against an immoral present and for a utopian future. This was the bill of goods Dr. Fadel sold to his followers. Followers he found like a farmer picking the fruits from various trees – careful not to mix those fruits together. From one of those trees he picked the ripened fruits that were Waheed and Rashid Mosaab.

Like most homegrown wannabe jihadists, the Mosaab brothers possessed a peculiar relationship with Islam. They were as estranged from Muslim communities as they were from western societies. They detested the mores and traditions of their parents, had little time for mainstream forms of Islam and cut themselves off from traditional community institutions. It was not through mosques or religious institutions but through the internet and Dr. Fadel that they discovered their faith and their virtual community. Separated from social norms, finding their identity within a small group, shaped by Dr. Fadel's black-and-white ideas and values, driven by a sense that they must act on behalf of all Muslims and in opposition to all enemies of Islam, it became easier for wannabe jihadists like the Mosaab brothers to agree to commit acts of horror and to view such acts as part of an existential struggle between Islam and the West.

Dr. Fadel had picked the fruit from several trees, but the Mosaab brothers were the most ripe. They also were the most indebted to the doctor. He had taken them out of poverty by giving them jobs in his oil fields. Eventually, their loyalty earned promotions to the administrative side of the business, and finally to the doctor's sponsored jihad.

Dr. Fadel arranged the visas and financing for the brothers to move to New York City and open a variety store in the borough of Queens. The doctor now had players in place to activate at the right moment. The Mosaab brothers turned out to be astute businessmen and four years later the store was thriving. They were successes in the capitalistic western society they had been taught to hate. This paradox presented a real problem for the entrepreneurs. Waheed, the deeper thinker of the pair, realized that there would someday be a moment of truth. As he and Rashid became more and more involved in capitalism, he knew that the day would come when Dr. Fadel would reach out and direct them to carry out an operation. Waheed was intuitive enough to realize that the operation would likely be suicidal in nature. Deeply engrossed in the life of a small business owner, Waheed was no longer looking forward to becoming a martyr. He would have to find someone to take his place in martyrdom. Waheed's search was brief, as he needed to look no further than his younger cousin Marwan.

Twenty-two year old Marwan moved with his family to Iraq in 1998. Before the war, his father's successful business earned enough--even during the difficult years when the West imposed economic sanctions on Iraq--to provide a good life for his family. Unlike many other Sunnis in Fallujah, Marwan's father had little love for Saddam's Sunni-led regime. Yet once the dictator fell, he turned against the Americans because after bringing Saddam down, he expected the Americans to leave – but they stayed. His father's negative political opinion of America was worlds away from becoming part of the jihad, but it was the opening that Waheed Mosaab needed. Marwan was learning-disabled and dropped out of school at age fourteen. He had few friends, but appeared to be content growing up around his parents and the family dog. According to his mother, Marwan was a peaceful soul who would not hurt a fly. In fact, she would regularly scold Marwan for bringing home stray dogs and cats he would find in the street.

Marwan's father saw no point in sending his simple-minded son back to school, only to have him fail. When the time was right, he would try to somehow get his intellectually limited son involved in the family business. In the meantime, his father tried to keep Marwan out of trouble by keeping him involved in his religion. When Marwan's father died suddenly of a heart attack, his protective shield was gone. Waheed connected with Marwan on Facebook, and it took only two months for the pliable, suggestible Marwan to be lured into jihad. Marwan's journey toward suicide murderer began with a new-found hatred of America as taught by his cousins.

For the deeply pious Marwan, his colleagues in the jihad were now closer to his heart than his family and few friends. He embraced the jihadist worldview of one global Islamic state where there was, in Marwan's words, "no alcohol, no music and no Western influences." He conceded that he had not thought deeply about what life might be like in such a state; after all, he wasn't a deep thinker and really didn't expect to live long enough to experience it.

Besides, he fought first for Islam, second to become a "martyr" and win acceptance into heaven.

Indoctrinating Marwan into the Jihad was the easy task facing the Mosaab brothers. More daunting would be getting him to America, especially, without the assistance and resources of Dr. Fadel. In fact, the brothers did everything in their power to ensure that the doctor never learned they were placing a pinch hitter in the martyr on deck circle. In analyzing their challenge, the Mosaab's realized they had a virtual smorgasbord of opportunities to choose from.

They could take the path of a temporary visa for Marwan, such as those issued to students and tourists. After all, the September 11th hijackers were originally allowed into the country on temporary visas. Overstaying a visa was not the only option for Marwan. Foreign-born Islamic terrorists had used almost every conceivable means of entering the country over the last decade. They had come as students, tourists, and business visitors. They had also been lawful permanent residents and naturalized U.S. citizens. They had sneaked across the border illegally, arrived as stowaways on ships, used false passports, or been granted amnesty. Terrorists had even exploited America's humanitarian tradition of welcoming those seeking asylum.

In the end, the Mosaab's used America's immigration policy in processing visas against them. The Consular Service had adopted a culture of service rather than skepticism, one in which visa officers were expected to consider applicants as their customers. Satisfying the customer - the foreign visa applicant - had become one of the service's most important goals, leading to pressure to speed processing and approve marginal applications. State Department procedures called for supervisory review of refusals, but not issuances. Thus, relatively inexperienced junior officers were trusted to issue visas but were second-guessed on refusals. Visa officers were judged by the number of applications processed each day and by their politeness to applicants rather than on their thoroughness in screening applicants. It was in this atmosphere that Marwan Abu Abbas was happily handed a temporary visa to enter the United States of America.

Marwan lived with the Mosaab brothers for two years. They found him the cheapest and filthiest one room apartment in the same building where they lived. They basically limited Marwan to two activities – working in the store and visiting the mosque. All the while, Waheed took the lead role of preparing Marwan to someday become the replacement martyr. Waheed put Marwan through a relentless program to discipline his mind and cleanse his soul. The training was mainly psychological and spiritual. Besides the Koran, he taught Marwan about the history of jihad, and about great martyrs who had gone before him. These things were meant to strengthen his will. One popular source of inspiration for Marwan was The Lover of Angels, by Abdullah Azzam, one of Osama bin Laden's spiritual mentors, which told stories of jihadis who died fighting Soviet occupying troops in Afghanistan. Marwan additionally listened to taped speeches that addressed subjects like the rewards that await warriors in heaven.

As a would be martyr, Marwan used his waiting time to take care of business like destroying any photographs of himself. Waheed taught Marwan that true Islamists regarded pictures as a sign of vanity and therefore were taboo. He also began to compile a list of the 70 people Islamic tradition says a martyr can guarantee a place in paradise. He had not yet written 70 names on his list because he did not know that many people. In fact, his list contained only the names of Waheed and Rashid Mosaab.

Some suicide bombers dig graves for themselves and leave instructions on the way they should be buried--generally with simple headstones. Waheed told Marwan not to worry about this ritual because if he was lucky his body would be vaporized leaving nothing to bury.

CHAPTER 4: THE COP

0755 hours – The Last Day: Police Officer Bobby Moylan filed out of District 4 with the rest of the second platoon, but skipped the normal socializing outside the command. Instead, he motioned for Steve Bryant to follow him directly to the uptown Lexington Avenue platform. Bryant was a rookie with less than a year on the job, and this would be the first and last time they would work together. Bobby and his partner stood in the center of the island platform ready to move in either direction. The 4 and 5 trains on the express track as well as the 6-train on the local track all stopped at Grand Central. After all the years Bobby still marveled at the mass of rush hour commuters who stood leisurely on the yellow tactile warning strip, literally inches away from arriving trains.

"Just one little push," he thought.

His train of thought went no further, however. He glanced at Steve and nodded towards the imbeciles standing perilously close to the edge of the platform.

"I don't have to worry about them anymore," he chuckled, as they inched closer to the waiting crowd.

The double doors of the express opened and people lunged out of the train even as new passengers pushed forward. Arguments started, and profanity seasoned them. Bobby and Steve elbowed and shouldered their way aboard, their uniforms receiving no special treatment from the crowd. People were crushed together and groped for handrails already crowded with hands.

"Watch the closing doors," shrilled a barely audible announcement over the loudspeaker. "The next stop will be Grand Central."

The train jerked forward, stopped, lurched several times, jerked forward again, then left the station. Steve Bryant was still not used to these typical New York City subway rush hour conditions. He surveyed the crush of pressing people and moved his head close to Bobby.

"God! How do they survive this day after day? They're like fucking cattle."

Bobby simply grinned and said "You'll get used to it."

It had been many, many years since a subway crowd bothered Bobby Moylan.

It was in a crowded schoolyard in the Jackson Heights section of Queens, on a crisp, fall day in 1965 that the FSC was formed. The six founding members were "Little" Donald Hanley, Eugene "Huge Head" Cassidy, Jimmy "The Hose" Dooley, Amy Giordano, Mary O'Brien, and Bobby "The Cop" Moylan. By height and girth, Donald Hanley was by far, the largest member of the group, but because he had an older brother, friends and family routinely referred to him as little Hanley. The moniker stuck, and to his friends, Don Hanley was simply "Little." Gene Cassidy's exceedingly large cranium resulted in the far less subtle nickname of Eugene Huge Head. Jimmy Dooley always wanted to be a fireman, and right up to the day he entered the FDNY academy he swore that "The Hose" referred to his firefighting aspirations. The reality of the nickname, however, was quite different. One late afternoon in May, the Our Lady of Fatima Schoolyard Crew, or FSC for short, was hanging out on their turf when "Little" suddenly looked at Dooley's prominent proboscis and announced, "Is that a nose or a garden hose?" The hose was born.

As for Bobby Moylan, Sister Ann Cecilia's fifth grade class was designated as the safety patrol, and had to provide safety patrol boys to make sure the first and second graders crossed the street safely coming and going to school each day. From the moment Sister slapped down the white safety belt with the shiny silver badge on Bobby's desk, he became "The Cop." Even at ten years of age, chivalry prevailed resulting in no nicknames for the female members of the crew.

The FSC really believed they were something special and that every kid in the fifth grade would be begging to join. They even went out and had FSC jackets made to properly put their coolness on display. As graduation from Fatima loomed in June 1969, the FSC had acquired no new members over the preceding four years. As a matter of fact, they lost a member when Huge Head's family moved to Maine after the seventh grade. After graduation, the FSC slowly began to go their separate ways. Little and The Hose went to Msgr. McClancy High School in Jackson Heights, while Amy traveled to St. Vincent Ferrer in Manhattan. Bobby and Mary attended Bryant High School, the local public school in nearby Woodside. That Bobby and Mary were the last of the crew to be hanging together was no surprise. As next-door neighbors on 82nd Street, they had been hanging out together since they were five years old.

Upon Graduation from Bryant High School in 1973, Bobby's potential career paths seemed limited. Thankfully, the war in Viet Nam was winding down, ending the military draft. Without the possibility of compulsive military service, Bobby had to enter the working world. His father, a union carpenter for over thirty years, had been able to get Bobby into Local 79, the laborers union. Bobby wanted no part of construction work, but his father issued a stern warning. Bobby was not going to be a bum, and if he did not find other legitimate work, he would be a laborer even if he had to drag Bobby by his collar to the construction site each morning. So, it came to pass that during the summer of 1973 Bobby began digging ditches and hauling construction materials at sites all around Manhattan. He hated the job.

One hot summer Saturday evening, Our Lady of Fatima's schoolyard hosted an impromptu reunion of the FSC. Little, The Hose, Mary and Bobby lounged on the concrete platform in the southeast corner of the yard that was known as the throne. As they enjoyed the mild early evening summer breeze, they sipped cans of Coors. Obtaining Coors beer in 1973 was a major coup. The premium beer did not appear in the New York market until 1987. In fact, it was only available west of the Mississippi River up until 1980. This lack of availability and publicity created a cult status among New York City's beer drinking population, making the acquisition of Coors, even just a six pack, a major event.

As the FSC chugged away and reveled in their good fortune, Little made a seemingly insignificant comment that would change Bobby's life.

"I just filed the application to take the transit police test." Little's head was pointing skyward, draining every last drop from the can.

. Bobby put his half-filled can down on the concrete throne and looked curiously at his friend. "What is the transit police?"

Little chuckled. "You mean you don't know that there are different types of cops in the city? The housing cops work in the projects and the transit cops are in the subway."

Bobby stared into space in deep thought. He could care less what a transit cop actually was, but he was beginning to see a potential path off the construction site.

Bobby probed a little deeper. "How old do you have to be to be a transit cop?"

Little popped open his last can. "Eighteen to take the test – twenty to be appointed."

Bobby leaned back on the bench. After several seconds of contemplation, he turned toward Little. "Are they still accepting applications?"

In January 1975, at the age of twenty, Bobby "The Cop" Moylan was thrilled to be appointed as a police officer with the New York City Transit Police Department. He wasn't overly thrilled to be a cop, as he never had any great desire to pursue law enforcement as a career. He was thrilled, however, to leave the construction site for the final time. Bobby soon realized, however, that he may have been acting a bit prematurely when he tore up his union card.

US economic stagnation in the 1970s hit New York City particularly hard, amplified by a large movement of middle-class residents to the suburbs, which drained the city of tax revenue. New York City was on the brink of bankruptcy.

Bobby graduated from the Transit Police Academy on June 25, 1975, but on the 30th of June, the city laid off an initial 15,000 workers, including 3,000 cops and 1,600 firefighters – 20% of the city's entire force. Some 26 fire companies were simply disbanded. By September, 45,000 workers had been laid off. The Transit

Authority followed suit and laid off thousands of transit workers, including transit police officers. Since the 3,000 man Transit Police Department was about one tenth the size of the NYPD, 300 transit police officers were proportionately laid off.

Bobby Moylan had been out of the academy for all of five days when he received his layoff notice. From July 1975 until November 1979, no police officers were hired or trained in the City of New York. The only "new" officers were those who had been laid off and were rehired over the next three years. Bobby and the other laid off transit cops caught a break that kept him off the construction site. The Transit Authority was able to offer all the laid off transit cops jobs as bus drivers and token booth clerks. It certainly wasn't ideal, but Bobby felt fortunate to be working for the next two years in a token booth at South Ferry in Manhattan instead of hauling rebar around the 52nd floor.

Bobby was rehired in 1977 and because he had never experienced a break in service with the Transit Authority, he did not lose any seniority. In other words, he still qualified for a twenty-year retirement based on his original appointment date.

0815 hours – The Last Day: The train doors opened at Grand Central. Bobby and Steve were swept out to the platform by the wave of exiting humanity. Freeing themselves from the flow of the crowd, they stood on the platform behind a stairway, allowing time for the masses to scurry up the stairs. Bobby drew in a deep, deliberate breath, savoring the familiar smells – that pungent formula combining steel dust, sweat, urine, and a pinch of vomit. These were the smells of the New York City Subway, and although there was no rational way to explain it, he was going to miss the aroma. When the crowd had momentarily dwindled, and before the next arriving train brought a renewed stampede, Bobby and Steve climbed the stairs to the huge mezzanine and strolled directly to booth R-241.

"Call us on, will ya?"

Steve immediately responded to Bobby's request by knocking on the bullet resistant booth glass and pointing to a phone just below the glass. The station agent pulled the hasp releasing a small door providing access to the phone.

"Moylan and Bryant on post at 0820 at booth R-241, take care."

Bobby stood several feet away and silently watched the dance – those daily gyrations of thousands of people crisscrossing the mezzanine from all directions, yet avoiding any collisions. Bobby silently stared at the dancers, while Steve had enough insight to remain silent.

Bobby "The Cop" Moylan soon realized how apropos his nickname turned out to be. With the same intensity he learned to hate construction work, he learned to love being a cop. He was assigned to Transit Police District 4, which at the time was located inside the Chambers Street IND subway station in lower Manhattan.

During his first few years on patrol, Bobby Moylan was extremely active, routinely coming in with the highest arrest totals in the district. The overtime pay associated with processing arrests certainly did not hurt his motivation.

Arrests for most misdemeanors could be adjudicated from the district, with the arrestee being issued a desk appearance ticket, or DAT, for a future court date. All felonies and some misdemeanors did not qualify for a DAT and were called "keepers", meaning the perpetrator remained in custody until arraignment, at which time the judge would either remand him to the Department of Correction, release the detainee on his or her own recognizance, or set bail. The arresting cop was also in a sense, in custody. During the 1980s, the arrest processing procedure was in the infant stages of reform, but it was still at times a very lengthy endeavor. During the 1970s, a cop could be lost for days processing an arrest, and the whole reason for the move to improve the process was to eliminate the exorbitant amounts of overtime cops accumulated due to the length of the arrest process. There was so much money to be made via arrest processing overtime that cops referred to keepers as "Trash for Cash", and "Collars for Dollars."

From the first day he put it on, Bobby Moylan loved being in uniform. As corny as it sounded, Bobby took the "protect and serve" police mandate seriously, and the uniform was the most visible manifestation of this credo. Veteran cops explained uniformed patrol work as 95% sheer boredom and 5% sheer terror. Bobby loved the action included in the 5%, but he also relished the other 95% of uniformed patrol. He loved walking his post and interacting with the people. To Bobby, wearing the uniform was akin to wearing a sign that read "I'm one of the good guys – I can help you." Whether it was providing directions, comforting a lost child, tending to a sick commuter, or providing an ear to someone having a bad day, Bobby never lost the thrill he received in just being out there every day in uniform, mixing it up with the public.

There is a paradox inherent in the philosophy of policing. Patrol is considered the backbone of the profession and is looked upon as the most basic and important aspect of police operations. For the overwhelming majority of cops, however, efforts to abandon this vital function begin on the first day of assignment to patrol duties, with the activities associated with patrol, such as arrests and summons writing, used as tools in the quest to obtain a specialized assignment as quickly as possible. Bobby Moylan was not in the overwhelming majority of cops. From his first day walking the platforms and passageways on the Broadway Nassau subway complex in lower Manhattan, Bobby fit into patrol work like the proverbial square peg in the square hole.

For most cops, the interim step before getting off patrol was getting assigned to a steady tour with steady days off. Bobby Moylan, however, was perfectly content to work the standard transit police rotating duty chart of four days working – two days off, rotating from days to midnights to afternoon tours of duty. As time went by, the other cops in the command would look at Bobby with a degree of curiosity. Why was he still rotating? What did he do to get punished to keep him rotating? No one with any time on the job was rotating, and they just couldn't accept the idea that Bobby preferred to work the rotating chart.

It is said that the more a person does something, the more proficient they become at the activity. Bobby Moylan was the poster boy for that axiom. Month after month and year after year he pounded the transit beat. It did not take many years for Bobby to become the unofficial resident expert on all things related to patrol. Bobby came to know the arrest paperwork and procedures better than the sergeant and lieutenant desk officers who were responsible for approving the paperwork. He also developed an expertise at spotting transit criminals, such as pickpockets, lush workers, bag openers, and sex abusers. Most importantly, he could look at a person and instantaneously tell that he was carrying a concealed firearm.

Bobby's positive attitude toward patrol was both refreshing and unique. The nature of policing makes it very easy to develop a cynical attitude toward both the public and the department administration. Not so with Bobby Moylan. He simply loved being a cop on patrol and his attitude reflected his love for the job.

Life on patrol taught Bobby a lot about himself. He was pleasantly surprised to find that he functioned at his highest level during an emergency. Crisis seemed to bring clarity, and situations never seemed to be clearer and the necessary action never more obvious than during a dangerous situation.

The first example of Bobby's clear headedness in a tight spot occurred when he had just over a year on the job. Bobby was working a 4 x 12 tour on a Wednesday night at the West 4th Street station in Greenwich Village. West 4th Street was a two man post and Bobby was assigned to work the shift with Joe Nolan. Joe was a tall, heavyset "Hairbag" with eighteen and a half years on the job. A hairbag is a term used for a grizzled veteran, but not in a complimentary sense. Whether legitimate or exaggerated, hairbags developed a persecution complex with a feeling that the only rewards garnered from aggressive police work were civilian complaints and department discipline. Hence, the typical hairbag resolved to do as little as possible while on patrol. For Joe Nolan, doing as little as possible translated into writing one summons a day, the minimum required to keep the commanding officer off his back and to ensure that he kept his steady 4 x 12 duty chart until he retired at the twenty-year mark.

On this Wednesday late afternoon, Joe's plan was to write one farebeat summons as soon as possible and then retire to the police room on the mezzanine for most of the remainder of the shift. As Joe and Bobby detrained onto the uptown upper IND platform at West 4th Street, Joe was in the classic hairbag uniform. His shirt was wrinkled and his shoes were unshined. It was also obvious that Joe had not found the time to shave before coming to work. Joe Nolan's personal hygiene did not bother Bobby Moylan, but there was something about his worn leather gun belt that did make him nervous. From the time they exited the door at District 4, Joe began a lament about the uselessness of the department authorized holster. Both Joe and Bobby wore the standard swivel type holster to house their Smith & Wesson, Model 10, 4-inch service revolvers. Joe continuously ranted that he found it impossible to get his gun out of the holster using only his right hand. Joe was referring to the difficulty he experienced with the "thumb break" locking mechanism on the holster. The lock had to be broken free with the thumb while the rest of the hand removed the gun from the holster. Bobby could feel a little bit of empathy to Joe's complaint because it was not easy to manipulate that thumb break correctly. On the other hand, Bobby had no problem operating his thumb break lock because he had practiced using it until he had acquired competency. As inconvenient as it might be to learn how to use the thumb break lock, its presence was critical. Transit cops, who spent vast amounts of time working in close quarters with masses of people, needed to maintain the security of their weapons. With the holster lock engaged, someone who made a sudden grab for a cop's gun would not be able to get the gun out of the holster.

Bobby tried to be diplomatic. "It just takes some practice Joe. Before you know it, it will be second nature."

Joe scoffed at this kid trying to tell him what is best. "I ain't got time for that kind of nonsense. Besides, I already found a solution – look." Joe effortlessly pulled his gun partially out of the holster several times.

Since he had obviously not magically acquired any expertise with the thumb break lock, Bobby asked the logical question. "How are you able to do that Joe?"

Joe smiled. "Easy, I removed the lock."

Bobby could not believe his ears as Joe explained. "I just worked on the lip of the lock with sandpaper until it no longer caught the cylinder. It's great, isn't it? Look how easy it comes out."
Joe repeated his partial unholstering of the gun.

Bobby was stunned with the demonstration, but he did not feel confident enough to call a senior man a moron. Of course, Joe could easily remove his gun from the holster without the presence of the lock, but so could anyone else.

Booth N83 was located below the subway entrance at Sixth Avenue and West 3rd Street. One of the anomalies of the West 4th Street station was that there was no entrance at West 4th Street – only West 3rd Street and West 8th Street. The turnstiles on the mezzanine fed two long declining passageways – leading to the uptown and downtown platforms, respectively. Joe and Bobby took off their hats and took up a position against the uptown passageway wall, approximately fifty feet from the turnstiles. The location may not have seemed very covert, but without their hats, and with the density of the scurrying afternoon rush hour crowd, the two cops were virtually invisible to anyone approaching the turnstiles.
"This shouldn't take long," Joe smirked.

Joe was correct because less than a minute later a figure vaulted the turnstiles and continued trotting into the uptown passageway. The figure came to an abrupt stop.

"Oh shit." The thirtyish male Hispanic was short, bald and muscular, with numerous prison tattoos visible on arms and shoulders uncovered by a blue tank top shirt.

Joe immediately went to work. "Gimme some ID."

The illustrated man handed Joe a social services identification card, and Joe began writing the summons. The male was not saying anything, but there was something about his agitated body language that was making Bobby uneasy. As Bobby stood watch a few feet away, he could not help but notice Joe's total tactical ineptness. Joe was completely engrossed in writing the summons and had never even given a precautionary glance at his subject. Even worse was Joe's stance. In the police academy, Bobby was taught to always face a subject with his body bladed so that his gun was protected from the subject by the rest of his body. Joe was standing at a right angle to the male with his holster containing his unlocked revolver fully exposed.

Everything happened so fast, but in Bobby's world, the scene had switched to slow motion mode. Without a word the tattooed man reached forward with his right hand and grabbed the grip of Joe's revolver. Joe's efforts to remove the locking mechanism had worked perfectly as the gun came right out of the holster. At the same instant the gun cleared leather with its barrel taking a path directly towards Joe's head, Bobby calmly reached forward with his left hand and grabbed the gun around the cylinder. That one moment seemed to go on forever as Bobby's hand clamped down on the cylinder with all the force he could generate. He could feel the cylinder straining to turn under his grip as the male pulled the trigger with all his strength. Joe Nolan reacted much like a deer caught in headlights – eyes as wide as silver dollars and no movement. Joe's frozen figure stared directly down the barrel of his own gun with Bobby's grip being the only factor saving him from a bullet between his enlarged eyes. Bobby kept the cylinder frozen with his left hand while his right hand correctly released the thumb break lock on his holster. In one fluid movement Bobby drew his revolver, punched it out to within an inch of the male's right temple, and used the slow steady trigger pull he had been taught in the academy. Blood and brains splattered the passageway wall. It was over.

Joe Nolan was finished as a cop. He applied for and eventually received a line of duty disability pension due to the psychological trauma of being so close to having his blood and brains decorating the passageway wall. Although Joe Nolan's career ended that day, the legend of Bobby Moylan was just beginning. Bobby received the department's Medal of Honor for saving Joe Nolan's life. The story was all over the media, touting Bobby as the hero subway cop. The Chief of the Transit Police visited District 4 to personally congratulate Bobby in the presence of the second platoon roll call. As a reward, the chief offered Bobby assignment to any specialized unit in the department. Bobby stunned the chief and the cops at roll call when he said his only request was to remain working patrol in District 4. The district commanding officer asked Bobby to at minimum pick a steady tour to work, but again he declined the offer, stating that he was very happy in the rotating chart.

Sometime around the time that the city's newest police hero was born, something else unexpected happened in the life of Bobby Moylan. Strangely, neither Bobby nor Mary could identify the precise moment that it happened. In retrospect, it probably should have been expected: They had worn the labels of neighbors, playmates, schoolmates, and best friends. They were inseparable. So why would it be unexpected when they added the label of lovers. They were married in 1980 and moved into a modest apartment in the same Jackson Heights neighborhood where the FSC had held court. Bobby and Mary were an ideal couple because they viewed most of life through the same prism. Their shared world view included a master plan for themselves that was far away from Jackson Heights, New York City.

Mary's older sister married a guy who was an executive with a medical supplies company on Long Island. When the company relocated to Winston-Salem, North Carolina, her sister also had to relocate. The couple settled in Mount Airy, a sleepy little town about forty miles northwest of Winston-Salem. Bobby and Mary visited her sister several times and fell in love with Mount Airy. The pace was slow, and the people were friendly. In other words, it was the antithesis of life in New York City. Bobby loved the fact that Mount Airy was the hometown of Andy Griffith and served as the inspiration for the fictitious television town of Mayberry. Bobby and Mary both agreed that Mount Airy was the perfect place to raise a family, so the plan was set. Bobby would complete his twenty years with the Transit Police and then retire with a nice pension, inflated as much as possible through all the overtime he could accumulate. By the time they started a family, the kids would still be young when Bobby retired and not traumatized by being torn away from established schools and friends.

0835 hours – The Last Day: Bobby turned to Steve. "C'mon, let's give this place the once over."

Bobby learned many years earlier that it was crucial to completely inspect a post the size of Grand Central as soon as possible after arriving. If they found a body lying behind a stairway, they would not face any scrutiny because they found it at the beginning of their tour. Any questions would have to be answered by the cops covering the post on the preceding tour.

They walked down the stairs and through the passageways that led to the 7-train platform. After walking the length of this island platform, they ascended an escalator that led to booth R-238, the street level entrance to the 7-train on 42nd Street near Third Avenue. Just as their heads rose to a level allowing a view of the booth, the first sight to behold was a gazelle-like vault over the turnstiles. The long, lean Black teen jumped right into them. He could have turned and jumped right back over and been in the wind, but instead he sighed and slightly smiled in recognition of his impending summons.

Even though there were still several hours remaining in his career, as far as Bobby was concerned, his summons writing career was over. Steve, on the other hand, was just beginning.

"Go ahead, write him." Bobby guided the teen to the side of the booth while Steve opened his memo book holder to retrieve a blank summons.

It was clear that the teen was going to be cooperative, but Bobby still stood several feet behind Steve and to his right keeping a watchful eye on the proceedings. So many things had changed over the years. It wasn't even really a summons that Steve was preparing. Years ago, the Transit Police had switched from writing *universal summonses returnable to criminal court for farebeat violations, to writing administrative summonses. TABS were Transit Adjudication Bureau notices of violations, and were returnable to the Transit Adjudication Bureau, a body set up by the Transit Authority specifically to adjudicate violations in the transit system. As Steve worked on the TAB Bobby reflected on how many other things had changed over his years on the job. He took a deep breath in acknowledgement of how so, so much had changed.*

Three minutes later the youth sprinted down the escalator with the pink copy of the TAB in his hand.

Steve closed his memo book holder and stuffed it into his back-right pocket. "I hope you don't mind me asking, but you seem to really love this job, so why are you pulling the pin?"

Bobby was amused by Steve's attempt to sound salty by using the common cop vernacular for retirement.

"I'm aging out." *The blank expression on Steve's face alerted Bobby that further explanation was required.* "New York State law mandates that police officers retire on their 63rd birthday - that's tomorrow for me."

Steve was genuinely surprised. Bobby's face had yet to lose its youthful character, and combined with the 6-foot 180-pound frame sculpted through thousands of miles walking, he could easily pass for fifty. In fact, if he got rid of the full head of gray hair no one would question that he was in his forties.

Steve was beginning to realize that he was entering a sensitive zone, and he wanted desperately to increase the comfort level of the conversation. "So, what have you got planned after tomorrow?"

Bobby's monotone "Dunno, haven't given it much thought." *only served to raise the discomfort level up another notch.*

Steve was trying to find some way out of this uncomfortable conversation. Three times he inhaled, and his mouth opened in a prelude to verbalization, but three times he caught himself before any words came out. Finally, he turned toward Bobby and meekly said "Happy birthday."

Bobby turned to make eye contact and smiled in recognition of someone desperately trying to find the right words in an impossible situation. "Thanks, Steve."

Bobby watched the people pass on 42nd Street, but his thoughts were elsewhere. "Plans" he thought. The irony was not lost. There was a time when his life was all about making plans.

1993 was the first time the prospect of retirement and relocation left the realm of the abstract and became something very real. With about two years until departure, real actions were necessary. Bobby and the family increased the number of trips to Mt. Airy to begin the process of house hunting in earnest. They also stopped in several times at the local school district, so they would have a thorough understanding of the process to enroll Kristin and Patrick. Bobby's brother-in-law had also introduced him to Tom McArdle. Tom was the chief of the fifteen-man Mt. Airy Police Department, and when he learned of Bobby's plans to relocate, he asked Bobby if he would be interested in joining his department. It seemed that one of Mt. Airy's finest was scheduled to retire in 1995, and Tom would welcome the opportunity to hire a seasoned police officer from New York City. Besides, Bobby was only going to be forty years old, and he still wanted to work. It might be fun to become a real-life version of Barney Fife.

As summer of 1993 turned to fall, Bobby would at times become melancholy when thinking about leaving the job he loved. He was going to miss all the people he had worked with over the years. Bobby was especially going to miss his current partner, Joey Galeno. The old saying "opposites attract" must have been true because Bobby and Joey were about as dissimilar as two people could be. Bobby was a stoic, mature, measured Irishman, while Joey was a loud, confident, sometimes arrogant Italian. Their partnership began in 1988 and even though retirement was still over a year away, Bobby was already feeling somber about leaving his partner.

Tempering Bobby's impending loss of the job he loved was the love of a new area of life – fatherhood. If he wasn't working,

Bobby was with Kristin and Patrick. Bobby was well into an especially enjoyable time of life because at six and four years of age, he was now fully engaged in being a playmate for his kids. On days off Bobby could be found driving throughout Queens searching for a new park with a new playset for the kids to enjoy. Every day when he entered through the apartment door from work, except after a 4 x 12 shift, he was greeted by laughing, smiling faces, with his next stop being the living room carpet for several hours of play time. Life was good for the Moylan family and only getting better.

Saturday, December 18, 1993 seemed to be little more than routine. Bobby Moylan and Joey Galeno patrolled the platforms, mezzanines, passageways, and stairways of Grand Central on the day tour as they had for the previous five years. It was too close to Christmas to commit the scrooge-like act of writing summonses, and with no rush hour to contend with, the only activities of the day were likely to be some aided cases and disorderly persons left over from holiday parties that began on Friday evening. Their main focus during patrol was going over their own holiday preparations. For Joey, this was the most important Christmas of his life. The present he had purchased for Marie was a diamond ring, which he hoped would update her status from girlfriend to fiancé. Joey was uncharacteristically nervous over the impending presentation of the ring. Even though he and Marie had been together for a little over two years, the subject of marriage had never really been discussed. As far as Joey was concerned, the ring was a big jump into uncharted territory.

For Bobby, this was a Christmas he could truly look forward to. He and Joey were in squad 6R. After five years as partners he had brainwashed Joey into remaining in a rotating squad. Since most of the major holidays, including Christmas, fell on regular days off, this year, squad 6R was considered the holiday squad. As far as Bobby was concerned, the schedule for Christmas 1993 could not be better. He and Joey would work a set of midnight tours and finish at 7:50 AM on Christmas Eve. They would be off on Christmas Day and the 26th, and did not have to be back to work until the afternoon of the 27th. Normally, every extra cent that came into Bobby's possession went into the bank as part of the North Carolina plan, but this year he made an exception. Kristin and Patrick had entered the years where Christmas was pure magic, and Bobby readily admitted he went way overboard in spending on their gifts.

At 3:30 PM Bobby and Joey stepped into the sparsely populated rear car of a downtown 4-train. Union Square and District 4 was the next stop, but they lingered on the Union Square platform for several minutes before slowly making their way toward the district door. The PBA contract allowed for ten minutes wash up time, but the quickest way to command the wrath of a desk officer was to enter the command earlier than 3:50 PM. An incoming platoon was much like a lava flow, very slowly progressing along its path. The cops would arrive at Union Square from all patrol areas of the district and then very slowly make their way toward the district with the goal of having the first cop burst through the door in front of the desk officer at exactly 3:50 PM. Bobby and Joey were the last two cops on the entry line and Joey paid no attention when Lt. Hansen told Bobby to stand by.

As the incoming platoon filed single file along the narrow walkway bordered by the wall of the command and the railing separating the administrative area, Joey's cop instincts picked up an unsettling feeling in the air. The administrative area was generally a cluster of noise and activity, especially around shift change. As Joey tossed his memo book into the wooden box he noticed an eerie silence on the opposite side of the railing. Beyond the silence, what troubled Joey most were the glazed looks in the eyes of everyone in the administrative area. Joey continued into the muster room, but before he could reach the locker room door he barely detected Sgt. Kowalski hailing him from behind in a voice better suited for the inside of a church

"Don't get changed yet Joey. I have to tell you something."

The nature of police work can routinely open the dark side of a person. As a result, cops regularly indulge themselves in very inappropriate, taboo, dark humor and subjects. For example, on one particularly boring day on patrol, Bobby and Joey debated how many five-year old children attacking them could they handle before being overpowered. Due mainly to his more macho instincts, Joey stated that the number was unlimited and that the kids would never overpower him. Bobby, however, was more pragmatic. He reasoned that after 25-30 kids were hanging on him, fatigue and the inability to move would overcome him. Only cops could have a serious debate on a subject like that.

On more than one occasion Bobby and Joey theorized that taking a bullet in the head was likely painless as you would probably never even feel it before everything went black. At that precise moment inside the commanding officer's office, Bobby Moylan realized that his theory was true. His current life had just come to an end and he was numb. He couldn't feel a thing.

The wakes became a political circus. Regardless of their true levels of sincerity, everyone right up to and including the mayor of New York City filed into Conway's on Northern Blvd. to pay their respects and offer their condolences to Bobby Moylan. The media could not have asked for a more heart wrenching and political story. A Queens mother driving home after Christmas shopping with her two beautiful young children is blasted by a drunk driver who blew through a red light at 60 mph. To further politicize the incident, the drunk driver had two prior DWI convictions along with a suspended license. Every politician and community leader wanted a chance to get in front of the plethora of cameras to express their outrage.

On Christmas Eve, the three coffins were lowered into the grave at Calvary Cemetery and the rest of the city went back to the business of celebrating Christmas. Bobby Moylan was still as numb as the moment Captain Doyle had broken the news to him. Numb was probably the best description of bobby's condition. After all, he was a cop and Irish, both identities making it all but impossible to show emotions outwardly.

The sun was high in the sky on a cloudless day. Bobby stood alone on the corner watching the approaching red Taurus. As the car slowly passed him the kids beaming faces were vivid in the front and rear passenger windows. Mary's face was not as clear in the driver's seat, but she appeared to be smiling.

"Hi daddy" both cheered and waved from the passing vehicle.

He begged Mary to stop but she couldn't hear him. Along with the booming crash and ball of yellow flame, he could hear the faint cries of "help us daddy."

He woke up shaking in a pool of sweat. An hour later Bobby sat on a bench in Gorman Park, across the street from his apartment. It was New Year's Day, 1994, and at that moment the park was a microcosm of his life – dismal and empty. His light windbreaker was totally inappropriate for the frigid temperature, but still shaken from the dream, he felt no chill as he stared at the swings and slides where he had watched Kristen and Patrick play countless times. Mary's` sister had gone back to North Carolina and at that moment on that bench, with only a couple of squirrels to keep him company, he never felt more alone. As the squirrels pranced around the bench Bobby understood the reality that emptiness was an actual physical pain - just as real as a migraine or the pain in the lower back or hips.

Captain Doyle told Bobby to stay out of work as long as he needed. What he needed, however, was not to stay away from District 4. In the simple life of Bobby Moylan two things gave him peace and pleasure - his family and being a cop. His family had suddenly and permanently been ripped away, so all he had left was being a cop. He would report back to work in the morning.

Every cop and supervisor inside District 4 at the beginning of the second platoon was sincerely trying to do the right thing. The awkward nature of the moment was due to the fact that no one knew exactly what the right thing was. Some tried to bury Bobby in emotional embraces while others went out of their way to avoid him from fear of doing the wrong thing. Joey did his best to treat the situation as just another day on patrol. They detrained onto the northbound Lexington Avenue platform and walked up the stairs to Grand Central's massive mezzanine. They took up a vantage point next to the turnstiles at booth R241 and watched the masses of the morning rush hour scurry past. Bobby took a couple of deep, deliberate breaths. He was aware of the reality of the situation. He was like a hard-core junkie who had just gotten a fix. The heroin no longer provided a high, but it was needed to keep the intense pain away. As Bobby continued to breathe in the subway environment, the intense pain gradually subsided.

1995 was the planned year of retirement, but there was no way Bobby Moylan could give up his fix. Joey had moved on. Due mostly to the impressive arrest record involving gun collars rung up under Bobby's tutelage, he had been assigned to the Street Crime Unit. The Transit Police Department had no Street Crime Unit, but a monumental event in New York City policing took place in 1995.

For approximately fifty years, New York City had been policed by three distinct police departments. The New York City Police Department patrolled the streets of the city while the Transit Police was responsible for the subways and the Housing Police patrolled the city's public housing projects. The pay, benefits, rank structure, and uniforms were identical, with the exception of each department's shoulder patch. After years of political infighting, on April 2, 1995 the Transit Police Department ceased to exist when it was merged into the NYPD. A couple of months later the Housing Police was also merged leaving one police department in the city containing both a transit bureau and a housing bureau. For ambitious transit cops like Joey, being a member of the NYPD opened up a whole new world of opportunities and he quickly jumped into street crime.

As far as Bobby Moylan was concerned, when it became known that he had no plans to retire, everyone wanted to do something for him. Very few cops with ten years on the job were still out pounding a uniformed subway beat, no less a cop approaching twenty years. The seemingly endless barrage came from all angles "Get off patrol" "Work in roll call inside the district" "work in an administrative unit at One Police Plaza" "work on the wheel at Transit Bureau HQ" "At least work in plainclothes in an anti-crime unit". All Bobby Moylan wanted and needed to do was to keep patrolling Grand Central. To get Captain Doyle off his back he grudgingly accepted one of his offers. He would still patrol Grand Central in uniform, but he would do it while working steady day tours with weekends off. Maybe now everyone would just leave him alone.

The fix he received from patrol only lasted for eight hours a day, and Bobby realized he would have to find other outlets for pain relief. Aside from an occasional beer, he had never been a big drinker, and he was determined not to reinforce an all too common Irish and police stereotype by sinking into a bottle to anesthetize his pain. Of one thing however, he was certain. He had to get out of the apartment. Every time he turned around he was greeted with a reminder of Mary and the kids. Bobby had not touched the kid's rooms, so conditions were exactly as they had been when they went Christmas shopping on that last morning. He thought he would find some comfort in this kind of suspended animation. To the contrary, it tore him apart even worse, as he could actually smell Kristin and Patrick on their clothes, sheets, blankets, and pillows. It was just too much to bear. He had to get out of the apartment and he only had two parameters to meet in a new place. First, it had to be closer to District 4 than the Jackson Heights apartment and second, it had to be walking distance from the subway.

At 6'2" the blond haired, blue eyed, fair skinned Bjorn Nielsen was every inch a Nordic male of Swedish ancestry. A twelve-year veteran and a member of the District 4 plainclothes anti-crime unit, Bjorn was affectionately known in the command as the Jamaican slum lord. This rather odd nickname was the result of his industrious nature. Much like a stereotypical new arrival from Jamaica, Bjorn was holding down several different jobs. Besides his full-time police career, Bjorn was somehow finding the time to drive a cab, work as a security guard, caddy at an exclusive golf course, and work an adult newspaper route. Bjorn sank every extra cent earned from his various revenue streams into real estate, and he was presently the owner of three residential properties in Brooklyn. The less than desirable locations of his homes combined with the multiple jobs gave rise to the Jamaican slum lord moniker. Bjorn was surprised and reluctant when Bobby inquired about the third-floor studio walk up he had for rent on Havemeyer Street.

He was unsuccessfully fishing for the right words before finally admitting "Bobby, it's a shitty area. You don't want that"

Bobby didn't care. The apartment was near the subway and in the shadow of the Williamsburg Bridge, which made it closer to Manhattan and District 4 that the Jackson Heights apartment.

In the days and weeks after the tragedy he had been visited by numerous counselors and chaplains from the NYPD, the Transit Police, the Transit Authority, and the local community. They all meant well, but Bobby failed to see how they did him any good. At least they had enough professionalism not to say "I know how you must feel." He lost count of how many times he had to endure that line. As with most everything else, Bobby held his emotions in check until he let loose on poor Stan Brodsky.

Stan had utilized a week of his 1993 vacation and all of his 1994 vacation so he could take his family to Florida to visit his parents over the holidays. Since cops are allotted 27 vacation days in a year, the second platoon roll call on February 11, 1994 was the first time Stan had seen Bobby Moylan since he lost his family.

Stan approached Bobby in the muster room with moist eyes and wrapped his arms around Bobby's shoulders. "I'm so sorry brother. I know how you must feel."

Bobby had unknowingly reached his breaking point. He lurched back to free himself from Stan's embrace.

"Do you Stan? Do you know how I feel? Were your wife and kids killed by a drunk?"

There was complete silence in the crowded muster room and Stan was stunned

"Don't ever tell me again that you know how I feel because you don't. Nobody knows how I feel."

Bobby departed District 4 without standing roll call and headed for Grand Central. Seconds after he was outside he was sorry for his outburst. Stan was a friend who had only good intentions. At the end of the shift Bobby was the one initiating the embrace as he apologized to Stan.

One of the chaplains, he thought it was the one from the Transit Authority, had said something that stayed with him. This chaplain told Bobby that the terrible fact of life was that the pain from losing his family would never go away, but that the deep grief would lessen. He did not understand the chaplain at the time but a few years later his comments were making sense. The pain and grief he felt in those immediate weeks following the loss had to subside because it would be impossible to carry on with daily life activities if it did not. If that intense grief did not lessen Bobby would surely have eaten his gun. So, the pain continued, but some of the edge was taken off with the passage of time. Passage of time, however, did not effect that dream, as Bobby was haunted by the recurring nightmare almost every night.

1996 became 1997 and the pain was still with him along with that horrible dream. There were minor differences in each dream, but the nightmare always ended with the helpless voices of two small children crying "Help us daddy."

Uniformed patrol was the best therapy he had, but Bobby desperately needed another source of pain relief. He discovered that source in a very unlikely manner. The Bedford Avenue station was not his nearest subway access. In fact, the L train at Bedford Avenue was over nine blocks away from his Havemeyer Street apartment. The long walk, however, was well worth the convenience of the L train. Upon boarding at Bedford Avenue, the train travelled directly into Manhattan and stopped at First and Third Avenues, before arriving at Union Square and District 4. The train ride was no more than ten minutes.

One beautiful fall afternoon in 1997 Bobby departed District 4 after his shift and followed his usual path to the island platform of the L train. Two minutes after he arrived on the platform, PA announcements alerted riders that L train service to Brooklyn was suspended. Being a transit cop, Bobby knew he had several options to get home. He could have connected to the J train to get to Marcy Avenue – the station that was actually closest to his apartment. He could have taken the 7-train into Queens and then re-connected with the L line. He could have simply walked back into District 4 and waited for L train service to resume. Bobby selected none of these options. He ascended from the subway station and sat on a bench in Union Square Park, contemplating the beauty of this late afternoon. Suddenly, a completely new option for getting home was formulating in his brain. Bobby rose from the bench and stretched. He began leisurely walking south through the park and onto Broadway. His leisurely walk took him from Broadway to East Houston Street to Delancey Street, and onto the Williamsburg Bridge. 3.5 miles later his stroll terminated at his Havemeyer Street apartment.

    Bobby could not put his finger on exactly what it was about the walk that had a positive effect, but the fact of the matter was it made him feel good. He knew little of the stress relieving endorphins that are released into the brain during exercise. All he knew was that his head was clear and he developed a sense of peace when walking. Most importantly, for that hour and twenty minutes that he was mobile, the pain lessened.

    From that day forward, Bobby Moylan never stopped walking. He began leaving early enough to walk the 3.5 miles to District 4 and on his days off he would spend hours walking through the streets and parks of Brooklyn and Queens. The walking naturally had a tremendous positive impact on him physically as well. Bobby had always been in half way decent shape, but he was never much of an exercise or diet guru. Like many cops, he could afford to lose some of the 220 pounds from his six-foot frame. Two years after he began walking Bobby leveled out at around 180 pounds without any changes to his diet.

    Bobby Moylan's twentieth anniversary on the job came and went with no recognition or fanfare. What was supposed to have been the beginning of a new life in North Carolina turned out to be another drizzling, lonely day with only his patrol time at Grand Central, as well as his pre and post work walk providing any peace. To Bobby, the calendar became a car slowly picking up speed. The days quickly became weeks, then months, then years. In what seemed like the blink of an eye, Bobby was faced with a stark reality.

New York State law required police officers to retire on their sixty third birthday, and this milestone was fast approaching. What would he do without the job? Of course, he could still walk, but how many hours a day could he roam the streets and parks of the city? The day of his approaching 63rd birthday seemed like a dark abyss, with nothing beyond that point. It was now more than twenty-two years since the day he lost his family, and Bobby had not progressed emotionally since that dark day. He had the job and his walking – that was it. It was because of the peace that uniform patrol brought him, he never even thought about taking a sergeant's test, and he kept refusing the continual offers from the various commanding officers of District 4 to work in a specialized assignment. Bobby's social life was virtually non-existent. He went out occasionally for a few beers, usually at a job-related racket, but the clear majority of his non-working, walking life was spent inside his apartment, watching TV or reading a book.

Of course, Bobby Moylan was human, and over the years he had several liaisons with females – a neighbor he met while walking in a local park and two female cops from District 4 – but there was never a girlfriend. After all the years he could just not bring himself to enter into a serious relationship with another woman. Bobby was certainly smart enough to realize he had serious issues to address. The inability to consider a female relationship and the fact that he was still regularly tormented by the recurring dream were certainly indicative of the need for professional assistance. No matter how bad things got, however, Bobby Moylan came from an Irish-American police world where psychiatry and psychology were simply not an option.

Although not romantic in nature, there was one female relationship Bobby Moylan entered into. Ellen Tomlinson was a dear friend. After Joey Galeno moved on, Bobby only had one other steady partner, and that was Ellen. As a rookie, Ellen underwent some tough times adjusting to life on the job. Bobby Moylan took Ellen under his wing and guided her on the path to becoming an effective patrol cop. It was obvious that Ellen was enamored with

Bobby and Bobby had strong feelings for Ellen as well. His never-ending grief, however, prevented him from acting on these feelings. In fact, it was because he felt so strongly about Ellen that he would not simply add her name as one of his female liaisons. Bobby and Ellen maintained their "best friends" relationship through the years as Ellen rose through the ranks of the department. Now, as Bobby's last day loomed, Inspector Ellen Tomlinson was the Commanding Officer of Transit Borough Manhattan.

1410 hours – The Last Day: The time had transitioned to the PM side of the day, as the final few sands of Bobby Moylan's career timer were draining. Bobby caught sight of someone inside the large glass window on the main concourse. He stopped and motioned for Steve Bryant to accompany him to the window.

Aaron Brown rearranged merchandise on the three levels of shelves. Bobby was glad Aaron was working because it would not have seemed right to end his career without saying a proper goodbye to his friend.

The New York Transit Museum Gallery Annex and Store opened on September 14, 1993 at Grand Central, in the terminal's main concourse. The Gallery housed a transit-oriented gift shop as well as a space for rotating temporary exhibitions. The Annex was the site of the Transit Museum's annual "Holiday Train Show", where an operating model train layout was displayed for the public. Fifty-eight-year-old Aaron Brown had been the manager of the Gallery since it opened. Bobby first met Aaron during early December of 1993, when he brought Kristin and Patrick into Grand Central on his day off to see the new Holiday Train Show.

Bobby found Aaron to be very personable, so during patrol he would routinely stop into the Gallery and say hello. It was a couple of weeks after a 1994 shoplifting caper in the store that Bobby learned a startling fact about Aaron. Five years earlier, Aaron Brown had lost his ten-year-old daughter to a drunk driver. Bobby felt devastated for Aaron, but he also felt a sense of excitement. Finally, he had found someone who really could understand how he felt. Although they never socialized or spoke anywhere other than inside the Gallery, Bobby treasured his friendship with Aaron. Conversations with Arron Brown were the closest that Bobby Moylan was ever going to get to actual therapy. Bobby never missed a day of dropping in for a few minutes of conversation, so it was only appropriate that Aaron be part of his patrol agenda on the last day.

The sight of Bobby Moylan entering the Gallery brought Aaron Brown's work on the shelves to an immediate halt as he called out his usual greeting,

"My brother from another mother," he happily announced, in ironic reference to the fact that Bobby was White while he was African-American.

Steve Bryant stood to the side while Bobby and Aaron embraced. "I was beginning to think you were going to retire without saying goodbye to me."

Bobby shook his head and completed the accepted manly hug with a few pats to Aaron's back. "No way brother. I have to say goodbye to you."

After several minutes of reminiscing, Bobby began to make his final exit, this time with a traditional handshake. "We have to get back on patrol. Take care brother."

Steve was already through the Gallery's door and Bobby was in the doorway when Aaron brought his exit to a halt. "Hey, you want to come work here?"

Bobby held the door open and turned toward Aaron with a perplexed look on his face. "What?"

"Sure," Aaron continued. "You can work full time or part time. We will work out whatever hours are good for you."

Bobby laughed while still in the doorway. He had no plans past his end of tour today, but he certainly never even thought about the possibility of working at the Gallery. "I don't know Aaron – maybe – I'll stop in next week."

The Gallery door closed, but quickly reopened with Bobby's head protruding inward.

"Thanks for the offer brother. I don't think you realize how important our talks have been to me."

Aaron Brown smiled. "I know you don't know how important our talks have been to me. Why do you think I offered you a job."

They both laughed as Bobby closed the door again. Bobby and Steve leisurely made their way back to the main mezzanine. Bobby's career – his life as far as he was concerned – could now be measured in minutes.

CHAPTER 5: THE LIEUTENANT

0605 hours – The Last Day: Lt. Joey Galeno activated a short burst of the siren on his unmarked Chevy Caprice. The siren stirred the armed security guard from his blissful sleep, and he lazily yawned as he pressed the button that lowered the Delta Barrier. As Joey drove past the bullet proof security booth he returned the wave of the guard, who was a retired NYPD cop he had worked with several years earlier. A minute later Joey eased the Caprice into his assigned parking space in the underground parking garage of 26 Federal Plaza in lower Manhattan. At this early hour the parking garage was as empty as the office of the JTTF. Joey fished his key ring out of his pocket and opened the door labeled COMMANDING OFFICER. He had a busy day ahead and he needed some quiet time to go over the status of his undercover operation in Queens. His undercover was coming in to brief him at 12:00 PM, and he needed to have his work wrapped up in time to be at District 4 at 4:00 PM for Bobby Moylan's walk out.

Joey poured himself a freshly brewed cup of coffee before settling in behind his desk. He opened a manila folder marked QUEENS 17-056 and flipped through the enclosed investigative reports. Joey had hoped to hide his absurd undercover agent in a meaningless mosque in Queens, but that was no longer possible. As improbable as it was, this mosque in Corona with a peaceful Imam and no prior history of radical activity was now hot. Three weeks earlier, Mustafa Hussein, a trusted informant from Joey's days in the Street Crime Unit, had contacted Joey with some startling information. An associate of Mustafa's, a member of a new cell, was looking to flip. Mohammed Islam explained to Mustafa that his conscious would not allow him to continue with the cell. Apparently, conscience was not Mohammed's only motivation, as he also wanted $10,000.00 for his information.

Joey stared for several seconds at the photo of Mohammed Islam. This was one scary looking dude, with the sinister sneer on his face and jagged scar running down the length of his right cheek. Joey studied the debriefing report. Mustafa insisted that a wealthy Qatari financier was going to move a small nuclear device into an east coast port via a cargo ship. New York Harbor was high on the *list of potential targets because Islam provided additional intelligence that the financier was working with two Qatari brothers named Mosaab. Further investigation revealed that Waheed and Rashid Mosaab owned a variety store in Corona, and that they were members of the nearby Masjid Al-Falah mosque. Joey's sole intent had been trying to keep his ridiculous undercover out of trouble when he assigned him to get inside that mosque. The worm had now completely turned, and Joey was dependent on getting solid information from his UC.*

The twelve o'clock meeting was going to be a high noon showdown. Either the UC was going to bring him some solid intelligence, or he would relieve him from duty – for his own safety and the safety of the population of New York City. The situation in Queens had him on edge. Joey closed the folder and smiled. His thoughts had momentarily drifted to later in the day. He shook his head in disbelief. Bobby Moylan was actually leaving the job after forty-two years. It just didn't seem possible to have an NYPD that did not include Bobby Moylan. Joey shook his head again. His 29 years on the job paled next to his great friend. Wow, he thought. had it really been 29 years.

10:30 on a Saturday night and groups of young bar hoppers began to flash their IDs at a popular Bay Ridge club. They were the regulars, the Italian Bensonhurst teens who came back weekend after weekend to socialize and flirt.

The girls, in their flare jeans, tight shirts, chunky boots and little black bags, looked like they just stepped out of Contempo Casuals. Their long, curly dark hair stiff with hair spray; their make-up, flawless, and their fingers, circled in flashy gold rings. Some stood shyly in the corner while others headed straight to the dance floor, jeering at each other in fierce competition.

The guys were modern versions of Danny Zuko and company in "Grease" wearing sweaters from Structure, baggy jeans and black boots underneath leather coats or bubble jackets. Large gold or silver chains surrounded their necks, and they wore their hair short, stiffly gelled or pushed back and spiky.

By midnight, they and their clones had packed the place, elbowing their way past each other to greet their friends. They gave each other "pounds" or kisses on the cheek. The DJ pumped up the volume.

Although many immigrant groups such as Russians, Asians, Greeks, and Arabs have been moving to Bensonhurst since the 1980s, on this Saturday night in 1986 the neighborhood was strictly Italian. It seemed like every young Italian male on the dance floor was a wannabe wise guy who had an Uncle Louie who was connected. Thankfully for twenty-one-year-old Joseph "Joey" Galeno, he had an uncle Paulie who was a detective with the NYPD. Joey loved his old man, but he had no desire to follow in his footsteps and take over the family barber shop. It was uncle Paulie who was the life of every family gathering with his tales of fighting crime in the big city. As Joey approached adulthood, he wanted what Uncle Paulie had, including the pinky ring, fat cigar, designer suit, and meticulously coiffed hair.

The stars and stripes were joined by the flags of New York City and the NYPD above the campus deck at 235 East 20th Street, marking the entrance to the New York City Police Academy. The eight-story structure with attached gymnasium dominated the landscape on the north side of 20th Street between Second and Third Avenues in the Grammercy Park section of Manhattan.

Joey Galeno emerged from the subway at Union Square at 6:45 AM and began the five-block walk to the academy. He walked north on Third Avenue and when he turned the corner on 20th Street, he stopped dead in his tracks. It was now 6:55 AM and the report time to be sworn in was not until 8 AM, but there before him was a single file line of approximately two hundred young men and women that stretched from the academy entrance almost to Third Avenue.

The momentary shock wore off and Joey took his place on the back of the line. By the time 7:45 rolled around, the line had turned on Third Avenue and had reached 22nd Street. At 7:55 a very tall, thin, baby faced male walked west along the sidewalk, apparently searching for the end of the line.

"Andy?" The tall male had obviously recognized an old friend and embraced the male in front of Joey on the line.

After the greeting and a few seconds of small talk, the male in front of Joey turned toward him, "I haven't seen this guy in years. Do you mind if he gets in the line with me?"

Joey could care less, "Knock yourself out my friend." Joey made a sweeping gesture with his right arm indicating that it was okay for the tall male to move into the line.

Moments later the line began to inch forward. It was 8 AM and Joey's NYPD career was about to begin. As he inched his way east along the sidewalk he could not help but wonder how long it would take him to obtain a gold detective's shield to go along with the pinky ring and cigars he planned on buying. As he got within view of the entrance, Joey could see several academy staff members standing on the sidewalk, funneling the new recruits into the building. Some of the staff were making notes on clipboards while others were barking orders to the new recruits as they passed. Joey was curious about one staff member in particular because it was not apparent to him what his function was. This tall, husky uniformed officer who looked to have at least twenty years on the job seemed to be making some type of count. As the recruits shuffled slowly toward the entrance, this crusty veteran was walking along the line, tapping the recruits on their shoulders and counting off numbers. As Joey drew closer to the front of the line he could finally make out the count. The veteran cop would count off seven recruits, then two, then one. He then repeated that count for the next ten recruits in the line. As much as he tried, Joey could not venture a guess as to the meaning of this 7-2-1 count off.

Joey was almost at the entrance when a new count began. The veteran cop began his count and reached seven when he tapped the shoulder of the tall recruit directly in front of Joey. Joey's tap received a one from the cop, with two going to the female directly behind Joey. A very short muscular male who was next in line received a one, and then the counting sequence began again. The line walked single file into the building and up the stairs to the fourth floor. As Joey emerged from the stairwell he could see that number's 1-7 in his group were being ushered into a nearby classroom. He and the female behind him, however, were diverted to a different room. Joey noticed that the short male who made up the tenth recruit in their count was sent to still another location. Joey sat and waited as the room slowly filled with new pairs of recruits.

At 9 AM a uniformed sergeant entered the room led by a police officer who shouted "Attention!" The recruits sprung to their feet and stood in silence. The sergeant stood at a podium and momentarily took in the sight of the recruits in front of him.

"Be seated." A big smile came to the sergeant's face as he made his welcoming statement, "Ladies and gentlemen, welcome to the New York City Transit Police Department."

"Transit Police?" Joey was stunned. There had to be some mistake. He didn't sign up to be a transit cop. Over the next twenty minutes Joey did not hear one word of the sergeant's speech. There had to be some mistake. Finally, the sergeant said someone would be in to begin all their paperwork as he began to leave the classroom. Again, the room came to attention, but Joey continued out of the room behind the sergeant.

"Excuse me sir, could I have a brief word – It's real important."

The sergeant spun to face Joey,

"I think there's been a mistake made here. I'm not supposed to be transit."

The sergeant chuckled. "You and about three hundred other transit recruits think the same thing." The sergeant continued, "I guess you never hear of tri-agency hiring, have you?"

The blank look on Joey's face indicated to the sergeant that an explanation was in order.

"Since 1982 the city has been using tri-agency hiring and training. Everyone takes one police test and all the recruits from NYPD, transit and housing train together in the academy. In tri-agency hiring, a 7:2:1 ration is used. For every ten police officers hired, seven go to NYPD, two to transit, and one to housing. Didn't you notice the cop on the sidewalk making a count? That's what he was doing. It was just the luck of the draw. You just happened to be one of the two allocated to transit in your group of ten."

The sergeant didn't even wait for the next question that he knew would be coming.

"If you don't want transit, you can leave, and go on the back of the eligible list. Maybe at some point your name will be reached again, but you know what?" The wide grin appeared on the sergeant's face. "You might get transit again."

Just then it hit Joey like a bolt of lightning. That tall, skinny jerk that he welcomed into the line in front of him. That guy became number seven in the group, forcing Joey into transit. If he had not been so magnanimous, he would be NYPD.

Newly graduated transit police officer Joey Galeno arrived at District 4 carrying his uniforms and equipment, as well a bad attitude. Six months in the police academy had done nothing to ease the sting of being assigned to the Transit Police Department. In fact, his academy training only fueled his negative attitude. Joey considered much of the training to be a tease. He received training in felony car stops, writing moving violation summonses, and investigating residential burglaries – training he would never utilize while stuck in the hole of the New York City subway system.

Two weeks after arriving at District 4, Joey's morale was still sinking – if that was possible. During his brief time on patrol, Joey's attitude towards the Transit Police had only been reinforced with assignment to a parade of hairbags whose idea of being a training officer consisted of showing him where the best cooping rooms were located.

On a Thursday evening, Joey was in a particularly foul mood as he entered the district. He was returning after two refreshing regular days off to begin his rotation of four midnight shifts. Before entering the locker room, he paused at the railing where a wooden shelf displayed the roll call assignments for the tour. Joey's eyes scanned the sheets until he found GALENO. He was assigned to work at Broadway-Lafayette with MOYLAN. Joey knew nothing about Police Officer Moylan, other than he was a veteran in the command, and likely just another in a long line of hairbags.

At 12:30 AM, Joey Galeno and Bobby Moylan stood on the quiet mezzanine adjacent to token booth N-78. They had been on the post for a half hour but had not spoken a word to each other. The silence was broken by two quick bursts of static on both their radios. Bobby Moylan immediately keyed the microphone he had clipped to the epaulet on his right shoulder.

"By the booth."

Joey shrugged his shoulders. "What's going on?"

"The sergeant is looking for us. That was him clicking on the radio".

"Great," Joey thought. "More great transit police work."

Sgt. John Henry Johnson emerged from the darkness of the stairway. Sgt. Johnson was a huge Black man who seemed to always be sporting a huge smile. Twenty-two years on the job had apparently not soured his attitude.

"Good evening boys. Beautiful night, isn't it?"

Bobby exchanged a salute with the sergeant while Joey followed suit with his own half-hearted version of a salute.

"Let me give you a scratch." Sgt. Johnson used the police vernacular for inspecting and signing a cop's memo book.

Bobby and Joey removed their memo book holders from their rear pants pockets and paged through their memo books, searching for the current page.

"You got the best teacher tonight kid. I hope you're learning from him."

"Oh yeah sarge, I'm learning a lot." The dripping sarcasm in Joey's voice was unmistakable, and Sgt. Johnson certainly received the message.

He was staring at Joey while addressing Bobby. "Do me a favor. Go upstairs to the car and get my pen."

"Sure," Bobby said while noting the presence of a pen conspicuously sticking out of the sergeant's shirt pocket.

When Bobby Moylan disappeared into the stairway, a transformation took place. Sgt. Johnson's large grin was replaced by an intimidating snarl. He loomed menacingly over Joey, his right index finger dangerously close to the tip of Joey's nose. At this moment, the last thing on Joey's mind was sarcasm. Joey Galeno was 6'1" tall and a well-built 225 pounds, but he looked and felt tiny next to the snarling Sgt. Johnson.

"Look shithead, I know all about you. You're mad at the world because you got transit. Poor you. If you don't like it – quit!"

Sgt. Johnson's eyes were widening and Joey was actually beginning to feel a bit nervous.

"Bobby Moylan knows more about policing than 99% of those gutter guards in the street. If you can't lower yourself to learn about transit policing, at least have the common decency to show some respect to a Medal of Honor recipient."

Sgt. Johnson might just as well slapped Joey across the face because the effect was the same.

Joey was stunned. "Medal of honor? But he's not wearing....."

Sgt. Johnson cut him off. "Bobby Moylan don't wear no medals or breast bars. That's who he is, and maybe – just maybe – you could learn something from him."

The jingling of keys from a gun belt announced the imminent arrival of Bobby Moylan from the stairway. The sergeant's huge grin returned as he quickly signed both memo books with his new pen. Moments later, the sergeant was gone and Bobby and Joey again stood silently on the mezzanine. Joey really didn't know what to do. The sergeant had shaken him, but his opinion of the Transit Police had not changed.

Bobby and Joey exchanged pleasant personal small talk as they went to the street to walk to the Bleecker Street side of the station complex. They emerged from the stairway just in time to see a White male with long dark hair crawl under the turnstile.

Joey reacted "Hey yo – come here – now!"

The male was about thirty years old and wore a dirty, baggy light jacket with equally dirty sweater and baggy pants, complemented by torn sneakers. With no train arriving, the male was trapped. He could either jump down to the tracks or comply with Joey.

Joey approached the male while barking additional orders. "Let me see some ID – now!"

The man began to reach toward his right pants pocket. Bobby Moylan nearly knocked Joey down while rushing by. In one fluid movement Bobby grabbed the man's right arm and pulled it away from his waistband. As the movement continued, Bobby used his control of the man's arm to force him down face first to the concrete platform.

Bobby straddled the man's back while calling out to Joey. "Gimme your cuffs."

Joey was trying to figure out what had just happened, while quickly complying with Bobby's request. Once rear cuffed, Bobby lifted the prisoner to his feet.

"This is how you handle a farebeat?" Joey's sarcasm had made a return appearance.

Bobby reached into the prisoner's waistband area and removed something. "No, this is how I handle a man with a gun."

Bobby displayed a silver 9mm semi-automatic pistol. For the second time in an hour, Joey was stunned.

Bobby continued, "Your cuffs are on him – You take the collar. Not bad – a month out of the academy and you got a gun collar."

"Thanks," Joey said while taking control of the handcuffed prisoner.

The shift left Joey Galeno with a gun collar and a question. Who was this guy Bobby Moylan?"

The following evening, Joey arrived in the district for his next midnight shift. He observed Bobby Moylan sitting on the muster room bench, paging through a newspaper.

Joey sat across from Bobby. "How did you know that guy had a gun?

Bobby kept reading the paper while he calmly explained, "The man's sweater was not color- coordinated with the rest of his outfit. When he walked, the front edge of his jacket was clinging to his right thigh, and as he walked, his right hand kept brushing his hip."

Joey was perplexed. "What the fuck are you talking about?"

Bobby chuckled. "If you're not looking for the clues you don't notice them, but if you're looking for them, they're so obvious they begin to jump out at you."

Joey's frustration with not understanding was growing. "How is this shit your spewing obvious?"

Bobby laughed a little louder. There was something about this big, arrogant kid with the bad attitude that he liked. "You need to develop a keen appreciation of body language. You have to start visually stripping everyone."

Now Joey laughed. "I can think of some babes I seen out there that I would like to visually strip – but I ain't visualizing guns."

They both shared a laugh as Bobby continued the lesson. He talked about picking out suspicious characters. The easy cases involved what Bobby called, almost dismissively, the "classic bulge." But Bobby pointed out that there were many less obvious hints. It might be discordant clothes, the inappropriate sweater or jacket worn in the belief it would conceal a firearm. It might be the stride.

He continued, "The vast majority of street criminals stick their guns in their waistbands, and when they walk, the leg on the gun side takes a slightly shorter stride, and the arm a shorter swing. Without thinking about it, everyone carrying a gun constantly reaches to touch the weapon, a security feel," he said, "And often they glance toward the gun. One of the most reliable clues appears when the carrier is getting in or out of a car, going up or down stairs or stepping off a curb: The hand automatically reaches to the waistband to adjust the gun. Running Also Makes It Easy."

Joey was impressed. "This shit is amazing. I'm gonna start looking for that leg stride trick right away."

Bobby held out his outstretched right hand in the universal stop sign. "No so fast boyo. The signs can be fleeting. It took me years to be able to pick out the shorter leg stride." Bobby continued. "Remember, there are legal issues here and you don't want to get jammed up. Stopping someone is easy to justify, but a frisk requires probable cause. When you stop a man with a gun, 99 out of 100 times he's going to do the same thing, He's going to turn the side that the gun's on away from you -- either several inches, just a quick turn of the hip, or halfway around. And the hand and arm are going to come naturally in the direction of the gun, in an instinctive protective motion. At that point you don't have to wait to see if he goes under the shirt for the gun or if he's just going to keep it covered. At that point you have all the right in the world to do a frisk."

Joey remained silent until he was sure Bobby was done with his lecture. "I'd really like to work with you some more to learn this sh…, technique."

Now Bobby had an opportunity to unleash some good-natured sarcasm in Joey's direction. "You mean it may be possible for you to learn something from a hairbag transit cop?"

Joey smiled. "I guess I deserved that." They both shared a laugh.

If ever two cops were not suited to be partners, it was Joey Galeno and Bobby Moylan. Bobby was ten years older than Joey and was quiet, reserved, and very measured in the actions he took. Joey was loud, confident, and tended to act impulsively. Sometimes you just can't rationally explain things, but there was some karma between them that clicked. Maybe it was the fact that they complemented each other so well, with Bobby's stoic, professional demeanor serving as a guide, and sometimes a restraint, for Joey's well meaning, but sometimes overly aggressive behavior. Most importantly, they both enjoyed each other's company on patrol. So much so that one Monday afternoon after the day tour, Bobby Moylan knocked on the commanding officer's office door.

"Remember when you asked me if I wanted to work a steady tour."

This was Deputy Inspector John Doyle's second tour at District 4. Ten years earlier as a new captain he had been assigned to District 4 just in time to see Bobby Moylan receive his Medal of Honor. When he returned to the district two years earlier and saw that Bobby was still in a rotating squad, one of the first things he did was to renew his offer of a steady tour.

"Sure I remember. What tour do you want?"

"I still want to rotate, boss. I just want to work with a steady partner."

"Who?" said Doyle..

"Galeno."

Deputy Inspector Doyle pushed back his chair and laughed. "Galeno? What do you want to work with that loudmouth for?"

Bobby shrugged. Doyle put his hands in the air in mock surrender. "OK. OK. You're the one who has to work with him."

Thus, began the odd but effective partnership of Bobby Moylan and Joey Galeno. As time went on the partnership grew into a full-blown friendship. When Joey started dating Maria, they would get together with Bobby and Mary several times each month for dinner, and Joey was stunned and brought to tears when Bobby asked him to be godfather when Patrick was born.

Besides learning to spot guns, Bobby also schooled Joey on the myriad of transit crimes he would encounter. It was during a midnight shift on the shuttle platform at Grand Central that professor Moylan opened the next chapter in Joey Galeno's subway crime education. The shuttle continuously made the short trip under 42nd Street between Grand Central and Times Square. At night, the train would sit at the platform for twenty minutes before commencing its run crosstown.

At approximately 3:00 AM, Bobby and Joey entered the lead car of the platformed shuttle train. Bobby stopped and pointed to the only occupant in the car. A well-dressed middle age White male was in a state of blissful sleep. Bobby drew Joey's attention to the only noteworthy factor regarding the male's appearance.

"See that?" Bobby pointed to the flapping, precision cut hole in the man's trousers. "That's where his wallet used to be."

Bobby stepped out of the car and looked up and down the empty platform. "There are lush workers out tonight working either here or Times Square."

A what?" Joey said, scratching his head. "Lunch workers?"

"No, no," Bobby laughed. "Lush workers – L-U-S-H." "It's like a lost art," Bobby continued the explanation, "It's all old-school guys who cut the pocket. They die off, and they do not seem to be replacing themselves."

Joey still had a confused look on his face so Bobby continued his lecture. "Lush workers date back at least to the beginning of the last century. During the 1920s, the New York Times described a lush worker as one who picks the pockets of the intoxicated. He is the just the old 'drunk roller' under a new name." Bobby continued "While the term technically applies to anyone who steals from a drunk, we usually reserve it for a special kind of thief who uses straight-edge razors found in any hardware store to cut the victims pockets."

Joey chuckled. "Geez, sounds like a god damn monster in a bedtime story. Don't drink, children, or the Lush Worker will get you."

Bobby also laughed and then reminded Joey of the business at hand. "OK, let's wake this guy and give him the bad news."

At 4:00 AM Bobby and Joey were back patrolling the shuttle platform. Bobby motioned for Joey to follow as he unclipped his key ring from his gun belt.

"Let's see if we can catch us a lush worker."

A darkened layup train was parked on the south side of the island platform. Bobby grabbed his train key, which was by far the longest key on his ring, and opened one of the doors of the layup. Inside the dark car, Bobby and Joey were virtually invisible to anyone on the lighted platform. A few minutes later the distant rumbling of an approaching shuttle train could be heard. The noise became louder and louder until the lead car emerged from the tunnel. Once stopped at the platform, a handful of passengers exited the train followed by the conductor and motorman. The platform was again quiet as Bobby and Joey studied the rear car of the shuttle from their hiding place.

A sleeping male was plainly visible sprawled across two seats. Movement inside the next car caught their attention. Someone was walking through the car. A moment later the moving figure was inside the rear car, cautiously making his way towards his sleeping prey. Bobby had his train key ready to open the door.

"Get ready," he whispered.

The predator stood above the victim, and started nudging him.

"What's he doing?" asked Joey. "Why the hell is he trying to wake him?"

Bobby maintained his focus on the event. "He's testing him – seeing how incoherent he really is."

The perpetrator then leaned into his sleeping victim. "That's it – he's cutting him – Let's move."

The layup train door slid open and Bobby and Joey were across the platform in a flash. Joey had the lush worker rear cuffed before Bobby had completely awoken the victim.

Joey took note of the long, even cut on the victim's trousers. "It's unbelievable he didn't cut this guy's leg wide open. He's like a surgeon with a razor blade, for God's sake."

The victim of the theft was a 23-year old male who had stayed way too late and drank way too much at an office party.

While the victim was still coming to his senses, Bobby turned toward the cuffed prisoner "How's it going, Blake?"

Jason Blake had 37 previous lush working arrests, three of these arrests being at the hands of Bobby Moylan. 48-year-old Jason Blake seemed relieved to see Bobby Moylan, and he immediately pled his case.

"For the record officer, I'm innocent tonight." Blake said that while sitting on the train he noticed the sorry condition of his own pants and being a handyman, he pulled out a razor blade to trim a ragged bit of fabric on his cuff. When Joey asked why he was sitting right beside the sleeping man on an empty train in the middle of the night, Blake shrugged and said no more.

While waiting for the car to transport them all to District 4, Bobby still wanted to continue Joey's training. "Hey Blake, you're one of a dying breed out here. Why don't you explain to the kid how a pro works?"

Jason Blake's chest inflated with pride as he described in detail how he, hypothetically, would rob somebody asleep on a train. First, he emphasized the importance of finding the right victim. "Whatever you're under the influence of has gotten the best of you," he said.

Blake said he was aware that the police used decoys who pretended to be passed out, but that a pro can spot them. "You can tell something's not right," he said. "Just because your eyes are shut doesn't mean you're sleeping."

"There are other clues," he continued "If he's slobbering on himself, he's not faking it."

In another reality, Jason Blake could have been a professor pacing the front of the lecture room, with Joey Galeno sitting in a cramped classroom desk, furiously scribbling notes as the professor imparted his knowledge.

"Michelangelo is quoted as having said, 'I saw the angel in the marble and carved until I set him free.' I study a slobbering drunkard the same way."

Bobby was shocked. "Michelangelo? My God, Blake, I never knew you were so philosophical."

Jason Blake ignored Bobby's sarcasm. For the moment, he was spewing with self-importance. "A good thief," Blake said, "will pass his hand around a victim's front and back pockets, patting them to divine their contents. Back pockets are tricky, but if the victim is really drunk, a simple nudge can help free a wallet. Front pockets are harder to reach into, and require the blade."

Now Blake got into the technical aspects of his work.

"Let's say he has deep pockets, with a wallet inside. You cut across the wallet, like making the letter U - Like a hook - lift the flap, and done."

The static and voices over Bobby and Joey's radios indicated that their transportation was upstairs. Bobby walked with the victim while Joey held the handcuffed Blake by his left arm. Joey was impressed with Jason Blake's work and explanation.

"How does a lush worker like you get so skilled using the blade?"

"You get better over time," Blake announced proudly.

As they rode up the long escalator, Jason Blake's chest deflated, and a defeated look came over his face. "If I was skillful," he said, "I wouldn't be here right now."

1995 was a bittersweet year for Joey Galeno. Under the tutelage of Bobby Moylan he had developed into an outstanding patrol cop. Joey's natural aggressiveness tempered by Bobby's maturity, knowledge, and communication skills produced the formula for a professional, effective police officer. Joey had completely accepted and grown fond of his role in the Transit Police, but he still realized that there were limits in transit to his career aspirations. Yes, he could try to become a detective or attempt to obtain assignment to the citywide plainclothes task force – but that was pretty much it. The NYPD had so many more specialized enforcement units that he would never be able to access.

Then came April 2, 1995. The day that would be forever known to old time transit police as the hostile takeover. This was the date of the police merger in New York City. At midnight the Transit Police Department ceased to exist with all its former members becoming part of the NYPD. While there was a sad aspect about having your police department go out of business, Joey quickly realized all the new opportunities potentially open to him as a member of the NYPD. Even though they had been partners for eight years, Bobby encouraged him to seek assignment in an NYPD specialized unit as soon as possible. Bobby told him that his impressive patrol record would be hard to overlook.

On May 15th, Joey sat at a conference table at One Police Plaza, wearing one of his favorite designer suits. On the other side of the table was a lieutenant and two sergeants from the Street Crime Unit. SCU was all about getting guns off the street, so it was appropriate that the lieutenant opened the interview with the most relevant question.

"How to you spot someone carrying a concealed firearm?"

The panel was not prepared for the dissertation that followed, based on years of study under professor Moylan.

"You need to constantly evaluate all eye contact, actions, mannerisms, and tones of voice. And monitor the way the subjects communicate and interact with each other, while you constantly scan the hands of the person or persons you are interviewing or challenging. Remember, quickly scan a subject's eyes and hands then scan the area around you, especially if you are working alone or with a partner who is inexperienced. Repeat this process until you complete the stop or field interview. Be careful when using this technique at night with a flashlight. Don't shine your flashlight on anything that will reflect the beam back in your face and damage your night vision. If anything, you should use your flashlight to damage a subject's night vision. Naturally, if a subject defies your instructions and moves or attempts to retrieve a weapon from a pocket or under his or her clothing you must take the appropriate action to protect yourself and other law-abiding citizens. If you are forced to pull the trigger to stop a threat from continuing to be a threat, your actions will be judged by how you adhere to the law and department policy."

Joey paused for a moment as if he was turning the page of a book.

"Yes, you can detect a concealed weapon with just a visual scan. But it's more likely that you will spot signs that a person has a weapon in his or her eyes or body language. Illegally armed individuals tend to give themselves away by trying to appear casual as they adjust their clothing to make sure their weapon is not protruding against their clothes. Evaluating body language can also be an extremely effective tool to use when you examine a potential suspect from a distance before you move in to conduct a field interview or stop. Just remember that you can't assume that even a jaywalker is unarmed. As you approach a subject, suspect, or violator you must be prepared to go tactical at a moment's notice."

No one on the panel had a follow up question as they silently stared at Joey Galeno draining his cup of water.

On June 1, 1995 NYPD Police Officer Joey Galeno was assigned to the Citywide Street-Crime Unit. SCU was a relatively small group of 100 to 150 carefully selected officers with outstanding records, who prowled the city looking for those carrying guns. Joey's years of learning to recognize criminal behavior up close and personal in the crowded subways under Bobby Moylan paid dividends with street crime as the unit made a virtual anthropological study of street criminals. They discovered that unlike many legal gun-carriers, they didn't generally use holsters, but instead stuck the gun in their waistbands. Because they constantly worried about the gun falling out, they'd walk in an unusual fashion. Thus, the gun-hunters looked for the subtle signs of behavior that would have escaped the notice of a regular police officer or civilian. If they spotted a suspected gunman, they wouldn't jump out of their cars with guns drawn. Instead, an undercover officer would quietly work his way up to the suspect and place his hand over the gun while other officers moved in, so nobody would get shot. The unit mastered the technique of conducting felony car stops, a tactic that has cost many police officers their lives. They never operated in a catch-as-catch-can fashion, but used choreographed tactics where several cars surrounded and halted a vehicle and officers took up designated positions around it.

Though many outstanding cops applied for a tryout with the SCU, only a certain number made it. Members of the squad had to vote on whether to accept the newcomer. This was very serious business for them because their lives might depend upon the individuals they were working with.

The success of the SCU prompted police brass to seek to expand it. The inspector in charge, a highly decorated street cop, argued against the proposal. He knew this kind of work wasn't for everyone. When headquarters ignored his advice, he resigned from the department. In 1997 the unit was expanded from 138 to 438 officers. Meanwhile Joey Galeno had passed the sergeant's exam and was promoted in December 1998. Joey's exit from SCU came in the nick of time because in February 1999, disaster struck. Four street-crime officers were searching for a rapist in The Bronx. As they closed in on a suspect, the male apparently feared a robbery and tried to move his wallet to his pocket. The officers mistook it for a gun and fired 41 shots, 19 striking the male. The officers involved in the case were young and inexperienced; they'd never worked as a team until that night. The local district attorney indicted them for murder, but they were acquitted. Shortly afterward, the entire Street Crime Unit was abolished.

Sgt. Galeno landed right back in Transit. He was assigned to District 20, which covered the subway lines in most of Queens. Fortune again smiled on Joey when a lieutenant's test was scheduled shortly after his promotion to sergeant. After a year of supervising subway patrol operations, Joey again found himself seated in a small conference room at One Police Plaza, being grilled by three captains.

In 1995 a commission on police corruption published a comprehensive report that levied some harsh criticisms on the quality of investigations conducted by the NYPD Internal Affairs Bureau. The easy part of the report was the conclusion that more experienced investigators needed to be assigned to IAB. The dilemma lay in how the NYPD was actually going to execute this recommendation. No cop wanted to investigate other cops and live with the police cultural stigma of being labelled a "Rat". The NYPD solved this problem by revamping its procedure for making assignments to its investigative bureaus. Instead of requesting assignment directly to the Detective Bureau or Organized Crime Control Bureau, sergeants and lieutenants would submit a generic request for assignment to an investigative bureau. Those police supervisors who passed a panel interview would be drafted to IAB. After a two-year commitment, the draftee was free to move on the OCCB or the Detective Bureau. With this policy, there would always be a fresh cadre of experienced, competent investigators passing through IAB. An additional benefit to this assignment policy was a reduction in the "Rat" stigma. Soon after the implementation of the policy it became common knowledge within the department that the only way for a sergeant or lieutenant to get to the detective bureau or OCCB was to put in two years as an IAB draftee.

Lieutenant Joey Galeno never felt comfortable in IAB, even with the reality that he was a draftee. Joey was assigned to group 26, the IAB unit covering corruption allegations in patrol borough Queens North. Every day Joey made the traffic filled trek from Bay Ridge Brooklyn to Long Island City Queens, and a non-descript office building on Northern Boulevard. On his first day at group 26 Joey hung a calendar on the wall of his cubicle and drew a big X through the current day. His two year countdown had begun.

At 7:00 AM Joey drew an X through day 381. He sighed deeply. There was still more than eleven months to go in his IAB sentence. Joey took note that his latest X was very sloppy and looked more like a letter from the Chinese alphabet. He resolved that he would begin using a ruler for his X tomorrow on 9/12/01.

IAB personnel were not detailed to Ground Zero, but Joey Galeno went there on numerous occasions on his own time. On several occasions he met Bobby Moylan on the site. Joey was elated whenever he met Bobby at Ground Zero. No matter how devastating the reality of the situation was, the presence of the calm persona of Bobby Moylan, a mere cop, always made Joey feel that everything was going to be alright.

The events of 9/11 prompted the NYPD to revamp its terrorism strategies. The most visible strategic change was the creation of a new Counterterrorism Bureau. The size and scope of the new terror fighting bureau required large scale personnel assignments at all ranks. With seven months remaining as an IAB draftee, Joey Galeno received another draft notice. This time, he was being assigned to the Counterterrorism Bureau

Joey Galeno found a home working counterterrorism. In the dangerous post 9/11 world he could think of no greater role in protecting and serving the citizenry. He was assigned to the newly constructed, super-secret office of the new Counterterrorism Bureau. When the secret was revealed to him, Joey was happy to find that the nondescript counterterrorism building was an easy commute from his Bay Ridge home. Personnel assignment policies had been thrown out the window in this instance. The police commissioner needed to fully staff the bureau with competent personnel immediately, so an executive committee was quickly formed to review personnel folders and recommendations. Overall, the plan worked, as the Counterterrorism Bureau quickly filled its ranks with seasoned, competent personnel like Lt. Joey Galeno. On the other hand, there was Inspector Richard Morgan.

Morgan had risen to his current rank via the most tried and tested method – knowing the right asses to kiss. To be fair, Morgan was not simply good at this method of advancement, he was an expert. Expert ass kissing had kept Morgan off patrol in cushy administrative assignments for most of his career. Now, for the first time, Richard Morgan needed to show an expertise in his job, which in this case was the executive officer of the Counterterrorism Bureau. Chief Foster spent most of his time at One Police Plaza, so the day to day business of the bureau was usually left to Morgan. Joey learned early on that the most important aspect of his job at the bureau would be to clean up the messes made by Inspector Morgan.

In 2004, Morgan was tasked to prepare a briefing for the Police Commissioner regarding active Islamic terrorist groups. Although he was not asked to, Joey reviewed a copy of the briefing before it was forwarded to the PC. Joey was filled with both horror and hilarity at what he read. The briefing mentioned that a new group had been formed in 2004. The group was a more militant offshoot of Al Qaeda called the Islamic State, or ASIS. Luckily, Joey didn't have anything in his mouth or he would have immediately spit it out. Obviously, the inspector meant to reference ISIS. ASIS was the American Society for Industrial Security and was one of the most highly respected private security organizations in the world. When Joey pointed out that he was about to notify the PC that ASIS was a threat to the nation, Morgan didn't thank him for the correction. He very nonchalantly stated, "It's just a typo – no big deal."

Joey saved Inspector Morgan from a far more embarrassing incident in 2006. Joey was sitting next to Morgan during a terror briefing that included the Police Commissioner, Chief of Department, Chief of the Counterterrorism Bureau, and Deputy Commissioner of the Counterterrorism Bureau. At one point Morgan started talking about the conditions at Gitmo, and how a lack of managerial oversight had led to the abuses. Joey was smart enough, and had enough experience with the inspector to realize that he couldn't underestimate Morgan's potential stupidity. He knew in an instant what was happening, and he jumped in uninvited to save Inspector Morgan from himself.

As ridiculous as it was, Joey realized that Morgan had mistaken the Guantanamo Bay detention facility in Cuba, known as Gitmo, for the Abu Ghraib Prison in Iraq. It was in Abu Ghraib where the well documented abuses of prisoners had taken place. Joey cut off the inspector in mid-sentence,

"Yes, Inspector Morgan is absolutely correct. The main problem at Abu Ghraib centered upon a lack of accountability due to poor management."

When the briefing was over, Morgan never even realized his error. The only thanks Joey received was a reinstruction not to interrupt him again. To this day, Morgan probably still believes Gitmo is the nickname for the Abu Ghraib Prison.

Morgan's ass kissing skills never diminished, and in 2008 he was promoted to Deputy Chief, and assigned to the Special Services Bureau. Joey was thrilled to be rid of Morgan, and he was especially happy that he was sent to SSB, where he couldn't do much harm overseeing Fleet Services and the Property Clerk Division.

Joey toyed with the idea of retiring when he completed twenty years, but as his twentieth anniversary approached, he tabled any retirement plans when he was assigned to the JTTF. The relationship between the FBI and the NYPD was never more critical than right after 9/11. The FBI-NYPD Joint Terrorism Task Force was one of the key instruments in the effort to protect the city.

The largest JTTF was in New York City. It operated out of 26 Federal Plaza and was commanded jointly by the FBI and the New York City Police Department. And for more than a decade – until the 1993 Trade Center bomb – it went without an international incident. The composition of the JTTF is always precisely 50 percent FBI agents and 50 percent NYPD detectives. Under the memorandum of understanding that established the task force, the FBI is the lead agency. The police members are sworn in as federal marshals to enable them to handle federal violations. A lieutenant oversees the police and an FBI supervisor oversees the agents. It is a choice assignment for cops and the task force members selected are always the cream of the NYPD. They tend to be senior detectives while the FBI members tend to be younger. They work in teams of two and are further divided into squads – one that deals with Islamic terrorists, one for domestic terrorism, and one for international terrorism.

The JTTF numbered no more than six cops and six agents in 1985. During the gulf war the commitment increased to about 100 / 100. By 1994 – after the Trade Center bomb – it had shrunk to thirty agents and thirty detectives. There had even been talk at One Police Plaza and 26 Federal Plaza about disbanding the task force entirely. After all, the Trade Center bomb was an isolated event, was it not? The came Oklahoma City and both the NYPD and FBI gave pause to the idea of disbanding the JTTF. Then, on September 11, 2001, the entire game changed.

Joey always heard about problems associated with working with arrogant, pompous feds, but Jay McGregor, the SAIC, or Special Agent in Charge, of the New York office, was a sweetheart for a boss. Just when he believed the negative stereotype associated with feds was all urban myth, Jay McGregor was transferred to Washington DC and in walked Ron Perkins.

The new SAIC had been with the Bureau for seventeen years, sixteen of which had been in various administrative assignments. Perkins injected new life into the stereotype. He was arrogant, pompous, sarcastic, and ill mannered. Joey believed Perkins was trying to compensate for his diminutive appearance. At 5'7" 150 pounds, with a receding hairline, Ron Perkins certainly did not radiate an imposing figure. Joey had matured and mellowed over the years, so dealing with a jerk like Perkins didn't bother him. What he could not tolerate, however, was the way Perkins treated the NYPD contingent of the office. To be fair, Perkins was ill mannered to all the members of the JTTF in the NYC office, including the FBI agents, but he was particularly condescending to the NYPD members.

Detective Terry Hansen was a good guy. Besides being an outstanding investigator, he was one of those rare guys who just seemed to always "get it." In a profession known for its cynicism,

Terry Hansen had a great attitude and would always go that extra mile. For a boss, Terry was a pleasure to have as a subordinate. Terry's performance did not suffer, even though he was going through a very tough period. Terry's ten-year old daughter had been diagnosed with leukemia and was undergoing chemotherapy treatments. Through it all, Terry rarely displayed anything but his usual upbeat demeanor and he was still a productive investigator in the unit.

At 1:15 PM on a Wednesday afternoon Joey returned to the office from a meeting at One Police Plaza. Before opening the office door he could hear Ron Perkins loud, obnoxious voice browbeating some poor soul, but when he opened the door he was stunned to see Terry Hansen on the receiving end of the verbal barrage. Perkins was standing at Terry's desk, right index finger pointing menacingly close to Terry's face. Terry sat in silence as Perkins ranted about turning in his reports on time, and that he would receive no special treatment.

The scene was just too much to take as the mature, mellow Joey Galeno was instantly transported back to the streets of Bensonhurst.

"Who the fuck do you think you're talking to?"

There was obvious fear in Perkins' eyes as he turned his attention from Terry to see Joey Galeno walking towards him. Fight or flight syndrome engulfed Ron Perkins, and he quickly made flight his choice. As he backpedaled away from the methodically advancing lieutenant, he tripped over a waste basket and sprawled on the floor on his back. Joey's advance terminated, and the audience of six in the office, including four FBI agents, broke into unrestrained laughter. Ron Perkins scrambled to his feet and staggered into his office, slamming the door behind him.

Joey would never have actually attacked Perkins, at least he would like to believe that. Regardless, the damage was done. The humiliated SAIC never brought up the incident again, and he never spoke to Joey Galeno again. Six months later when he was transferred to the Personnel Division in Washington, he vowed to the few friends he had that he would get even with Galeno.

CHAPTER 6: THE UNDERCOVER

0830 hours – The last Day: Jimmy Boy Craig sat at the kitchen table, staring at the assortment of papers laid out in front of him. The walk to and from the mosque combined with a second cold shower and multiple cups of coffee had finally tamed his hangover to a point where he could concentrate. Nothing of any significance has occurred during the Morning Prayer, although with his head still throbbing he couldn't be certain if he would have recognized something substantial. Now, back in his studio apartment, he took deep, deliberate breaths while scanning the assortment of papers laid out on the table in front of him. The papers represented months of his accumulated notes during his undercover assignment. He shook his head in disgust as he shuffled through all the different size papers – some torn and some crumbled up. He desperately wished that his organizational skills were on level with his intellectual prowess, but rifling through the wide assortment of papers was empirical evidence of his disorganization.

Jimmy Boy began stacking papers into categories. One pile consisted of any interactions he had with the Mosaab brothers. The next pile was for anything to do with the Mosaab's creepy cousin, Marwan. Jimmy also created a pile for papers relating to the Iman at the local mosque. His frustration was growing. He couldn't just dump every other paper into a miscellaneous category, but he could not spend all day figuring out different categories. In less than four hours he would be at the JTTF, sitting in front of a sure to be pissed off Lt. Galeno, and he needed to have a complete, concise report of his investigation ready to deliver. The kitchen window adjacent to the table was open six inches, and a sudden breeze blew his categorized piles back into a disorganized mess on the table and floor.

"Fuck." He placed his right hand to his forehead and closed his eyes. How the hell did he ever end up here?

In the early hours of August 2, 1990, more than 100,000 Iraqi troops moved tanks, helicopters and trucks across the border into Kuwait. Iraq maintained the world's fourth–largest military and had mobilized an overwhelming invading force. Within an hour, they reached Kuwait City, and by daybreak, Iraqi tanks were attacking Dasman Palace, the royal residence. The Emir had already fled into the Saudi desert, but his private guard and his younger half–brother, Sheik Faud al–Ahmad al–Sabah, had stayed behind to defend their home. The sheik was shot and killed, and according to an Iraqi soldier who deserted after the assault, his body was placed in front of a tank and run over.

Ali Al Salem Air Base was situated inside Kuwait approximately 23-miles from the Iraqi border. The air base was the last to be overrun during the Iraqi invasion. On August 3 Ali Al Salem was the only air base not occupied by Iraq. A small number of Kuwaiti regulars, staff officers, and the base commander, General Alaa Fasil, stayed to fight and organize resupply missions from Saudi Arabia. When it became apparent that the end was fast approaching, General Fasil ordered his executive officer, Colonel Ahmed Al-Fadhill and two junior officers to sneak out of the base and take up residence in a private home approximately a half mile from the base. By the end of the day, Ali Al Salem had been overrun. Upon discovery by the Iraqi military, General Fasil was hanged from the base flagpole by Iraqi troops. The remaining Kuwaiti military personnel were lined up outside the old Kuwaiti officers' club and shot.

The Kuwaiti government-in-exile was one of the most effective governments to ever operate. From Taif resort in Saudi Arabia, Sheikh Jaber set up his government so that its ministers were in constant communication with the people still in Kuwait. The government was able to direct an underground armed resistance made up of both military and civilian forces and was able to provide public services to the Kuwaiti people who remained, such as emergency care through the funds that it had saved from oil revenues. Colonel Al-Fadhill was the highest ranking military officer remaining inside the occupied country. The colonel and his two aides spent the remaining months of the occupation hidden in the empty appearing home, while keeping watch on the activities at the air base and transmitting intelligence information to the government in exile.

Saddam Hussein gambled that the remainder of the Arab and western worlds would ultimately choose to ignore his incursion into Kuwait, but as evidenced by the resulting Operation Desert Storm, he had made a gross miscalculation. On January 17, 1991, eight American AH-64A Apache attack helicopters destroyed part of Iraq's radar network in Desert Storm's first attack. CWO James Craig was piloting the lead Apache in the attack on the radar site.

On February 24, 1991, after 39 days of a devastating air campaign, the U.S. led coalition began to liberate Kuwait and systematically destroy most of Iraq's army. One hundred hours was all it took. Four days of a stunning display of speed and technology. Symbolic of the total devastation of the Iraqi military was the Highway of Death. Officially known as Highway 80, Coalition aircraft and ground forces attacked retreating Iraqi military personnel attempting to leave Kuwait via the six-lane roadway on the night of February 26–27, 1991, resulting in the destruction of hundreds of vehicles and the deaths of many of their occupants. Between 1,400 and 2,000 vehicles were hit or abandoned on the main Highway 80 north of Al Jabra. Several hundred more littered the lesser known Highway 8 to the major southern Iraq military stronghold of Basra. The scenes of devastation on the road were some of the most recognizable images of the war, and it has been suggested that they were a factor in President Bush's decision to declare a cessation of hostilities the next day.

Jimmy Craig was again at the lead of a squadron of Apaches, contributing to the destruction along the Highway of Death with his load of Hydra 70 Flechette rockets and Hellfire missiles. As the destruction along Highway 80 neared completion, Craig's squadron was directed away from the shooting gallery. Coalition forces, led by a contingent from the Kuwaiti army, were about to assault Ali Al Salem Air Base. Jimmy Craig and his Apaches were to supply close air support for the assault.

The operation wasn't much of an assault. The Iraqi military personnel occupying the base had commenced their run for the Iraqi border hours before Jimmy's attack squadron swooped down on the base. Once the Coalition ground forces declared the base secure,

Jimmy Craig and his squadron of Apaches became the first Coalition aircraft to land at the newly liberated air base.

After strafing the fleeing Iraqis along the Highway of Death and the immediate rush to the air base, Jimmy Craig needed a break. More specifically, he was looking for something to eat and someplace to sit down and relax. A Kuwaiti soldier pointed to a building at the far end of the air field that he identified as the officer's club. Jimmy reasoned that the officer's club was as good a place as any to search for his sustenance and rest, so he began the quarter mile trek across the vacant field.

Jimmy had no idea of the security measures that had been instituted by the ground forces, so he experienced some trepidation when he observed the pickup truck enter through the southern gate and drive along the tarmac in his direction. His curiosity became concern as the truck continued to come towards him. Jimmy stopped and released the snap on the holster of his 9mm pistol. He released his right hand from the pistol grip when he detected a hand waving out of the passenger window of the truck. Jimmy could further see that the friendly hand was attached to a smiling, equally friendly looking face.

Colonel Al-Fadhill reached to shake Jimmy's hand, but the handshake was obviously not sufficient, as the colonel continued forward until he held Jimmy Craig in a warm embrace. Colonel Al-Fadhil was returning to his command after months holed up in the house down the road. Jimmy Craig was the first American the colonel had run into upon entering the air base, and his emotions were getting the better of him as he tried to express his gratitude. Jimmy Craig realized at that moment that he had just made a new friend, but he had no idea the extent to which this friendship would affect the rest of his life.

Twenty-eight-year old James Craig was the product of working class parents in Boston. His police officer father was able to save enough money to finance Jimmy's education at the relatively inexpensive Framingham State University. Jimmy Craig knew exactly what he wanted to do with his life, and it wasn't to follow his dad into the Boston Police Department. Jimmy wanted to fly.

Flying aircraft is a coveted career in the United States armed services, and the process to become a military pilot is a competitive one. Most candidates need at least a bachelor's degree to apply. The exception is the Army, where the fleet consists mainly of helicopters rather than fixed-wing aircraft. Becoming a helicopter pilot in the Army does not require higher education or prior enlistment, a perfect combination for twenty-year old Jimmy Craig, who was too restless after two years of college to think about two more years of academia. Jimmy was accepted into the program and was on his way to Fort Rucker in Alabama to become a helicopter pilot recruit.

Before even thinking about getting behind the controls of a helicopter, Jimmy had to complete warrant officer candidate school. A warrant officer is a technical expert who specializes in a particular battlefield skill, such as flying choppers. Unlike commissioned officers, they continue working in their specialty, rather than moving up the chain of command. When CWO Craig led his squad of Apaches into the Ali Al Salem Air Base he had approximately six months remaining in his enlistment and had not decided whether eight years would be enough for his army flying career.

After the liberation of Kuwait, Jimmy's Apache squadron remained stationed at the air base. Jimmy had quickly become the favorite American of the base commander, newly promoted General Ahmed Al-Fadhill. At the conclusion of the war, Kuwait was desperately seeking military heroes to glorify to an adoring population. Since the hero pickings were somewhat slim, the heroic hiding of General Al-Fadhill in the house down the road from the air base was good enough to warrant hero status. Being close friends to a national hero provided benefits to Jimmy Craig. The two most important benefits were an introduction to the royal family and an introduction to Farah, General Al-Fadhill's daughter.

National hero status provided some unique advantages to General Al-Fadhill, primary of which was access to the royal family. Kuwait is a constitutional emirate with a semi-democratic political system. The hybrid political system is divided between an elected parliament and appointed government. The Constitution of Kuwait, approved and promulgated in November 1962, calls for direct elections to a unicameral parliament. Kuwait's judicial system is the most independent in the Persian Gulf region and the Constitutional Court is widely believed to be one of the most judicially independent courts in the Arab world. Sheikh Jaber al-Ahmad al-Sabah was the Emir of Kuwait and the third monarch to rule Kuwait since its independence from Britain. The Emir ruled over a large royal family, the most prominent member being the Emir's successor, the crown prince. Newly minted hero General Al-Fadhill quickly became a favorite of the crown prince, and by proxy, the generals great American friend also became close to the crown prince.

During October, 1991, Jimmy Craig reached a crossroad. In a week he would be returning to the United States to be discharged from the army. The only lukewarm plan he had for moving forward was the brainchild of his father. The Boston Police Department was holding a civil service test for police officer and his cop dad had filed an application for Jimmy, allowing him to sit for the exam almost immediately after returning to the USA. Jimmy still wanted to fly, but his father was pushing hard to convince him that with his experience he would have no problem getting assigned to the Aviation Unit once he was a cop.

The real source of Jimmy's apprehension, however, was not home in America. Jimmy had developed a very slow-moving relationship with the general's daughter, Farah. The general was thrilled about the blossoming relationship and did everything he could to encourage the ties between his daughter and his American friend. Now, a week away from leaving Kuwait, Jimmy Craig had to admit that he was in love with Farah. Jimmy's attraction was certainly understandable, considering Farah's big, almond-shaped sparkling green eyes framed with thick lashes complimenting an hourglass figure comprised of a tiny waist and generous hips, with a long, beautiful glossy black mane, all packaged in a sultry olive complexion.

A relationship between a Christian American and the daughter of a Kuwaiti general was not that farfetched. Hero status was not the only unique aspect of General Al-Fadhill. As a majority Muslim nation, Christianity in Kuwait was a minority religion, accounting for 10%-20% of the country's population, or 650,000 people. Kuwait's Christians were divided into two groups. The first group were Christians who were native Kuwaitis numbering approximately between 200 and 400 people. General Al-Fadhill was part of this small group. The second group, who make up the majority of Christians in Kuwait, are expatriates from various countries around the world.

Kuwait's somewhat liberal view on women's rights, in comparison with other Arab countries, was another factor allowing the relationship between Jimmy and Farah. Women in Kuwait were among the most emancipated women in the Middle East region, experiencing many changes since the discovery of oil. They had a long history of official political and social activism which started in the 1960s and continued today. In the 1950s their access to education and employment increased dramatically.

Even with the progressive policies in the country, the general realized there were many obstacles to be faced by a Christian female in Kuwait. He realized that much of his career success involved being in the right place at the right time, but his Christianity created a ceiling to his family's upward mobility – even for a national hero.

Three days before his scheduled departure, Jimmy wished he could speed up the clock to terminate the misery of his never-ending goodbye to Farah. On this night Jimmy was accompanying General Al-Fadhill and Farah to the palace of the crown prince for a farewell dinner. Jimmy had no idea of the conspiracy that was underway.

After the meal had been consumed, the prince brought the plot to fruition. "So, Jimmy, what are your plans when you get home?"

Jimmy rambled on for about a minute about the Boston Police Department, but it was clear to him that no one was really paying attention to him.

When Jimmy's ramblings were concluded, the prince continued, "How would you like a job as my personal helicopter pilot?"

Jimmy sat in stunned silence. Farah let out a shriek of delight and the general let out the satisfied laugh of a successful conspirator. There was no way that Jimmy could refuse the offer.

Jimmy was flying again, and for pay much more than offered by the US Army. To say his salary for being the prince's pilot was good was an understatement – it was great.

As far as General Al-Fadhill was concerned, the conspiracy reached its successful conclusion on June 2, 1992, when Jimmy Craig and Farah became man and wife. On May 10, 1993, James Patrick Craig entered the world. From day one everyone referred to James Patrick as "Jimmy Boy"

The year 2000 found significant changes on the horizon in the Craig household. Jimmy Boy was thriving in school, and it seemed like almost daily new examples would emerge revealing his academic gifts. His father, however, was growing restless. He missed Boston, and no matter how successful Jimmy Boy was in school, Jim Craig wanted his son to have a full life in America. Seven years in Kuwait was enough if Jimmy Boy was still going to have a childhood in the United States.

Jim Craig received no resistance whatsoever regarding his family relocation plan. To the contrary, the significant forces in his life were all for the move. General Al-Fadhil had retired from the military in 1999, so besides Farah and Jimmy Boy, the move to the USA would also include the general and his wife. With the prospect of having her parents close by, Farah lodged no protests to the move. The crown prince was also very supportive of the move. The prince had decided to invest in a chain of luxury apartment buildings in the northeast United States and he wanted Jim Craig to manage these properties. Jim Craig could not have asked for more. He already had a good amount of money set aside from his years flying for the prince, and now he was landing into another excellent salary upon returning to America. Jim thought he was dreaming when presented with the prince's final going away gift – a newly constructed duplex in the very upscale Back Bay section of Boston.

Jim Craig tended to believe that the family move to America was General Al-Fadhill's master plan from the moment of their first hug on the tarmac because the duplex contained four bedrooms, certainly large enough for the general and his wife to live comfortably with the Craig's. The general, however, would only smile slyly and wink when asked of his conspiracy.

Jimmy Boy was a little over seven years of age and an American citizen when he first entered the United States. A child born abroad to one U.S. citizen parent and one alien parent acquires U.S. citizenship at birth under US law provided the U.S. citizen parent was physically present in the United States or one of its outlying possessions for the time period required by the law applicable at the time of the child's birth. Jimmy Boy met the citizenship requirements based on the fact that his US citizen father had been present in the United States for at least five years, with at least two of those years being after the age of fourteen.

Jimmy Boy adapted very quickly to his new life of privilege in America. His dark hair and eyes, as well as his tan complexion labeled him as one of the thousands of 'Black Irish' in the Boston area. Every now and then, in just the right lighting conditions, his mother's Middle Eastern features would break through, but for the clear majority of the time, Jimmy Boy Craig appeared to be Boston Irish through and through.

Jimmy Boy may have been the only son of Erin in Boston, however, who spoke fluent Arabic. Arabic is spoken by almost 200 million people in more than 22 countries, and is the official language of Kuwait. English is widely spoken, however, so from the time he could talk, Jimmy Boy was bi-lingual. Jimmy Boy's Arabic fluency continued in America due to the fact that his mother, and grandparents spoke Arabic regularly around the house.

Jimmy Boy continued his academic achievements in Boston, and a battery of IQ tests revealed he was at near genius level. His advanced intellect fit well into his upper crust lifestyle, and as far as his mother and the general were concerned, Jimmy Boy was part of an elite class that should not have to mix with the riff raff. Jimmy Boy's dad and paternal grandfather kept him grounded and refused to let him develop an obnoxious elitist attitude. Jimmy Boy loved being around his paternal grandfather, and as he grew older he loved to hear stories about his time as a Boston cop.

When the time for college rolled around, Jimmy Boy's finances and grades made the choice easy – Harvard. Choosing a major, however, was not so easy. He decided to pursue a degree in History and Literature because it seemed as good as any bachelor's. Jimmy Boy had no interest in entering the world of business, finance or academia. Patrick Craig's tales of the Boston PD had made a lasting impression with Jimmy Boy, and much to the chagrin of his mother and the general, he wanted to pursue a career in law enforcement. Some inbred elitism had rubbed off on him, however, so there was no way Jimmy Boy Craig could lower himself to become a run of the mill local Boston cop. Only the most elite law enforcement organization would be good enough for Jimmy Boy, so he set his sights on the Federal Bureau of Investigation.

Jimmy Boy's intellectual prowess served him well, as he began to methodically plan his march to the FBI beginning during the summer before entering Harvard. The first action he took was to analyse the eligibility requirements for FBI special agent. Jimmy Boy went through the requirements one by one

- Be 23 to 36 1/2 years old. – Not a problem. He could begin the application process when he graduated Harvard at age 22. By the time he underwent all the pre-employment processing he would have reached the qualifying age of 23.

- Meet the Special Agent physical fitness standards. - Again, no issue. Jimmy Boy had blossomed into a very athletic 5'10" 175-pound lean body.
- Possess a minimum of a U.S.-accredited bachelor's degree. – A degree from Harvard, no less, and undoubtedly with a very high GPA
- Have at least three years of full-time work experience - This requirement was going to take some thought.

In fact, it took seven months of thought until Jimmy Boy discovered Freedom Ventures Inc., a contractor working with the defense, security and intelligence community sectors, offering a range of services, including translation in languages such as Arabic, Farsi and Pashto. FVI, as it was called, had an office in Boston where Jimmy Boy worked full time from 4 PM x 12 AM sitting at a desk translating documents into English. Not only did this job give Jimmy Boy the required experience for FBI employment, but as an added bonus, he received a secret clearance.

Jimmy Boy was fully aware that the FBI liked candidates with Juris Doctorates, CPAs, and other advanced degrees, but this type of additional education would require additional years of study. Restlessness was a trait Jimmy Boy had inherited from his father. Just as his dad did not have the patience for the last two years of college when he could fly helicopters with two years completed, Jimmy Boy had no time for additional years of academia as long as he had an alternative. He knew that applicants who were lawyers, CPAs and PHDs may be viewed as having a symbolic full house, but as far as Jimmy Boy was concerned, he was playing with a royal flush.

Whereas advanced degrees in law, business, science, and engineering were highly sought after by the FBI, foreign language speakers were gold. In the days of the radical Islamic terrorist threat, a native Arabic speaker was pure gold. A complicating factor, however, was that a Kuwaiti born native speaker would most likely be hired as a special agent specifically to perform undercover work, but that path would put him in the best position to be hired. This undercover career path was filled with potential roadblocks and dangers because for all intents and purposes Jimmy Boy Craig was a White, Christian American who would stick out like a sore thumb in most Islamic environments. Still, this career plan seemed feasible and the quickest route to the FBI. Jimmy Boy realized he needed a second opinion, and that opinion had to be from someone he trusted.

The sun was just beginning to set on a beautiful fall afternoon when Jimmy Boy turned his new BMW X5 onto Elred Street. The car had been a birthday present from his parents - actually from his mother - a reminder of his privileged status. He stopped at the curb in front of a tired looking cedar shingle cape cod style home. The house was 75-years old and looked substantially to be in its original condition. The door of the detached garage was open. The contrast in lighting conditions made it difficult to see the interior of the garage from outside, so as he approached the threshold, Jimmy Boy shouted a greeting.

"Gramps - you in there?"

A large figure came out of the shadows.

"Right here Jimmy Boy."

Patrick Craig, still sturdy looking and vibrant at 70 years of age came forward sporting a huge smile while embracing his grandson.

When seven-year old Jimmy Boy Craig arrived in America he referred to his grandfather as Seedo, the Arabic slang for grandfather. Patrick Craig had first seen his grandson in person when he visited Kuwait when Jimmy Boy was four years old. When Pat Craig exited the aircraft and made his way through the jetway to the terminal, he was met by his son, daughter-in-law and grandson. Upon catching sight of Patrick, Farah nudged Jimmy Boy forward, directing him to give his Seedo a big hug. Patrick instinctively recoiled, thinking that Farah may have been referring to a body part. Once settled back in the USA, Patrick Craig reminded his son that they were in America and that he would no longer respond to Seedo. From that moment forward, Patrick Craig became Pop-Pop. Pop-Pop was acceptable to Patrick, but when Jimmy Boy reached his teenage years, he found Pop-Pop totally unacceptable. Teenage

Jimmy Boy would cringe whenever his father, in mixed company, would call out to him "Don't forget to call Pop-Pop later." Jimmy Boy had to come up with a less juvenile name, so whether his grandfather liked it or not, he became gramps.

Gramps emerged from the refrigerator holding two cans of Old Milwaukee beer.

"Old Milwaukee?" Jimmy Boy scoffed.

"Easy lad," Patrick responded. "This beer won an award in 2001 at the Great American Beer Festival."

Jimmy Boy picked up his can and stated very sarcastically, "An award winner - wow."

Gramps realized Jimmy Boy was on to him. "Alright already - it's cheap."

Two Old Milwaukee's later, Jimmy Boy had completed laying out his career plan to Gramps. Pat Craig placed his empty beer can on the kitchen table.

"Look Jimmy Boy, I worked narcotics for more than five years and I learned that with the right scam, any undercover can get over."

Jimmy Boy intently listened as his grandfather continued.
"It's more about what you know than what you look like. You have to be completely prepared for the environment you are entering."

Patrick pointed out the kitchen window toward the flagpole in the center of his front yard. Just below Old Glory waved the red and white banner of the Boston Red Sox.
"We love the Sox, right?"

"Damn straight." Jimmy Boy declared with a burst of New England pride.

Patrick continued, "What if you had to go undercover in a crowd of Red Sox fans in a pub across from Fenway. You could go into that environment wearing a Sox cap and jersey, but if you don't know who Bucky F'ing Dent is, you're finished."

Pat Craig alluded to the light hitting shortstop of the hated New York Yankees who had ended the Red Sox 1978 season with a home run during a playoff game at Fenway Park. It mattered little what Bucky Dent's real middle name was. From the moment the ball cleared the Green Monster on that October afternoon all of New England bestowed him with a new middle name.

Gramps leaned forward and patted Jimmy Boy's forearm. "Let's face it Jimmy Boy, it's not going to be easy for a shanty looking soul like yourself to get over as an Arab, even with your background and language skills. You are going to have to know everything there is to know about that Muslim religion if you are going to pull it off."

Jimmy Boy pulled away from the curb on Elred Street completely energized. In his mind, he was now initiating OPERATION BUCKY F'ING DENT. He knew his grandfather was correct in stating that he had a lot of work to do on his own to realize his FBI dream, especially if he was going to use his Middle Eastern background as his main selling point.

Among his many academic proficiencies, Jimmy Boy was one of those people who just seemed to naturally pick up languages. Being completely fluent in Arabic, he had no trouble establishing fluency in Farsi and Pashto within eighteen months. He also visited the Islamic Center of Boston in Wayland and picked up a copy of the Koran. From that day forward, Jimmy Boy had no recreational reading other than the Koran. Jimmy Boy quickly believed he had a thorough understanding of the Koran, but he wanted to put his knowledge to the test. During his senior year in college he was able to enroll in an Islamic history class. He genuinely wanted to learn more about the faith, and he also wanted to see how well he could maintain scholarly discussions on Islam.

In other words, Jimmy Boy wanted to make sure he could walk the walk and talk the talk. Jimmy Boy quickly established that he had a deeper understanding of the topics being discussed than quite a few of the other Muslim students.

During one class, Jimmy Boy dominated the discussion with his in depth knowledge of Islam. When class was over, two young ladies in hijab were outside the class complaining about the White guy talking smack on Muslims. Jimmy Boy was going to engage them, but thought better of it. Instead, he just walked off with his white skin and a better understanding of what he may be up against. Jimmy Boy picked up a lot about Islam during that semester, but the most important lesson was administered by the two girls in the hall. It was not going to be easy for lily white Jimmy Boy to pull off a charade as a Muslim.

When Jimmy Boy first contacted the mosque to explain his hopes of attending a prayer service, he was surprised with how he was greeted with openness to the idea. The pleasant sounding woman answering the phone confirmed that Jimmy Boy was more than welcome to attend a service and immediately offered to set up an appointment with the local imam and a member of Islamic Society leadership to provide him a more comprehensive first experience with the faith.

With his visit to the mosque scheduled to begin late in the morning, Jimmy Boy rose early and left his house with plenty of time to make the trip to Shawmut Avenue. Jimmy Boy was almost thirty minutes early for his appointment, and he hoped he wasn't interrupting any other events at the center. As he approached on the sidewalk, Jimmy Boy noted that the three-story red brick building looked like no church he had seen, nor did it resemble any of the ornate mosques he could recall in Kuwait. As a matter of fact, the site looked like a run of the mill small apartment building found all over Boston. Jimmy Boy quietly entered through the door and into an empty, quiet space. Near a doorway in front of him rested signs asking visitors to remove their shoes and directing people to the mosque entrance. In response, Jimmy Boy slid off his footwear and placed them on a nearby shelf before slowly walking past the breach of the mosque doors. In the space outside the mosque relics and artwork lined the walls. Their rhythm was only broken by the periodic posting of flyers that made mention of religious group meetings, events, and the center's impacts on the local community. In silence, Jimmy Boy read about the Mosque for Praising Allah's outreach and its mission to spread peace and knowledge to its fellow citizens.

After taking a quick look at the mosque interior through a series of nearby windows, Jimmy Boy walked back toward the mosque entrance and heard some soft voices from a hallway around the corner. Realizing that likely meant there was a reception area on the second floor, Jimmy Boy put his shoes back on and ascended the stairway where he was met by a man and two women carrying on a conversation in a nearby office. Doing his best not to interrupt, Jimmy Boy introduced himself to the group. With a smile, one of the women responded to his remarks.

"Yes, James, I remember your voice. I was the one that spoke to you on the phone. Please come in."

Despite his early arrival, it was clear the mosque was happy to accommodate Jimmy Boy, which made him feel comfortable.

The female from the phone stated, "You can wait here with us for a little while, and when the imam or the executive director become available I will let you know,"

Jimmy Boy nodded and thanked her before turning his attention to the glass of water now resting on the table in front of him.

Jimmy Boy sat in the office for a few minutes sipping at his glass until a man emerged from a room behind him.

"Hello, James?" he said as Jimmy Boy turned in his chair to meet him, "I'm Othman, the executive director of the Mosque for Praising Allah. I understand you are interested in learning more about Islam?"

Jimmy Boy confirmed that was the case and rose from his chair, extending a hand to meet Othman's.

"Please, come to my office, and we can talk for a bit," he said with a gentle tone and a smile. "I'd be happy to answer any questions you might have."

With that, Othman guided Jimmy Boy to his office and offered him a chair in front of his desk. Taking a seat in front of him on the same side of the desk, Othman began the conversation simply.

"So, what brings you here today?" he asked with sincerity.

Jimmy Boy commenced his well-practiced speech regarding his intentions to learn more about the faiths of the world and especially his desire to gain more experience with Islam. Jimmy Boy's remarks were met with acceptance and understanding, which led Othman to give him a brief background on the origins of the religion and the main tenets of the faith. Explaining Islam's ties to Christianity and Judaism before it, Othman took time to explain the life of Muhammad as one of many prophets among Jesus, Abraham, Moses, and others that have significance in Islam. As Jimmy Boy listened to Othman, he began to feel remorseful with the deceit he was committing. But what else could he do. Was he going to explain to Othman that he aspired to become an FBI agent, and that he wanted to learn about Islam to allow him to work undercover in the Islamic community? Not likely.

Othman's explanation was full but concise, and it revealed more insight about Islam in the first few minutes than Jimmy Boy had obtained in all his independent study.

"Well," Othman sighed while tapping his desk, "It's time for the service."

After thanking Othman for his time, Jimmy Boy found his way down to the mosque and took a seat against a wall toward the middle of the sanctuary. Around him, men were steadily trickling into the space and going through their ritual prayers as they entered and found a position in the vast carpeted space. As the crowd grew, the imam took to the front of the room and began speaking about a variety of topics all focused on being better people, better citizens, and better neighbors in the name of God. The imam's message continued to resonate through the mosque as a man approached the front of the room to begin the call to prayer before a room of people now filled to capacity. The beautiful sounds of Middle Eastern melodies carried through the space, prompting all those in attendance to rise for the collective prayer. As the mosque fell quiet with the end of the call to prayer, Jimmy Boy watched as each person in the room around him simultaneously committed a series of actions leading into a bow. As quickly as they reached the ground, the group rose back to their feet to complete the prayer to God with a final act of praise before the ceremony came to an end.

Eventually, Jimmy Boy moved toward the door and found his way back toward the mosque entrance. With the afternoon hurrying along and some unfavorable weather scheduled to move in, he decided to start his journey home. On his way out of the mosque, he parted the crowd of jovial men and women to find Othman once more. Catching him between conversations, Jimmy Boy thanked him once more and did his best to express the impact his time at the mosque had on his perspective. Othman immediately expressed his joy at the fact the experience had been so positive and proceeded to offer him his hand for one final handshake.

By the time June 2015 rolled around, Jimmy Boy had set his career table as best as he could. He was about to graduate from Harvard with a 4.0 GPA and a BA in History and Literature. Additionally, he had completed just over three years of bonafide fulltime employment with a secret clearance for FVI. It was time to apply for the FBI.

As the months passed, Jimmy Boy was very happy with the progress of Operation Bucky F'ing Dent. The only thing he could not control was the fact that he did not look very much like a Middle Eastern Muslim. To the contrary, he looked more like he just stepped of the stage as an extra in Riverdance. As far as Jimmy Boy was concerned, however, his appearance was small potatoes. He would not address that issue until he absolutely had to.

It was 11AM on a Saturday morning, and Jimmy Boy lay paralyzed in his bed. He had spent his night off from work barhopping Irish pubs with friends from Harvard, and the large quantity of beer consumed had contributed to this temporary paralysis. Jimmy Boy seldom drank to excess, but the evening's festivities celebrated his twenty third birthday, so he made an exception and indulged.

Jimmy Boy didn't stir when a knock on his bedroom door was followed immediately by the entry of his father. "Mail's in. the elder Craig stated while tossing and envelope on Jimmy Boy's chest. Jimmy Boy groped for the envelope with this right hand and pulled it close to his face. The return address read simply "Federal Bureau of Investigation, Washington, DC." Jimmy Boy placed the envelope back on his chest and stared at his father. Mr. Craig stared back without a word.

They gathered anxiously that first July morning, the 50 members of class "16-03," In the first of many traditions they would encounter at Quantico, the recruits, still dressed in their dark civilian suits, were asked to stand and describe their backgrounds and explain why they wanted to join the FBI. For many, the amphitheater-style classroom was not a surprising destination. Thirty students -- 60 percent of the class -- had been in the military or law enforcement, traditional recruiting grounds for the FBI. But others came from the highly educated nontraditional backgrounds the Bureau has tried to emphasize. There was a biomedical engineer with a doctoral degree in pathogenesis, a lawyer from a white-shoe Manhattan law firm who was taking a 75 percent pay cut, and a college professor from Georgia with a doctorate in forestry. There was also a twenty-three-year old from the highbrow Back Bay section of Boston who was born in Kuwait and spoke fluent Arabic, Farsi, and Pashto.

On a tour of the academy their first night, the recruits had passed by a reminder of the FBI's mandate to fight terrorism -- two 10-foot black granite towers formed in the shape of the World Trade

Center and bathed in soft light. At the base sat a jagged stone from Ground Zero and a concrete piece of the Pentagon. On the ground nearby rested a blue metal fragment of the airplane that crashed in Pennsylvania.

Everywhere the students went in the ensuing 4 1/2 months there were also reminders of the FBI's past and the culture into which they were being initiated. The street leading into the sprawling academy was named Hoover Road. A portrait of the agency's controversial first director, J. Edgar Hoover, hung in the reading room named after him. On the walls near the cafeteria and gym were posters of famous FBI movies. The one from "The FBI Story" was autographed by its star, Jimmy Stewart.

A few days into the course, Jimmy Boy and the other recruits received a pointed lesson that whatever their backgrounds, there could be no doubt about what they had signed on to do. It was an FBI tradition called "Reality Check." For the next hour and a half, a firearms instructor told the recruits -- by now wearing FBI-issue uniforms of blue polo shirts, khaki pants and hiking boots -- that there were to be no questions and that they were only required to listen. The instructor showed the class a collection of handguns he had removed from the academy's gun vault. The first was the partly melted remains of a .40-caliber Glock 22 that had been carried by an FBI agent who rushed into the World Trade Center.

"You are volunteering to put yourself in harm's way," the instructor said. "When everyone is running away from danger, you must run toward it."

The Glock was followed by a 9mm Smith & Wesson with a bullet hole through the middle. The gun belonged to a special agent who was killed with another FBI agent during a gun battle in Miami in 1986. Then a 9mm SIG Sauer that a criminal wrested away from a female agent at D.C. police headquarters in 1994. He shot her in the head.

The instructor then asked the recruits to look under the firearms manuals in front of them. Everyone who found a slip of paper with a name and age scrawled on it was to stand and read them. The 16 names read off were of agents killed in the line of duty who once sat in the same room. To reinforce the message, a grainy black-and-white video of a South Carolina highway trooper pulling over a car was played. In seconds, the video ended with the trooper being shot by the driver and screaming into a radio for help. A gurgling sound could be heard through a microphone the officer was wearing.

The trainees stared in stunned silence.

"Think about this over the weekend," the instructor told the recruits. "Make sure this is the job for you. If it is, I'll see you next week."

A female recruit named Lisa resigned after "Reality Check." It had taken so long to get to the FBI, but after the firearms class, she knew she had to leave. It hit her that being an FBI agent also really meant being a cop.

"Orders," another ritual, sent a different but equally powerful message about the FBI and the agents who serve in it, particularly to Jimmy Boy Craig. During the first week of class, recruits had been asked to rank preferences for their first assignments among the FBI's 56 field offices. Five weeks later, at Orders, they very publicly learned their fates.

By tradition, recruits had to go to the front of the room and tell their classmates their first choice before receiving the sealed envelope with their assignments. Each one then had to open the envelope, call out where he was going, collect himself and pin his picture on a giant map of the United States.

One woman said she wanted Honolulu and the class laughed. She didn't get it. Another asked for Atlanta but received Washington. One trainee muttered under his breath, "Boy, I didn't see that coming," as he pinned his photo on New Haven, Connecticut. On the map, clusters of pictures were concentrated on each coast, with 18 of the trainees headed to New York, Washington or Los Angeles. But most of the class was scattered across the country, from Anchorage to Kansas City. Every three to five years, they must be ready to pick up their families and move again. Jimmy Boy had selected his hometown of Boston, and based on his life of privilege, he was somewhat stunned when he had to place his pin on New York City.

None of the recruits, including Jimmy Boy, complained. They were becoming part of the FBI culture, ready to serve wherever the bureau sent them. One new agent went to a two-man office in Montana and another to a five-man office in Victorville. Twelve went to the Washington Field Office, known as WFO.

Jimmy Boy was destined for the Joint Terrorism Task Force in New York City. When Jimmy Boy expressed his surprise at the JTTF assignment, a Supervisory Special Agent from Alabama who was overseeing the Orders Ritual stated in a pronounced southern drawl,

"With your credentials son, where the heck did you expect to go?"

One day in September, the class waited in a muddy yard behind the gym for "OC Spray," remembered by Jimmy Boy as the worst day of training. He stepped forward and stood ramrod straight in anticipation. The instructor raised a canister of a derivative of cayenne pepper known as oleoresin capsicum, or OC. Pepper spray. From four feet away, the instructor let loose a big burst. Jimmy Boy choked, coughed and gagged.

"Open your eyes!" the instructor screamed. "Open your eyes!"

To pass, Jimmy Boy had to open at least one eye, protect his gun from a trainee trying to grab it and force the trainee down spread-eagle onto the ground before yelling "FBI! Don't move!"

One by one, the sprayed trainees, hunched over in agony, were led away to rinse their swollen faces and red-rimmed eyes. The point of the exercise was not merely to toughen them; the instructor wanted them to understand what OC spray felt like before they used it on someone else and to know that they could survive if it's used against them.

The next day, there was "Bull in the Ring," an ordeal designed to bring the recruits face to face with the old-fashioned culture of toughness that has long been part of the FBI. Jimmy Boy, throughout his protected upbringing and private school experiences had never actually been in a real fight. That was about to change.

Wearing boxing gloves, headgear and mouth guards, they were arranged in five circles in the academy gym, according to weight.

"We're classmates, pals and friends," an instructor told the trainees. "But for the next hour, we're not. Just don't quit. Do not turn your back. It's going to hurt. It's not fun. You can't duck. You have to survive. Work your way through it. Keep going."

Jimmy Boy stood in the middle of the circle, surrounded by nine other trainees. One man moved into the circle and sent his fist into Jimmy Boy's face. He took the punch and tentatively hit back. He hit Jimmy Boy in the shoulder and kept pounding. Then he backed up and another trainee moved in and began pummeling Jimmy Boy. For two minutes, he took and threw punches. The instructors ordered them to do it all again for another two minutes each. Afterward, they had to punch each other as hard as they could while fighting on the ground. The "Rocky" theme song was blaring.

Jimmy Boy jabbed cautiously at Michelle, the former corporate lawyer. He was uncomfortable punching a woman, especially one who had become a good friend.

"Hit her harder," an instructor yelled.

Inside an interview room, Jimmy Boy casually chatted with an actor playing "Pat Taylor," an employee of a defense contractor building top-secret radar systems. It was week twelve. While their instructors watched them on video monitors, the trainees were learning how to elicit confessions.

The recruits received 70-hours of instruction on what is perhaps the most critical FBI skill: the art of interviewing and interrogation. FBI agents rarely use their guns or get into street fights, but they do spend most of their time talking to people. In the most basic sense, an agent's job is to get information that can be used to solve crimes or stop terrorism.

Jimmy Boy asked Taylor, suspected of stealing a blueprint to sell to a North Korean intelligence agent, about his family, job and two children. The Washington Redskins came up and Jimmy Boy said that he was new to the area and not a Redskins fan. In a room nearby, several FBI instructors groaned and laughed. Great way to build a rapport with someone from around here, they joked. Despite the Redskins comment, Jimmy Boy seemed to connect with Taylor, showing respect and learning about his life. He smoothly asked him to sign away his Miranda rights.

After leaving the room to let Taylor stew, Jimmy Boy returned, removed his jacket and rolled his chair closer to Taylor. Using information gleaned from the interview, he now had to go for the confession.

"At this point, he needs to move in," said an observing instructor. "Invade his comfort zone. Let him smell the chili he had for lunch so he can't think straight."

Jimmy Boy said: "Now, Pat, I understand you are a single father. You have a lot of responsibility and you have a lot of bills. I understand that, Pat."

Taylor tried to say something, but Jimmy Boy cut him off. The trainee is supposed to show who's in control with a 10-minute monologue.

"Listen to me, Pat," Jimmy Boy said. "You took the prints simply because your son needs more money. I understand that. If I were a father, I would do almost everything for my kids, I really would."

The technique is called "rationalization" and expresses sympathy with the suspect. But Jimmy Boy finally got the confession by bluffing with a blank videotape that he said captured Pat in the act.

"That's a risky move," the instructor said. "If there were a video machine in the room, the suspect could have called Jimmy Boy's bluff."

During week 17, with the end in sight, the trainees lined up to take their final firearms exam at the outdoor range. Each had to fire a gun from four positions at four distances, 150 shots in all. To pass, each trainee had to put at least 120 shots in the target. Handling a firearm came easy to Jimmy Boy, and he very effortlessly qualified with an expert designation.

When he finished, Jason, a 25-year-old Army lieutenant planning to get married the day after graduation, had a sinking feeling. There were not as many bullet holes in the target as he had hoped. A somber instructor carried over his scored target. Jason had failed by one shot. Tears filled his eyes. He knew what that meant: He would not graduate with his class.

Growing up in small-town Kentucky, Jason was familiar with guns and cut from the traditional mold of an ideal FBI agent. He won a Bronze Star in combat in Iraq. He was the top scorer in the final physical fitness test. He peppered his language with "Yes, Sirs" and "Yes, Ma'am's" and described himself as a Type A personality. Jason was immediately placed with a new class and given special instruction. If he failed the next firearms qualification test, he would be out. Jimmy Boy was thrilled when he learned that Jason had passed his firearms qualification a month later.

For Jimmy Boy and his classmates, there was one more firearms exercise -- FATS -- a firearms training simulation. In a darkened room, with classmates sitting behind, each trainee was called forward to face a movie screen with a video simulating a potential crime unfolding. The trainee had to decide whether to shoot. Act too quickly and an innocent person could be killed. Hesitate and it could be the trainee.

It was Jimmy Boy's turn. On the video, his partner knocked at an apartment door looking for a fugitive's girlfriend. But the suspect himself opened the door. Jimmy Boy's partner pulled his gun. Lunging, the suspect took away the gun and the two men rolled on the ground, fighting for it. Jimmy Boy, who had never fired a gun before Quantico, leapt onto a table. His heart racing, he shot at the suspect, who was still on the ground tussling with his partner. The suspect's girlfriend suddenly appeared at the door. Jimmy Boy yelled for her to stay back. It happened so fast that it was hard to see where the bullets landed.

The lights came on. The instructor felt Jimmy Boy's pulse, to comic effect. Then the instructor became serious. "Did you shoot your partner?" he asked.

Jimmy Boy's face fell. "I don't think so," he said.

When the computer simulation was rerun in slow motion to track each bullet, it was clear: Jimmy Boy had missed his partner and killed the criminal with a shot to the head. His classmates cheered.

On the morning of December 1, parents, grandparents, spouses and children streamed into the huge FBI auditorium. It was graduation day. Class 16-03 lined up for a photograph with the FBI Director, who swore members in as special agents.

"We are on the front lines for America," he told them. "Will *you* develop the source that provides the intelligence we need to disrupt a terrorist plot? We must continue to change because the terrorists certainly will."

They walked down the long glass-enclosed corridors for the last time. They crossed the grassy quad, past the granite twin towers and the piece of United Airlines Flight 93. They headed toward the gun vault, where their firearms instructor was waiting for them.

Eighteen weeks earlier, he had gone into the vault to get something to show the class: the burned Glock 22 handgun that an agent had carried into the World Trade Center. Now, he handed each of them something of their own. A brand-new Glock 22.

The new graduates were given leave for a week before reporting to their new duty stations, so Jimmy Boy was going to accompany his parents back to Boston before reporting to the JTTF in New York City. Jimmy Boy had one more stop to make before departing Quantico.

Special Agent in Charge Ron Perkins responded with a disinterested "Come in," to the knock on his office door.

Jimmy Boy entered the office but remained silent as the middle age male behind the large oak desk remained focused on the contents of a manila file folder while extending his right index finger in the universal sign for "wait." Finally, the folder closed on the desk and Ron Perkins got a good look at Special Agent James Craig. At first, Jimmy Boy thought he detected outright horror on Perkins' face, but that was quickly replaced by a serene smile.

"I'm in charge of personnel assignments, Agent Craig, and I always personally meet new agents being sent to undercover assignments."

Jimmy Boy acknowledged with a slight nod of his head as Perkins continued,

"I have to say…you don't exactly look the part to be able to infiltrate a radical Islamic cell."

Jimmy Boy did not react at all as Perkins continued probing.

"You do speak Arabic, Farsi, and Pashto, don't you?"

"Yes sir."

"And you were born in Kuwait to a Kuwaiti mother, right?"

"Yes sir."

Ron Perkins sat back in his chair and continued to eye the new JTTF undercover who looked like he would be better suited to infiltrate the St. Patrick's Day Parade. Perkins pushed his chair back and began to rise.

"You will report to Lieutenant Galeno of the NYPD. He is in charge of the NYC JTTF." Perkins extended his hand to Jimmy Boy, who thought he detected an evil sneer to Perkins' smile

"Good luck. You are perfect for this assignment agent Craig."

Fresh off a week of rest and relaxation in Boston, Jimmy Boy Craig felt energized. He pushed through the revolving doors at 26 Federal Plaza and strode confidently toward the elevator that would take him to the office of the New York City Joint Terrorism Task Force. He was convinced he could successfully carry out Operation Bucky F'ing Dent, and he actually looked forward to explaining his plan to his new boss. Jimmy Boy was alone in the elevator as it began its ascent. He reached into his suit jacket pocket and glanced at a piece of paper. He just wanted to make sure that he had his bosses' name right – NYPD Lieutenant Joseph Galeno.

Fifteen minutes later, Jimmy Boy concluded the speech regarding his undercover plan. He sat back in the chair with a look of satisfaction on his face. On the other side of the desk, Joey Galeno's face was quite different. He wore an expression that was a mixture of amazement and horror. Lt. Galeno's first words completely deflated Jimmy Boy.

"What the fuck does Bucky Dent have to do with anything?"

Joey Galeno cupped his hands over his mouth and stared at this figure in front of him. He had been waiting months for a desperately needed undercover that could work Islamic terror cells. His frustration was boiling over.

"I don't believe this. I gotta get someone inside these Islamic cells, and they send me Seamus Finnegan."

"Who is Seamus Finnegan?" Jimmy Boy innocently inquired.

Joey exploded. "How the fuck do I know who Seamus Finnegan is. All I do know is that you are better suited to be Seamus Finnegan than you are to be Abdool Farad."

"Who's Abdool Farad?"

"Just shut up!" Joey commanded.

Joey was still trying to wrap his brain around this situation. This couldn't be what it appeared to be. For a moment, he even considered the possibility that he was on a hidden camera television show.

"You're really my UC," Joey said, hoping there would be a change to the previous answer.

"Yes sir," Jimmy Boy responded.

"Just stand by a moment Agent……..", Joey fished through the papers on his desk looking for the transfer order.

"Craig sir." Jimmy boy ended Joey's search by providing his last name.

"Yeah, Craig. Just wait a minute". Joey dialed his phone.

"This is Lieutenant Galeno, JTTF New York City. I need to talk to someone in charge of personnel assignments."

Approximately thirty seconds later Joey's nightmare was revisited.

"SAIC Perkins. May I help you?"

Like a bad dream, the specter of Ron Perkins had materialized. Joey was momentarily stunned. He looked at his phone receiver, then at Agent Craig, then back to the phone. Finally, he addressed the inevitable.

"Hey Perkins, this is Galeno in New York City."

Ron Perkins feigned joy at hearing from Joey. "Lieutenant Galeno – this is an unexpected surprise. How have you been?"

Joey was not up to playing any games.

"Cut the shit Perkins. I have Agent Craig in front of me, so I think you know exactly why I'm calling."

Joey may not have been in the mood for games, but Ron Perkins was thoroughly enjoying playing his.

"Whatever do you mean lieutenant? I thought you would be thrilled to get a new UC."

"You know exactly what I mean, you asshole. I'm not looking to infiltrate the IRA. How is this kid going to get over in a mosque?"

"Please listen to me Lieutenant Galeno." It was obvious Ron Perkins was enjoying every moment of this conversation.

"Special Agent James Craig is uniquely qualified for this assignment. He was born in Kuwait, speaks fluent Farsi, Arabic, and also Pasto I think, and he is an expert in the Koran."

Joey's blood pressure was rapidly rising, and he was not about to let Perkins enjoy his moment.

"Listen to me Perkins. I'm going to be an expert in kicking your ass all over Washington DC. You better hope no one gets hurt because of this kid."

Joey slammed the phone down and now had to focus on a very anxious looking Jimmy Boy Craig. Joey began to feel bad for this kid.

"Look kid, I know this isn't your fault, but I need someone to get inside a mosque. How are you going to get over as a Muslim?"

Jimmy Boy tried to sound confident. "I can do it sir. I know I can."

Joey and Jimmy Boy stared at each other, both wondering who would speak next. Finally, Jimmy Boy broke the silence.

"I'm going to let my whiteness work for me. I'm just a brother in the cause who happens to be white. Think about it. Who in his right mind is ever going to send a white guy into a mosque undercover?"

Joey had little to no faith in this argument, but what else could he do.

Jimmy Boy strolled along Atlantic Avenue, searching for #195. He thought it would be easy to pick out an Arab bakery, but now he wasn't so sure. The entire Avenue was lined with Arab coffee shops, groceries, restaurants, and music stores. Jimmy Boy was relieved to see the green awning clearly marked 195. The remainder of the sign read DAMASCUS BREAD AND PASTRY SHOP.

Ceiling fans rotated at a much slower pace than the workers behind the counter who were filling boxes and bags with cakes and pastries at a non-stop, frantic pace. Opposite the counter, on the other side of the clean, white tile floor were three small tables, with two chairs pressed tightly at each table. At one table sat an elderly couple sipping coffee. The wave from a man at the next table caught Jimmy Boy's attention.

Mustafa Hussein was a player. He wasn't a thug or a big-time crook. He was a hustler who would do almost anything to make a buck, including stretching the limits of the law if he had to. Most importantly, Mustafa Hussein knew the pulse of the street. Mustafa's parents were illegal aliens from Syria, but when he entered the world on DeKalb Avenue in a delivery room at the Brooklyn Hospital center, Mustafa Hussein became a red blooded American citizen. Joey Galeno had met Mustafa while he was assigned to Street Crime. Mustafa became a paid CI, or confidential informant for Joey, and his information resulted in several significant gun arrests. As time went on, Joey came to trust the information supplied by Hussein, as being more reliable than the information garnered from the NYPD Intelligence Division. When Joey's police beat changed from guns to terrorists, he maintained contact with Mustafa. Although Mustafa had no links to organizations associated with terror groups or cells, he still provided real value. For Lt. Joey Galeno, Mustafa Hussein was like a mobile microphone. Every day he roamed the streets, coffee shops, social clubs, and mosques in New York City's Islamic communities – listening.

Mustafa's present mission was different. Today, he was to be a coach. Joey Galeno had asked him to meet with an undercover, and to provide some pointers on staying alive. Mustafa had been a bit confused by this assignment, but the situation became crystal clear when Jimmy Boy Craig entered the bakery.

Mustafa shook his head and laughed while motioning for Jimmy Boy to sit.

"I never thought the boss had much of a sense of humor, but this is hilarious." Mustafa chuckled in English.

Jimmy Boy stared at the bearded, long haired, greasy looking figure in front of him, having a good laugh at his expense. He was not amused, but he was prepared for this moment, as he commenced a diatribe in perfect Arabic that included the expressions KESS IKHTAK and KESS OMMAK.

Jimmy Boy knew that most insults and Arabic swear words and expressions center on the family and in some instances combine parents and siblings in one curse or insult. KESS IKHTAK literally means "your sister's vagina." This pretty much bashed Mustafa's honor because Jimmy Boy was referring to his sister's genitals. KESS OMMAK built on the previous insult, and literally means "your mom's vagina." This was the common equivalent of "fuck your mom." This was an escalation from the sister insult because Jimmy Boy didn't know if Mustafa had a sister, but he definitely had a mother. Jimmy Boy finished his speech by calling Mustafa a giggling son of a bitch, then sat back in his chair and waited for a response.

The rage in Mustafa's eyes quickly dissipated, replaced by a look of admiration.

"You're Arabic is good – real good." Mustafa pushed a fresh cup of coffee toward Jimmy Boy. "I'm sorry for how I reacted, but it was kind of shocking to see a pasty faced white boy who is supposed to infiltrate an Islamic terror cell."

Over the next thirty minutes Mustafa heard the history of Jimmy Boy Craig, from Kuwait to Boston, to New York City. Finally, it was time for Mustafa's advice.

"Look, my friend, this will not be easy for you, but I believe you can pull it off." Mustafa continued, "Your language ability and knowledge of Islam is better than any Muslim I know."

He motioned the worker behind the counter for another cup of coffee.

"Embrace your whiteness – don't run from it. Make your script as close to reality as possible. You were born in the Middle East to an Arab mother and a White father and make up your story from there. Maybe you came here as a student – you can fill in those details."

Mustafa put down his cup and pointed his right index finger at Jimmy Boy. "Remember, don't leave any blanks in your cover story – have the details in your mind as if they really happened. You will automatically come under suspicion because of how you look. You will have to win their trust, wherever you go."

Before they parted company on Atlantic Avenue, Mustafa extended his hand. "Good luck brother."

Jimmy Boy shook his hand and rather sheepishly stated, "Sorry about what I said earlier. I'm sure your mother is a very nice person."

Mustafa laughed loudly as they disappeared in different directions.

Jimmy Boy had another stop to make on this day. Jorge Espinal, an NYPD detective with the JTTF had pulled him aside after his meeting with the lieutenant. He motioned for Jimmy Boy to follow him into the men's room and cautiously performed a visual check under the doors of each stall to make sure they were alone.

"I know they told you not to carry while working undercover, but that's bullshit. I used to be a UC, and let me tell you brother, the most important thing is to be able to protect yourself out there."

"What kind of gun did you carry?" Jimmy Boy whispered.

Jorge responded in an equally low tone. "A custom piece made specifically for undercover work."

Jorge reached into his pants pocket and handed Jimmy Boy a creased, stained business card. The card read ACTIVE FIREARMS, MEDFORD, NY, HERBERT STROMEYER, OWNER.

Jimmy Boy took Ahmed Al-Fadhill as His UC name because he thought it would be easier to remember his grandfather's actual name, especially in a stressful situation. The JTTF leased a 2015 Hyundai Accent for him, which he promptly registered in his UC name.

Jimmy Boy pulled the Hyundai to the side of the road on Jericho Turnpike. He looked at the worn business card and at the sign on the store. It was the correct address, but this storefront sign read ANTIQUES. This antique store was the only sign of life in this area of Suffolk County, Long Island. Directly adjacent to the east side of the store were the remnants of an ancient gas station. Jimmy Boy mused that most of that old gas station was probably for sale inside the antique store.

The drive out to Medford had taken well over an hour, so he saw no harm in entering the store to see what happened to the gun shop. Just like in an old movie, the wooden door creaked and a bell rang announcing Jimmy Boy's entrance. Jimmy Boy stood in the doorway and took in the array of "Antiques" that were piled in just about every available space in the store. Using the word antique was being kind, as Jimmy Boy actually believed he was staring at multiple piles of junk.

From behind one of the larger junk piles came a low, subdued voice.

"Be with you in a second." Several seconds later a man emerged from the junk and extended his hand.

"Herb Stromeyer. Nice to meet you."

Jimmy Boy's first impression was that one of the antiques had crawled off a pile to say hello. Herb Stromeyer was a relic from another era. He appeared to be at least 70 years old, medium height and thin build. He had long, dry, wiry, kinky grey hair and an unkempt grey beard to match. His skin had an ashy tone, no doubt due to years of avoidance of animal proteins. His long hair was pulled back into a pony tail and partially secured by a multicolored headband. He wore an ill-fitting dirty white t-shirt with a large peace sign emblazoned on its front. Equally ill-fitting ripped jeans led down to much worn looking sandals. Jimmy Boy had seen pictures of hippies at Woodstock in 1969, and he now appeared to be standing in an antique shop shaking hands with an antique hippie.

"I'm sorry to bother you," Jimmy Boy began. "There used to be a gun store here that one of my friends recommended."

The handshake was in overtime as Herb responded. "Who recommended you?"

"Jorge Espinal."

"Oh wow, how is that spic?" Herb had suddenly come alive. His new found energy and use of a racial slur had taken Jimmy Boy off guard. For an instant he believed this old hippie may have recently taken speed that had just kicked in.
Herb continued in his animated fashion.
"I got a real special custom piece for ol' Jorge."

Herb's words brought Jimmy Boy back to the matter at hand. "You mean this actually is a gun shop?"

"Absolutely partner. I been getting into antiques over the years, but I still have my federal firearms dealers license."

Herb's eyes widened in anticipation as he asked, "What do you need?"

Jimmy Boy explained his assignment and his need for a covert compact undercover weapon. Jimmy Boy could almost see the light bulb appear over Herb's head as he sprinted towards the back room of the store, returning in less than a minute holding a small box. As herb opened the blue box he started describing its contents. He wasn't just providing a description. As Jimmy Boy listened, he felt as if he was listening to a high school friend passionately describe a night of sex with the head cheerleader.

"I got just what you need." Herb sang while displaying the box. He opened it like the prideful owner of a rare coin.

"This is the base model NAA Mini five shot Revolver, daddy-o."

Jimmy Boy realized he had never heard a real human being use the term daddy-o before, but he continued to focus on Herb's description.

"It is made of stainless steel and features bird's head style wooden grips. It's all steel but it only weighs about 4 ounces unloaded. It's got a 1-1/8 inch barrel with a fixed half-moon front sight milled above the barrel. It's real small but it packs punch with a .22 magnum round."

He handed the gun to Jimmy boy. He examined the weapon, but was concerned by what appeared to be the lack of a rear sight

"What about its accuracy? There looks like there is only a little notch for a rear sight":

"Fuck accuracy, daddy-o – this is a chin gun baby. You gotta get this barrel right up under a dude's chin and -Badda Boom".

He put his right index finger under his chin and symbolically shot himself. He took the gun back from Jimmy Boy,

"And here's the best part. The grip is foldable, and I got a belt clip for it."

He very efficiently folded the grip, attached the belt clip and stuck it inside the front of his dirty jeans. It fit directly over his belt, taking the place of his real belt buckle. Jimmy Boy loved it.

An hour later Jimmy Boy entered his room at the Holiday Inn near LaGuardia Airport. He went directly to one of his suitcases and rummaged around until he found his belt with the removable buckle. He carefully replaced the buckle with his new firearm and then stood for an extended period of time assessing himself in the mirror. No matter how hard he stared he could not see any evidence of a gun secreted in his belt. Better yet, as he moved about the room, he felt no difference in his belt area. He couldn't even feel the presence of a firearm. For the next hour Jimmy Boy stood in the middle of his hotel room, learning the art of the quick draw with his new covert belt gun. With complete customer satisfaction, he blurted out a tribute to Herb Stromeyer. "Way to go, daddy-o."

From that moment forward, regardless of what he was wearing, Jimmy Boy always wore his special belt. Before long, it had become so much of a routine, he would forget about the special nature of the belt. There were a couple of occasions where he was attending sporting events with friends from Boston, and he had forgotten the nature of the belt. Once at Yankee Stadium and another time at Madison Square Garden, Jimmy Boy was just about to be screened at the metal detector when he suddenly remembered about the belt he was wearing. On both occasions he was able to leave the metal detector line and discreetly seek out an NYPD cop to identify himself and the contents of his belt.

Joey Galeno leisurely leaned on the railing, taking in the warmth of the late afternoon sun. The view of Lower Manhattan from the Brooklyn Heights Promenade always took his breath away, no matter how many times he had been there. Made famous by cameo appearances in movies like *Annie Hall* and *Moonstruck*, it was one of the most romantic spots in New York City, and had been the destination for thousands of first dates, wedding proposals and anniversary celebrations. Joey felt good standing in the exact spot where he had proposed to Marie.

The messy divorce ten years earlier had been all his fault. His affair with a female cop from the Counterterrorism Bureau and subsequent lack of remorse had so alienated his wife, that when he finally lost his arrogance, it was too late. Marie would never take him back and would never forgive him. In fact, she did everything in her power to make life difficult for her ex-husband. Her lawyer was ruthless when it came to alimony and child support, and she went out of her way to upset his visitation rights. Joey had visitation with his eight-year old daughter, Danielle, every other weekend. It was bad enough that his job responsibilities disrupted some of these visitation periods, but Marie seemed to come up with excuse after excuse to cancel a weekend visit. Sometimes Danielle would have a fever, and at other times she needed to stay home to study for a test. Ultimately, Joey would back off. No matter how much it hurt not to see his daughter, he refused to allow Danielle to become collateral damage in a war with Marie.

Joey let out a low, frustrated laugh as he looked out at the river. He had become very much like his good friend Bobby Moylan. The main focus of his life now revolved around the job, and he could not think of a life without it. He shook his head in self-disgust. If only he had some of the same moral character as Bobby Moylan. Regardless, standing at this exact site where he had proposed still managed to make him feel good.

One-third of a mile long, the Promenade offered a vista of the Statue of Liberty, the Manhattan skyline and the majestic Brooklyn Bridge. Lined with flower beds, trees, benches and playgrounds, the promenade was a favorite destination for tourists, joggers, strollers, families and lovers.

Joey's happy memories were disrupted by Mustafa's voice.

"Why do we always have to meet here boss? It's not healthy for you to keep living in the past. Forget about her already."

Joey stepped back from the railing. "Just shut the fuck up and tell me how it went."

Mustafa took a step back and raised his hands in mock surrender. "OK, OK – I know I shouldn't go there."

"What about my UC," Joey stated impatiently.

"He's a smart kid – real smart. He walks the walk and talks the talk better than most of the brothers I know, but…."

"I knew there was going to be a BUT," Joey responded sarcastically.

"But, I just don't know if he is going to be able to overcome his look. On one hand I would say you would be getting him killed by sending him into certain mosques. But on the other hand, if I were a player, and this kid walked into my mosque, I might say that he looked so outlandish, that he couldn't be an undercover."

Joey looked out toward the Statue of Liberty while Mustafa probed. "So, what are you going to do?"

Joey shook his head. "It's not worth the risk of getting him killed, so I am going to hide him somewhere where he will be safe."

"Where might that be?" Mustafa inquired.

"Where you tell me." Joey shot back.

Mustafa took two steps back and put up his hands up again. "Where I tell you? I don't want the blood of this kid on my hands."

"You just told me he's a smart kid. C'mon, you know the lay of the land in this entire city. There has to be some shitty mosque where there's nothing radical or controversial going on."

Mustafa took in the scene of Lower Manhattan and shrugged. "Well, I guess…"

"You guess what?" Joey pressed.

"Well, there is this small mosque in Corona, Queens where my uncle used to live. The Iman has been there forever and he's a real peaceful Muslim, just what you Americans want. Nothing is happening there. Send the kid there. Maybe he can teach the Iman a thing or two about Islam."

Joey again stared out at lower Manhattan, unsuccessfully trying to suppress memories of his past life. "OK, I guess I'm stuck with him. See if you can find an apartment near the mosque we can rent for him."

"You got it boss."

Joey pointed his right index finger directly at Mustafa's nose. "And don't be an asshole. Make it a cheap apartment."

Mustafa chuckled. "Of course boss. Cheap is my specialty."

Joey was back to focusing on the skyline. He continued talking, but Mustafa wasn't sure if he was addressing him or talking to himself.

"I have to send him to the confidential ID section of OCCB to get him fixed up with fake ID. We already got him the car."

Joey turned again making it clear that he was now addressing Mustafa. "I understand he's using his grandfather's name as his UC name."

"That's smart, boss. I told you he was a smart kid." Mustafa stated. "If he gets into a tight spot, the last thing he needs is to be fishing for some fake name he never heard before."

Joey continued, "You must have made a real impression on him, or at least scared the shit out of him." He pulled a piece of paper from his pants pocket – unfolded it, and began reading. "Ahmed Al-Fadhill was born in Kuwait to a Kuwaiti mother and an Irish father. His father had immigrated to Kuwait from Dublin to work in the oil fields. His father was killed when Ahmed was two years old in an oil field accident. His mother changed his name to her family name, making Ahmed Al-Fadhill the only name he has ever known. He was able to get a student visa to study at

Framingham State University in Boston, but after two years he dropped out. Around the same time he learned that his mother had died in a car accident. With no real family in Kuwait, he decided to stay in America. When his student visa expired he became an illegal alien, so he decided moving to New York City would be the safest place to blend in with the population."

Mustafa nodded his head. "Not bad. I told you he is a smart kid. What about a job?"

Joey returned the paper to his pocket. "We're getting him set up working off the books as a messenger in Manhattan. If he needs to, we'll have an office for him to report to and we won't have to worry about anyone trying to verify employment because he's an illegal working off the books."

Mustafa again nodded in approval. "Sounds good boss."

Joey replied sarcastically, "Yeah, now I just have to keep him alive."

0920 hours – The Last Day: Jimmy Boy finally had all his loose papers separated into some type of logical categories. He picked up the pile he had titled "Mosaab Brothers". It had only been eight months since he walked into the Masjid Al-Falah Mosque. He picked up a crumpled piece of loose-leaf paper and smoothed it on the table. These were the notes from his first visit to the mosque.

Jimmy Boy arrived just before lunchtime prayers. He wore the short, rounded prayer cap known as a "taqiyah." He was also sporting a "thobe", the white, ankle-length robe worn by Muslim men. To add realism to his charade, Jimmy Boy reminded himself to refer to his robe as a "dishdashi", the term used for the robe in Kuwait. After signing in he was asked to remove his shoes, and was shown into the main room in the mosque, where he was told he was welcome to observe the prayers taking place. Jimmy Boy was struck by how familiar it all felt. The sight of the last few people hurrying in, followed by a few latecomers. The sight of a young worshipper, late teens, discreetly checking to see he had turned off his smartphone. The crying of a child during the worship. These were all sights and sounds that were very familiar to Jimmy Boy – not from his visits to the Mosque for Praising Allah – but from St. Cecilia's church in Back Bay.

Jimmy Boy realized, of course, that the format of prayer did feel very different than St. Cecilia's. The call to prayer that precedes the service for 15 minutes was designed to act as a reminder that worship is imminent, much like St. Cecilia's bells. The services were led by Iman Ahmed Hamshoo, who had led worship at Masjid Al-Falah for over 35 years.

Over his next several visits to the mosque, Jimmy Boy began to feel completely at ease. He met the Iman and several of the community leaders, and no one questioned his appearance. There was only one person making him feel uncomfortable. During his first visit, and at every successive service there was a male staring at him. Just the prospect of someone staring was enough to raise the discomfort level, but this guy had a real creepy appearance. During the services Jimmy Boy would attempt to avoid eye contact, but whenever their eyes would meet, this male would smile through a mouth devoid of most of its teeth. He also had those crazy eyes Jimmy Boy had read about where the white portion of the eye is visible all around.

The act was becoming routine as Jimmy Boy hit the sidewalk on National Street after his sixth visit to the mosque. His departure was halted by a voice behind him.

"Hey, wait."

Jimmy Boy turned to see the creep jogging towards him.

"I'm Marwan. What's your name?"

Marwan was sporting his usual toothless smile and crazy eyes. In outdoor lighting conditions, Jimmy Boy could get a much better view of his new friend, and it only served to reinforce his creep assessment. Marwan appeared to be a couple of years younger than Jimmy Boy. He was short, very thin, with long, black hair and an unkempt beard. Jimmy Boy identified himself and resumed walking, with Marwan keeping pace beside him. Jimmy Boy said nothing as Marwan carried the conversation with non-stop ramblings in Arabic in a strange, sing-song pace. Jimmy Boy came to the conclusion that Marwan's voice and personality perfectly fit his creepy appearance. Jimmy Boy was beginning to perceive that there was something really wrong with his new friend. He may actually be mentally challenged, or possibly just the stupidest person he had ever met. The ramblings were non-stop and not connected as Jimmy Boy kept walking and tried to figure out a diplomatic way to ditch the creep.

"You want to be my friend?"

"We're the same age."

"I don't like the Iman"

"I'm going to blow up the city"

"I'm hungry."

"There are no pretty girls at the mosque"

Jimmy Boy stopped in his tracks. "What did you say?"

"There are no pretty girls at the mosque"

"Before that," Jimmy Boy probed

Marwan appeared confused. "I'm hungry?"

Jimmy Boy waved his hand in a circular motion. "Keep going."

Marwan stared into space with a blank expression prompting Jimmy Boy to provide assistance. "Something about the city."

A very dim light bulb appeared to turn on in Marwan's head. His crazy eyes and toothless grin returned as he proudly stated, "Oh yeah, I'm going to blow up the city someday."

Jimmy Boy resumed walking and tried to react as if Marwan had just told him his favorite food. "Really? When are you going to do that?"

"As soon as my cousin tells me". Marwan was rambling again.

"I'm a holy warrior."

"Death to the infidels"

"I'm a martyr"

Jimmy Boy began to tune the ramblings out as he continued walking. This creep was just a simpleton who was playing jihadi, just like a little kid would play army – nothing more.

Jimmy Boy didn't think it was worth mentioning Marwan to Lt. Galeno in his weekly briefing to the JTTF. As a matter of fact, he made every effort to avoid contact with the creep. His avoidance strategy worked well for three weeks, but on a Saturday afternoon, Jimmy Boy strolled down 103rd Street, heading towards the elevated subway line. Jimmy Boy's march to the train was interrupted by an all too familiar creepy voice.

"Hey, Hey, over here."

Jimmy Boy reflexively turned in the direction of the voice. Across the street he could see Marwan standing in the doorway of a store, frantically waving him over. With no other alternative available, Jimmy Boy crossed the street to greet his friend. Jimmy Boy realized that a quick greet and depart would be difficult once Marwan retreated inside the store. He would now be forced to enter the store.

As he approached, Jimmy Boy reflected that he had never been inside this variety store. It looked very typical in the neighborhood, with an old, worn awning, and dirty windows filled with cheap merchandise and signs announcing bargains. As Jimmy Boy stepped into the store, it took a moment for his eyes to adjust from the sunlit street to the dimly lit store interior. Marwan was in full creep mode, complete with crazy eyes, toothless grin, and rambling voice. He was pointing toward Jimmy Boy while addressing someone behind the store's counter.

"This is my friend. This is my friend. He wants to blow up the city too."

A nervous laugh accompanied the man emerging from behind the counter.

"My cousin is somewhat – you know." The man stated in perfect English while making a circling motion with his right index finger around his right ear – the universal sign for a nut.

"I understand." Jimmy Boy responded while shaking hands with Waheed Mosaab. Waheed released the handshake and apprehensively sized up his cousin's new friend.

"Forgive me brother, but you don't look very much like a Muslim."

Jimmy Boy related his entire story to Waheed, complete with tales of Kuwait, his Middle Eastern mother, his language skills, and his knowledge of Islam. After fifteen minutes of conversation Jimmy Boy was convinced that he had won Waheed's confidence. His chest swelled with pride. Jimmy Boy had successfully identified the middle name of Bucky F'ing Dent.

Jimmy Boy was about to make his exit from the store when another man emerged from the back room.

Waheed called out to Jimmy Boy. "Wait a moment brother, I want you to meet someone."

Jimmy Boy shook hands with Rashid Mosaab and received the same apprehensive, suspicious look.

Waheed tried to allay his brother's fears. "Ahmed is a friend of Marwan's. I talked to him and he is alright."

As Jimmy Boy departed, Waheed Mosaab ended the conversation where it had begun.

"My cousin is not smart. In fact, he is an idiot, and he talks a lot of shit. You understand, right."

"Of course," Jimmy Boy reassured Waheed while shaking his hand.

Five minutes later Jimmy Boy leaned over the edge of the elevated platform, looking for the next Manhattan bound 7-train. Jimmy Boy was still swelling with pride. Even though the Mosaab brothers gave no indication of being terrorists, he had successfully pulled off his Islamic charade. Gramps and Mustafa Hussein would be proud.

As distasteful as he found it, Jimmy Boy did everything he could to enhance his friendship with creepy cousin Marwan. After weeks of circulating at the mosque, Marwan's wild boast of blowing up the city was still the only information he had obtained that even remotely qualified as intelligence. Hanging around with Marwan meant hanging around at the variety store and the Mosaab brothers.

Jimmy Boy spent most of his time in the store sparring with Waheed. Sparring was an appropriate description because like two cautious boxers, Waheed Mosaab and Jimmy Boy Craig, AKA Ahmed Al-Fadhill, spent most of their time together probing and jabbing at each other, looking for an opening.

From Waheed's perspective, it was absurd that this white guy suddenly showed up at the mosque and in the neighborhood, buddying up to his idiot cousin. On the other hand, this same white guy named Ahmed had all the answers. Ahmed spoke better Arabic than he did, as well as speaking Farsi and Pasto, and his depth of knowledge of the Koran and Islam put Waheed to shame.

Waheed really wanted to believe Ahmed Al-Fadhill was legitimate, because if he was, what a prize he could be. During many of their probing conversations Ahmed had expressed sympathy for the jihad, and Waheed drooled at the prospect of having a real live "apple pie" American white boy to use in an operation. He just wasn't sure enough to take their conversations to the next level.

As time passed, Waheed utilized the radicalization process as taught to him by Dr. Fadel He knew that a critical part of radicalization is the way the message is socialized, and becomes a central part of everyday conversation. During every one of Jimmy Boy's visits to the store, Waheed would always probe him by bringing up news items reflecting how Muslims were being oppressed and mistreated throughout the world, and trying to judge

Jimmy Boy's level of outrage. Waheed was trying to foster an "Us vs. Them" perception to force Jimmy Boy to come down on one side or the other.

Waheed also knew that for this type of socialization to work best, the conversation should be contained, with any contrary messages being kept at bay. Therefore, there was never any alternate point of view present – only Rashid and Marwan to reinforce the jihadist doctrine. Jimmy Boy did not want to seem too eager to take the bait, so he would never just declare "Death to America." He tried to maintain a somewhat neutral point of view while attempting to make it clear that he was coming down on the "Us" side of the equation. Jimmy Boy's attempt at a veneer of neutrality was routinely jumped on quickly by Waheed with attempts to make him feel guilty and potentially ostracized.

As for Jimmy Boy, Waheed was an enigma. It was clear in their conversations that Waheed was sympathetic to the jihad and that he supported terror activities. Jimmy Boy just could never get over that next hump. Was Waheed Mosaab just a loud mouth sympathizer, or was he involved in operations or know operators. He just couldn't get the conversation to the next level.

CHAPTER 7: THE INSPECTOR

0845 hours – The Last Day: *The unmarked blue Caprice emerged from the darkness of the underground parking garage of One Police Plaza. The transition from darkness to bright sunlight caused Inspector Ellen Tomlinson to momentarily squint. With her vision fully adjusted to the light, she directed her driver to head back to the office. Compstat hadn't been too bad this morning. As Commanding Officer of Transit Borough Manhattan, Ellen was responsible for Districts 1, 2, 3, and 4. Overall, crime was down in the Manhattan transit commands, but the Chief of Department still managed to rip into Captain Tom Foster, the CO of District 1, for not having the right answers regarding a pickpocket pattern at Times Square. Ellen made a note to talk to Captain Foster. The remaining activities of the day, however, made Compstat seem insignificant. Bobby Moylan had pled with her not to stage any fanfare or ceremonies for his last day. For the most part she would honor his wishes, but whether Moylan liked it or not he was going to get the "walk out", where the entire command would line the path leading out of the district to form an honor guard for his last walk out of the command.*

Ellen was also going to make it her business to stop by Grand Central to see Bobby on patrol one last time. Ostensibly, visiting Bobby on post on his last tour was the right thing for a borough commander to do. It was also probably her last shot at pushing her much more personal agenda.

The best word to describe Ellen Tomlinson's passage to adulthood was "typical." She grew up in the typical Long Island middle class town of Massapequa in the typical two-parent, two-child household. Ellen always received good grades in school, but she was never the smartest in her class. She also possessed athletic ability, playing basketball and softball through high school, but she was never the star on any of her teams. Ellen also matured into the pleasant "girl next door" type, but would never be confused for a prom queen. She once heard a boy in one of her high school classes refer to her as mildly attractive, and she still wondered whether the comment was a complement or an insult.

Ellen stayed at home and commuted to Hofstra University to pursue a degree in psychology because she really could not think of anything else to do at the time.

Ellen loved both her parents, but one of the real shining spots in her childhood had been her relationship with her father. Ellen adored Jack Tomlinson. Janice Tomlinson had acquired the role of the disciplinarian to Ellen and her brother Thomas, while Jack was more of a buddy to the kids. As a detective with the New York City Transit Police Department, Jack Tomlinson worked long, challenging hours, but he always managed to be there for his kids. On more than one occasion when Jack had to work during one of Ellen's softball games, miraculously, when Ellen stepped to the plate she would suddenly hear his voice cheering from the stands.

In 1993, Ellen was sleepwalking through her third year of college when tragedy struck. She came home from classes to find her home filled with somber friends and family. Before anyone said a word she quickly scanned all the faces. He wasn't there. At that moment Ellen knew the news she was about to receive. Her beloved father was dead – victim of a sudden, massive heart attack. Ellen was devastated by the loss of her dad.

Upon graduation from Hofstra, Ellen put her psychology degree to work via employment with the American Automobile Association. Five days a week from 4 PM to 12 AM she sat in a cubicle in a call center counselling motorists requesting roadside assistance. She hated the job.

It was 7:55 PM and the never-ending stream of rude, lost, disabled, and stranded motorists had resulted in the predicable headache.

"I'm very sorry sir, but our personnel will change your tire, but you have to supply the spare tire." Her ears were still ringing from the barrage of insults as she signed off the phone system and removed her headphones. Thank goodness it was time for her meal break.

Ellen sat alone in at a table in the quiet, empty lunch room. Biting into her apple caused her headache to flare up, but at least she didn't have to deal with the phone for an hour. The throbbing in her head subsided as she drained a bottle of cold, refreshing water. She walked across the room and flipped the empty, plastic bottle into the trash container. As she returned to her seat, Ellen picked up a newspaper that had been left on an adjacent table. She still had forty minutes remaining in her break, and since she didn't feel like taking a nap, Ellen leisurely paged through the paper seeking anything that might catch her interest. It was not a news article that made her stop flipping pages. It was an advertisement on the bottom of page eighteen TAKE THE TEST – JOIN THE BEST - BECOME A TRANSIT POLICE OFFICER.

Ellen had never thought about becoming a cop, and her mother would join her father in the grave if she ever thought Ellen was considering a career in law enforcement. To Ellen's mom, the cause of Jack Tomlinson's heart attack was crystal clear. It was the stress and long, irregular hours that had killed her husband. Ellen could not turn the page away from the advertisement. Just seeing the words TRANSIT POLICE made her think of her dad, and that made her feel good. It made her feel even closer to her dad when she filled out the application and subsequently took the police officer exam. Ellen was convinced that it was through her dad's intervention that the letter notifying her that she scored a 99% on the exam arrived in the mailbox at a time that her mother was not home.

Over the next several months, Ellen covertly passed all the physical, medical, and psychological testing required for police officer appointment. Completing all the steps necessary to become a transit police officer made her feel close to her dad, but now there was nothing left to do except to return exclusively to her mundane existence in the call center and wait.

Ellen sat up quickly in her bed, startled from the nightmare. She took a few deep breaths while trying to remember the dream. Her only recollection was of a phone ringing and her mother shrieking. Before she could delve any further into her memory, her brother's voice accompanied pounding on her bedroom door. The clock on her night table came into focus – 5:55 AM. Ellen took a deep breath and rose from her bed. Throwing open her bedroom door, she was met by her brother's solemn look and shaking head.

"What's going on?"

Thomas continued shaking his head. "You need to go downstairs right now. She's going crazy."

Ellen threw on her robe and hurried down the stairs, realizing now that her mother's screams had not been a dream. Her mother was waiting in the middle of the living room. Ellen noted her mom's red, wide eyes, and flaring nostrils. Was this indicative of rage, fear, or a combination of the two? She could not tell. Taking her eyes off her mother's face, Ellen noticed the telephone receiver in her mom's right hand. There was no more shrieking. Her mom's voice was not much more than a whisper.

"It's for you."

Ellen put the phone to her ear apprehensively.

"Hello."

"Is this Ellen Tomlinson?"

"Yes." Ellen responded.

"This is police officer Addison, Transit Police applicant investigation unit."

Ellen could think of nothing to say, except to repeat, "Yes."

"Report to 300 Gold Street in Brooklyn at eight o'clock Monday morning in business attire to be sworn in as a transit police officer."

Ellen still could only repeat her previous responses "Yes."

"OK, see you Monday."

Ellen finally came out of her trance. "Wait a minute. Why are you calling me at this hour?"

Officer Addison chuckled slightly. "Oh yeah, sorry. We make these calls really early on a Friday morning to give the candidates the opportunity to quit their jobs today."

"Oh, OK, Thanks." Ellen lowered the phone away from her ear.

Her mom had not moved a muscle. Not a word was spoken as Ellen brushed by her to hang up the phone. Janice Tomlinson was still statue-like as Ellen returned to the stairs and began her ascent. Two steps into her climb, Ellen stopped and turned.

"I don't know what to say mom, but I'm going to do this and I hope you support me."

Her mom remained silent, but Ellen noticed a transformation take place. The rage and fear on her mom's face were gone, replaced by a look of profound sadness.

On January 17, 1995 Ellen Tomlinson picked her way through the pedestrian traffic on the busy sidewalk. She could not afford to be late on her first day, and still had to navigate most of the approximately one mile on Flatbush Avenue before arriving at the Transit Police Academy Ellen realized that she could have cut the length of her walk significantly by utilizing the subway, but she was a Long Island girl who spent very little of her 23 years on earth in the five boroughs of New York City. She had virtually no experience with the New York City Subway system, which is why she chose to take the Long Island Railroad commuter railroad into the Atlantic Terminal in Brooklyn, and then walk the rest of the way to the academy.

Ellen was a bright girl, and the irony of a transit cop not knowing anything about the subway system was not lost on her. She slightly slowed as she turned off Flatbush Avenue onto Gold Street. She then picked up steam again, but only momentarily, as she quickly came to a stop in the midst of several small groups of young men and women, all dressed in business attire. Everyone seemed to be just standing on the sidewalk and street waiting.

Ellen sought out a nervous looking female standing by herself and asked "Is this 300 Gold Street?"

The nervous young lady smiled slightly and nodded. Ellen took a long look at the site. This building looked like no police academy that she had ever envisioned.

300 Gold Street had seen better days. The structure was a 6-story building located in downtown Brooklyn, near the intersection of Flatbush Avenue and Tillary Street. The building was erected sometime around 1900, and it had functioned as a shoe factory until the Transit Police took it over during the 1950's. Several of the Department's administrative units had offices in the building, and several classrooms had been built to house the Transit Police Academy.

Beginning in the late 70s the NYPD, Transit and Housing Police Departments all trained their recruits together at the New York City Police Academy at 235 East 20th Street, in the Grammercy Park section of Manhattan. In an effort to stifle the ever-increasing drum beat calling for a merger of the police departments in NYC, the Transit Police pulled out of the NYC Police Academy and established their own academy at Gold Street. January 1995 was the fifth class of transit police recruits to be trained at this new Transit Police Academy. It was also the last class. Neither the recruits or the instructors knew that on April 2nd, everything would change. The police merger suddenly made Ellen and her classmates members of the NYPD, and they finished the last two months of their recruit training at the New York City Police Academy in Manhattan.

Ellen sat proudly in Madison Square Garden. The graduation ceremony was going to start in a few minutes, and while she waited she reflected on the past six months of academy training. Had it really been that long? It seemed like only yesterday she was breathing heavily making that first hurried walk along Flatbush Avenue. Thoughts of the academy faded. Sitting proudly in her brand-new dress blue uniform, Ellen had one dominant thought on her mind – her dad. Sitting there amongst a sea of blue, she just knew Jack Tomlinson was smiling down on her. She felt good.

The ceremony included speeches by the Mayor and Police Commissioner. There was also a speech by the class valedictorian, who just happened to be the nervous looking female who verified the location of 300 Gold Street on the first day. Out on the street, Ellen made the rounds hugging and congratulating classmates. Coming out of a four-person group hug she turned to find Thomas and her mom in line for the next hugs.

Thomas took the initiative. "Congratulations sis."

Her brother backed away leaving Ellen facing her mom. Both of them seemed a bit hesitant in moving forward, but they ended up in an embrace.

"Congratulations honey."

"Thanks mom."

Ellen began her withdrawal from the embrace, but her mom pulled her closer and whispered in her ear.

"Your father is so proud of you."

There was no progression in emotion. Ellen moved immediately to sobbing as she held her mother close. Ellen finally released the embrace and wiped her eyes with tissues supplied by Thomas. As she dabbed at her wet, red eyes, she could not help but notice the expression on her mother's face. It was the same look of profound sadness she had seen six months ago on the morning of the phone call

Ellen was assigned to a rotating squad in District 4, the Transit Bureau command at Union Square in Manhattan. She quickly settled into life on patrol. She wanted to learn the job as quickly as possible. Ellen Tomlinson wanted to be a good cop.

The small shop on Bleecker Street, just east of Lafayette Street was named Cosmopolitan Coffee. To most of the cops in District 4, the coffee shop was known by the nickname given to its owners – the Las Vegas Brothers. Vito and Tony Amelio loved their little shop, and they loved the fact that cops liked to stop in regularly. Vito and Tony were basically nice guys who liked socializing with the cops in their shop. They certainly weren't thugs or crooks. The problem with the Las Vegas Brothers was their inability to resist a good scam. From pyramid schemes to phony slips and falls, Vito and Tony were always looking for an angle, even if it crossed the line from somewhat unethical to outright illegal.

Police officer Lazlo Storm was a unique individual who did not fit the mold of a typical cop. Whereas the overwhelming majority of New York City cops lived in the surrounding suburbs, Lazlo resided in a studio apartment in Greenwich Village. He also fancied himself a thespian and had appeared in several off, off, off Broadway productions. It was likely the actor in him that prompted his legal name change from John Crump to Lazlo Storm.

When Ellen Tomlinson arrived in District 4, Lazlo Storm had thirteen years on the job and was somewhat of a cult figure inside the command. The other cops loved it when Lazlo would debate a sergeant at roll call with his elegant Shakespearean tone. Lazlo was tall and lean with perfectly coiffed hair. He was always impeccably dressed, and the fact that he spoke and dressed like he was acting in one long never-ending play only seemed to endear him to the other members of the command. The cops of District 4 loved Lazlo Storm.

Lazlo worked steady day tours and was given Broadway – Lafayette as a steady post. The Broadway – Lafayette subway station complex was actually two stations, including the Broadway – Lafayette IND station and the Bleecker Street IRT station. The station was a dual patrol post, but Lazlo did not have a steady partner. Every day, Lazlo patrolled Broadway – Lafayette, and made frequent stops into the Las Vegas Brothers, which was four storefronts east of the stairway to the Bleecker Street station.

It was during her third week assigned to the district that Ellen Tomlinson perused the second platoon roll call and observed that she was assigned to Broadway – Lafayette with PO Lazlo Storm. The morning was uneventful as Ellen and Lazlo patrolled the platforms and mezzanines during the rush hour. Although routine, Ellen had to admit that Lazlo's frequent soliloquies on his philosophy of life made the morning quite entertaining. For all his quirks, Lazlo really was an engaging, likeable fellow.

By 10 AM the rush hour herd had significantly thinned, prompting Lazlo to suggest that a break was in order. After entering a personal in their memo books, Ellen followed Lazlo up the Bleecker Street stairs, past several storefronts, and into the Cosmopolitan Coffee Shop. The small shop was empty and Lazlo promptly introduced Ellen to the two gentleman behind the counter in typical Lazlo style.

"Officer Tomlinson, it is my unique privilege to introduce you to the royal family of Bleecker Street – I give you Tony and Vito – the fabulous Las Vegas Brothers."

Ellen resisted the urge to stand and applaud, and instead smiled, nodded, and said hello. Ellen found the coffee to be exceptional, as she carefully sipped while listening to the Las Vegas Brothers very excitedly show Lazlo a baseball that was filled with autographs. She heard Tony brag that the ball contained every important player from the 1961 Yankees, including Mantle, Maris, Berra, and Ford. Ellen found it somewhat odd when she thought she heard Lazlo tell Vito that he needed five of these autographed balls.

The only other customer who entered during her coffee break was a small nerdy looking guy named Petey, who immediately engaged Lazlo and the Las Vegas Brothers in conversation regarding the availability of single signed Mickey Mantle baseballs. Ellen finished her coffee and attempted to pay, but the Las Vegas Brothers would have none of that. As Ellen and Lazlo strolled back to the station, she couldn't help but think what a nice little coffee shop that was and what nice guys Vito and Tony were. Little did she realize that she was knee deep in a Las Vegas Brothers scam.

Approximately two weeks after her introduction to the Las Vegas Brothers, Ellen Tomlinson exited through the steel door of District 4 after completing a day tour, joining the throng on the Union Square subway station mezzanine to begin her usual trek home. The journey took her down to the uptown R train where she exited at 34th Street and ascended to the street. One long block west later and she descended the escalator into Penn Station. Even though she knew from past experience that her 4:42 PM train to Massapequa would be on track 9, she waited like the hundreds of other commuting zombies, silently staring at the huge Penn Station timetable board. When the moment of truth was at hand and track 9 appeared on the board, Ellen and he rest of the Massapequa crowd would make a mad dash toward track 9 to lay claim on the best seats for the commute home.

On this day, however, her trance-like stare at the board was broken by a voice to her immediate left.

"Hi Ellen, Can I speak with you for a minute?"

Ellen reflexively turned her head to see that the request had come from a very pleasant looking fortyish female. The female had medium length blond hair and was dressed in business attire. She also discreetly opened a leather case in her right hand, displaying an NYPD sergeant's shield.

"I'm Christine Hoffman, from Internal Affairs, and this is Joe Keenan."

With the slight twitch of Christine's head to the left, Ellen became aware of a similarly aged male standing next to Christine, also discreetly displaying a sergeant's shield. Ellen had not yet uttered a word as Christine continued.

"I don't want you to miss your train, so is it OK if we ride out to Massapequa with you?"

168

Ellen had still not responded when track 9 appeared on the board next to the 4:42 to Massapequa, prompting a halt to all conversation while the dash to the train commenced. Each car on the M7 style Long Island Railroad cars had a couple of rows of seats that faced each other. This alignment allowed a group of four commuters to sit in a convenient conversational group. Christine led the way into one of the middle cars of the ten-car train and walked directly to one of these face to face seating alignments. Ellen and Christine faced each other in the window seats while Joe occupied the seat next to Christine. Social mores would ensure the privacy of their conversations because even though this was a rush hour train with commuters jammed tightly into all the vestibules in the car, it would be too socially uncomfortable for a stranger to plant himself in the lone empty seat of Christine, Joe, and Ellen's social circle.

At 4:45, the 4:42 began to move at the snail's pace mandated by the speed restrictions present in the tunnels around Penn Station. Suddenly, fear struck Ellen like a hard slap in the face. Her daily race to the train had somehow masked the fact that she was now sitting with two sergeants from Internal Affairs. She had no idea what they wanted with her, but it couldn't be good.

Joe was completely silent while Christine made some remarks about the incompetence of the Long Island Railroad. Ellen's apprehension was rapidly rising, and she wished Christine would just can the small talk and get to the point. Most importantly, Ellen wanted to know if she was in some type of trouble. Ellen let out a deep sigh of frustration when she perceived that the small talk was continuing when Christine asked if she was a sports fan. A few seconds later, however, Ellen realized that the query was the beginning of the main event.

Christine began the tale just as the train emerged from the tunnel into the late afternoon sunlight of Queens. Two years earlier, the FBI identified a major problem threatening the entire sports and celebrity memorabilia market. The Chicago Division of the FBI initiated a sports memorabilia fraud investigation targeting a group of individuals who forged, fraudulently authenticated, and distributed Chicago athletes' autographed memorabilia, including Michael Jordan. The case resulted in the conviction of fourteen individuals in five states involved with forging and distributing forged memorabilia. Information developed by the Chicago FBI's "Foul Ball" investigation suggested that the problem might be national in scope.

Christine elaborated that while it was impossible to definitively estimate the percentage of forged memorabilia, most industry experts conceded that over half of the most sought-after athletes' and celebrities' autographed memorabilia was forged. Industry experts estimated that the autographed memorabilia market in the United States was approximately $1 billion per year. In 1993, the FBI in San Diego utilized information from Operation Foul Ball and other sources to institute an undercover operation designed to infiltrate the nationwide memorabilia fraud network.

Christine told Ellen that the key evidence in this investigation were recorded statements which provided evidence of the individuals' involvement in forging, fraudulently authenticating, and/or distributing the materials. In Operation Bullpen, referred to as Phase I, the San Diego Division of the FBI conducted well over 1,000 consensually recorded audio and video tapes. During the consensually recorded conversations, numerous co-conspirators made incriminating statements which illuminated the nature and common practices involved with sports memorabilia fraud. As an example, Christine cited how one of the conspirators liked to joke to the undercover agent how Babe Ruth still has one arm out of the grave signing autographs.

Ellen's head was spinning. What did celebrity autographs have to do with her? She got her answer as Christine continued the story. A total of 18 searches were conducted in 12 states, resulting in 36 additional convictions. It was in several of these recorded statements that the names of the Amelio brothers surfaced. It seemed that the primary business being run out of the Cosmopolitan Coffee shop was not serving excellent coffee in the front of the store. Rather, the real action was taking place in the back room where the Las Vegas Brothers would spend hours signing phony autographs on baseballs, footballs, photos, and anything else they thought memorabilia enthusiasts would buy.

PO Lazlo Storm was not an actual partner with the Amelio's, but he had seen the money to be made, and was in essence, granted a franchise by the Las Vegas Brothers to operate his own phony autograph operation. Petey, the other male Ellen had observed in the shop talking about the autographs, was not another scammer or conspirator. Petey was actually an undercover FBI agent who was on his way to bringing down the Las Vegas Brothers scam operation, as well as fifteen other operations throughout the New York City Metropolitan area.

Ellen's near panic produced an involuntary stutter as she attempted to declare her innocence

"But I didn't…I had no idea…."

Christine leaned forward and placed her right hand gently on Ellen's left shoulder in a gesture of support. "I know you are not involved in this Ellen."

Ellen melted into her seat as her muscles relaxed with Christine's words.

"I'm going to need your cooperation, Ellen."

Ellen's muscles began to tense again as she realized what cooperation would entail. The train rolled at varying speeds for the next 50-minutes through Queens and Nassau counties before terminating in the eastern Nassau County town of Massapequa. During the trip Christine explained to Ellen that the FBI was arresting thirty-five people in the New York City area, and that the Las Vegas Brothers and Lazlo Storm were among that group. Ellen knew exactly what was coming next as Christine very unemotionally said that Ellen would have to testify regarding her observations of the autographed baseballs in the coffee shop.

Ellen knew she could not feign ignorance because the FBI undercover agent had seen her sitting in the shop in the presence of Lazlo and the Las Vegas Brothers. Ellen detrained at Massapequa, while the Internal Affairs sergeants moved to the other side of the platform to catch a train back to Manhattan.

As she fumbled for her car keys in the railroad parking lot, a feeling of impending doom came over her. Ellen Tomlinson was only a rookie cop, but she knew well what the repercussions of her actions would be. No one would care about her testimony against the Las Vegas Brothers, but Lazlo Storm was a different story. Lazlo was a popular brother in blue, and regardless of what he did, police culture would deem Ellen's actions to be much worse.

A month after her train ride with Internal Affairs, Ellen Tomlinson was becoming a basket case. The FBI arrests that included Lazlo Storm and the Las Vegas Brothers had been all over the news. Lazlo and the brothers subsequently accepted a deal to plead guilty to misdemeanor fraud charges to stay out of jail. Tony and Vito Amelio could ultimately return to serving their excellent coffee. Lazlo Storm, however, was finished as a cop. The plea bargain deal had spared Ellen from having to testify at a public criminal trial, but she still had to appear as a witness for the department at a department hearing that resulted in Lazlo's termination.

There are very few secrets inside a police station house, and once the word spread of Ellen's testimony, she was an instant pariah. It mattered little to the other cops that she really had no choice in the matter. Ellen was still on probation and could be fired without any reason. The presence of Petey, the FBI undercover, meant that if she tried to say she did not see or hear anything related to the autographs inside the coffee shop, she would be just as finished as Lazlo Storm.

There are concepts not covered during police academy training that are more deeply engrained in the police culture than any laws and procedures. One of the strongest cultural concepts was that the worst thing a cop could be was a rat. Cops who were murderers or thieves could ultimately be forgiven of their sins – but not a rat. After her appearance at Lazlo's hearing, Ellen was instantly ostracized by the other members of District 4. No one wanted to work with her, and very few cops would even talk to her. This informal method of punishment was having its desired effect, as Ellen had reached the point where she was just about ready to resign.

On a rainy Tuesday morning her ordeal seemed to be reaching its climax. Ellen sat alone in one corner of the muster room, waiting for the second platoon roll call to begin. As was the norm, none of the other cops acknowledged her presence during the usual pre-roll call hijinks and banter. Why this day was any different was unclear, but Ellen felt herself losing her grip. Despite her best efforts, tears were welling up in her eyes, and she could not halt her hands from shaking. This was about to become her last day, as she eyed the entrance to the female officer's locker room in the distance. The only thing stopping her dash to the locker room was the finality of the act. Ellen knew that if she changed out of uniform and went home, she would likely never come back. Her body was beginning to rock forward in anticipation of rising from her chair, when much like her surprise introduction to Christine Hoffman, she was startled by a voice from her left.

"Collins just banged in sick, you're working with me today at Grand Central." The calm, steady voice belonged to Bobby Moylan.

His intervention momentarily squashed her emotions, and she continued her rise from the chair, but this time in response to the sergeant's call of "fall in."

Thirty minutes later Bobby and Ellen stood on the mezzanine near booth R-241, watching the morning rush hour crowd's daily dance. Ellen decided to break the ice and bring up the five hundred pound gorilla standing next to them.

"I'm surprised you're willing to work with me."

Bobby responded in his usual steady tone. "Why wouldn't I want to work with you?"

"Because I'm a rat." Ellen responded.

Bobby maintained his calm demeanor, but turned his head to make eye contact with her. "Do you think you're a rat?"

Ellen never expected to be asked her own opinion, and she hesitated for a moment before responding. "No, I don't think I'm a rat."

Bobby turned to face the passing throng of humanity on the mezzanine "That's all that's important, isn't it?"

Ellen also turned to face the crowd. In one instant, Bobby Moylan had made her feel better about herself than she had for the entire previous month.

Having a respected veteran like Bobby Moylan request to work with her provided Ellen with some instant credibility – but it was not enough. The haters in the district were still going to label her as a rat, and Bobby knew it. The following morning Ellen scanned the roll call and was pleasantly surprised to see that she was assigned to work again with Bobby Moylan.

Ellen stared at the roll call sheet, contemplating her good fortune, when a voice from behind startled her.

"What's the matter – you don't want to work with me?" Bobby Moylan smiled slightly as he continued walking toward the male locker room.

Ellen was flustered, responding with disjointed sentence fragments even though Bobby was out of earshot. "No, fine, just checking meal time, checking post conditions."

She put her head down and walked toward the female locker room, hoping she had not actually sounded as stupid as she perceived. Forty minutes later Ellen and Bobby stood on the Mezzanine at Grand Central, watching the passing crowd.

"I spoke to the captain yesterday," Bobby said while continuing to focus on the passing sea of humanity.

"Oh?" Ellen wasn't certain what to say, but she certainly did not want to repeat her disjointed act from earlier.

"Yeah, I said I wanted you as a steady partner and he said OK."

Ellen stared straight ahead and said nothing.

Bobby turned his head toward her. "Is that OK with you?"

Ellen shrugged. "Sure."

She strained to control her emotions. It took all of her self-control to keep from embracing him in a display of thanks.

As the weeks passed, so did Ellen's silent treatment. With Bobby Moylan as an ally, slowly but surely most of the cops in the command began to warm up to her. Ellen was aware of Bobby Moylan's tragic story. It was impossible to work in District 4 and not have heard this terrible tale. Standing together on the Grand Central mezzanine, however, was the first time she had actually had personal interactions with him. The attraction was instantaneous. Despite a significant age difference, every day, a new box on the Ellen Tomlinson "perfect man" checklist seemed to be marked. Of course, she found Bobby pleasant to look at, but that was purely secondary. Ellen was a classic movie buff, with her favorite actors being John Wayne and Gary Cooper, the epitome of what is known as "the strong silent type." Ellen quickly placed Bobby Moylan into this same category – a man who conveyed his resolve and power through a sturdy, deliberate silence.

Every day Ellen's attraction to Bobby became stronger, and she didn't fully understand this phenomenon. She spent much of her home time stretched on her bed, searching her college psychology books for an explanation. Perhaps it was her primitive desire to find a mate who appeared mentally strong, confident and physically attractive in order to have healthier children. This theory suggested that such men have facial features that display the 'Dark Triad' of personality traits - Machiavellianism, narcissism and psychopathy, and women who want children show a clear preference for these features because, like natural selection among animals, it indicates strong genes and good health, both mental and physical. Ellen released an incredulous chuckle, but she kept reading. Another chapter asserted the truth of the stereotype that any given girl would prefer to date the captain of the football team instead of the captain of the chess team. The former is bigger, broader, and more physically fit. Back in the day, this was the kind of guy that would spear boars or kill bandits. The page ended with a quote regarding the female perception of power

I learned several major things about power that day, the most significant being that girls are attracted to it."

"Interesting," she thought, flipping the page to see who made such a deep, profound comment on human behavior.

-The Sandman: Friendly Neighborhood Spider-Man Annual

"You have to be kidding me," she said out loud while slamming the book shut. A few seconds later, however, the pages were turning again.

She stopped at the beginning of chapter twelve. She nodded her head and tapped the page with her right index finger. Here was another possible explanation for her infatuation with Bobby. For decades, experts believed women flocked to silent types because of their aloof and mysterious nature - but new research suggested it is because the trait is actually an ultimate sign of masculinity. On average, women talk three times as many words each day than men, and their brains are wired to recognize this trait. When a woman meets a man who talks a lot, they consider them to be more feminine and less attractive, yet men who use shorter words and speak more concisely were more attractive because they appeared more masculine. Ellen stared out her bedroom window while contemplating the theory. Bobby Moylan – man of few words. Maybe it was all part of the profile that attracted her to him.

There was no way for Ellen to finish her psychological research without addressing the obvious. When she found the page she was seeking, she read aloud.

"While previous research has suggested this to be the case, these controlled results show for certain that the quality of a daughter's relationship with her father has an impact on whom she finds attractive. It shows our human brains don't simply build prototypes of the ideal face based on those we see around us, rather they build them based on those to whom we have a strongly positive relationship. We can now say that daughters who have very positive childhood relationships with their fathers choose men with similar central facial characteristics to their fathers."

The book slammed shut – this time for good. Was Bobby Moylan a father figure? She wasn't sure. And if it turned out that her attraction to Bobby was based in her love for her dad – was that something to fear or embrace. Ellen shook her head while heading to the bathroom. She was more confused than when she opened the psychology book.

As time passed, Ellen showed herself to be a quick learner and was fast becoming an able patrol cop. Bobby was glad he had made the decision to help her during her tough time. He truly liked her enthusiasm and enjoyed working with her.

Bobby was always trying to get Ellen experience in the various aspects of transit policing. On this particular day shift, Bobby requested that he and Ellen be allowed to work the tour in plainclothes so he could show her how the world of pickpockets operate. They stood leisurely on the sidewalk of 42nd Street, just outside the entrance to the Chase Bank. Ellen got flashbacks to her professors at Hofstra with the manner in which Bobby explained pickpockets.

He explained to her that pickpocketing in America was once a proud tradition, rich with drama, and celebrated in culture, singular enough that its practitioners developed a whole lexicon to describe its intricacies.

"Thanks professor," she sarcastically muttered under her breath as she waited to start performing some plainclothes police work.

Bobby wasn't finished with his class, however. He drew a deep nostalgic breath.

"Pickpocketing is more or less dead in this country. In a way you had to respect the skill of some old-time picks, but it's a lost art form."

"Art form?" Ellen questioned, "They're crooks."

"I know," Bobby responded, "but you have to respect the skill of some of the old-time picks. Robbing someone at knifepoint takes no skill, but lifting someone's wallet without them knowing...." Bobby's sentence trailed off, but Ellen got his point.

"Times have changed," Bobby continued. "The subway used to be the happy hunting grounds for pickpockets – sometimes alone and sometimes in teams. Some of these teams were your classic skilled organized gangs, targeting wealthier riders, then 'bag workers' who went for purses, and 'lush workers' who targeted unconscious drunks. There were also fob workers out here."

Ellen cut in, "What the heck is a fob worker?"

"A fob worker is a subspecies of pickpocket who works his way through train cars using just his index and middle fingers to extract coins and pieces of paper money—a quarter here, a buck there—from riders' pockets. They weren't greedy, and they never got caught. Bit by bit, fob workers could make up to $400 on a single subway trip; then they'd go to Florida in the winter to work the racetracks."

"Wow, I never realized the extent of this." Ellen responded with a genuinely surprised look.

"Yeah," Bobby continued, "Most of the pros trained in South America, and if they were any good, they came to New York," Bobby continued with a touch of pride. "In the subways, we had the best there were. For a time, pickpocketing in areas like Times Square was out of control. I made tons of arrests during the 80s."

Bobby continued looking straight ahead and provided a caution to Ellen as he spoke.

"Don't make any sudden movements, but there is a guy to my right in front of the food cart – see him?"

Ellen attempted to be as casual as possible in her observation. "The Hispanic middle age guy in the blue blazer?"

"Yup."

"And?" Ellen stated, seeking more information.

"And...I know that guy. He is part of a crew. This is your lucky day officer Tomlinson. It appears that we are going to have some real pick action."

Ellen had been excited about the opportunity to work out of uniform, and she was especially excited at learning about the potential action, but Bobby's lack of movement was frustrating her. The morning rush hour was in the subway below, yet they were leisurely sipping coffee on the street.

She could restrain herself no longer. "If there's action downstairs, what are we doing up here?"

At that precise moment Bobby nodded toward a male exiting the bank and in his usual measured, even tone stated, "We're doing the same thing Mr. blue blazer is doing - waiting for him."

The fifty-something year old male in the gray business suit hurried down the stairs, through the turnstiles, and onto the mezzanine of the Grand Central subway station. Fresh out of the bank with his wallet in his back pocket, the mark was blithely unaware that he'd stumbled into the clutches of a practiced jug troupe. Bobby motioned for Ellen to take up a position next to him in front of the florist shop.

He leaned into her "Watch."

A voice near the turnstiles shouted, "Look out for pickpockets,"

The verbal warning prompted the mark to feel his back pocket to make sure his wallet was still there. A male in his twenties on the other side of the mezzanine heard the verbal signal, visually identified the mark and wiped his brow, signaling to an attractive female who began walking toward the mark. She bumped into him, and while the startled mark apologized for his clumsiness, Mr. blue blazer swept noiselessly past with a balletic grace and made the dip, slipping out the wallet, dropping it into a newspaper and passing it to another male wearing a black beret.

For the first time there was a sense of urgency in Bobby's voice. "Let's go – before he gets rid of it."

Bobby was on the beret and had him cuffed before he knew what hit him. The rest of the crew was long gone. That's how it worked in this game. Once the police checked in it was every man or woman for himself.

Bobby kept a tight grip on the handcuffs while calling out to Ellen, "The mark….get the mark."

"What?" Ellen was confused.

Bobby knew from years of experience that most pickpocket victims never realized they had been victimized, so it was important to get to the victim before he disappeared onto a rush hour train.

Bobby's voice expressed a touch of frustration "The victim….the guy in the gray suit…don't lose him."

Ellen took off down the stairs to the northbound Lexington Avenue line platform and returned two minutes later with the mark in tow. The man was still in a state of disbelief that his wallet had been taken right out of his pocket.

Bobby produced his portable radio from his inside jacket pocket.

"4 crime to central K"

"Go with your message 4 crime"

"4 crime with one under requesting transportation vicinity booth R-241."

"10-4, 4 crime."

Bobby led the prisoner by holding the cuffs "Let's go wait for the car by the booth."

When they arrived at the booth Bobby turned towards Ellen and for the first time this day, a wide grin filled his face

"This is a great collar, officer."

Ellen realized that Bobby was going to let her take this felony arrest. Ellen was ecstatic to get this arrest on her record.

"Thanks, Bobby, I never thought I'd collar a pro pick pocket."

Bobby smirked. "Pro…who said anything about pros? This crew are not pros."

Ellen could not help but be a little bit deflated, as Bobby took his trip down pickpocket memory lane

"There's no sense of craft anymore. Nowadays youngsters haven't got it- no patience- no discipline- they don't want to spend the time to learn, so they hit some poor old lady over the head and grab her purse. This mope here is a pick, but he is far from a pro."

Simply by chance, Bobby and Ellen exited the district at the same time. Gentleman that he was, Bobby held the heavy steel door for Ellen as they both turned left on the crowded mezzanine and headed towards the stairs near booth A-54. Ellen began fumbling for her car keys while Bobby kept walking towards the stairway to the L train.

"See you tomorrow partner." Bobby's voice trailed off as he continued walking.

Ellen had her keys in hand, but before she exited through the turnstiles she stopped and made an about face.

"Hey Moylan – you wanna get a beer?"

Bobby stopped in his tracks. "Why not."

As they strolled south on University Place, Ellen was feeling increasingly self-conscious. Her decision to ask Bobby to go for a beer had been completely spontaneous, and now she was very concerned about what she considered to be the unkempt appearance of her face, hair, and clothing. When they entered the Cedar Tavern on Tenth Street, she excused herself and made a dash for the ladies' room. Gazing into the mirror she lamented that there was not much she was going to be able to do about the current condition of her hair and face. Ellen shook her head in disgust. If only she could have five minutes in her own bathroom.

Ellen was already very attracted to Bobby Moylan, but this was the first time she spent time with him socially, and she was nervous. As the minutes turned into hours, Ellen was delighted to discover that her attraction continued to grow. Inside the dimly lit, sparsely populated Cedar Tavern, with the jukebox providing the background atmosphere, Bobby Moylan outside of work was everything she had hoped he would be. He was personable, confident, and displayed a great sense of humor.

After three hours of great conversation, interrupted by cheeseburgers and a few beers, they were back on the sidewalk, approaching Ellen's car parked at Union Square. Bobby started to take a few steps toward the subway entrance and repeated his line from three hours earlier.

"See you tomorrow partner."

The beer absorbed into her bloodstream made it impossible to allow Bobby Moylan to just walk away.

"Hey, where are you going? You know it's not safe to be riding the trains alone after dark," Ellen declared with a big smile. "At least let me drive you home."

Bobby turned and returned the smiled. "You talked me into it."

Traffic leaving Manhattan was still extremely heavy, even after the traditional afternoon rush hour had concluded. As Ellen's Toyota crawled onto the Williamsburg Bridge, Bobby joked that he may have been able to walk home faster. Ellen laughed because she heard Bobby laugh, but she really had not heard his comment. She was too busy anticipating what she thought was about to happen. Spending the afternoon with him – the conversation – the closeness – the beer. Ellen wanted Bobby Moylan badly. Following his directions off the bridge, Ellen soon found herself creeping along Havemeyer Street. Bobby pointed to his three story walk up, and Ellen was thrilled to see a legal parking space directly in front of the one hundred year old building.

Once parked, there was a moment of awkward silence before Bobby recited his line for the third time.

"See you tomorrow partner."

Ellen was stunned. A million thoughts raced through her mind. Bobby was already out of the Toyota, but just before he slammed the door, Ellen leaned over to the passenger side as far as she could.

"You're not going to invite me in?"

Bobby hesitated, and then re-entered the vehicle. He closed the door and sat silently for a long moment, staring straight ahead. He turned toward Ellen and sighed.

"No, I'm not going to invite you in."

Ellen had no idea how to respond, and she could already feel the tears welling up in her eyes. Bobby gazed downward. He couldn't stand to see her imminent breakdown.

"If I invite you in, I know what's going to happen."

Ellen was straining to maintain some composure and dignity. "I'm OK with what happens."

Bobby made eye contact again. "You are a wonderful girl, Ellen. You're a great partner and it certainly doesn't hurt that you are gorgeous."

Tears were now running down blushing cheeks. "So, what's the problem? I don't understand."

"I just can't Ellen. It's been three years since..." his voice trailed off.

The genuine torment present on his face was only making him more attractive to her.

"It's Ok Bobby. I'm not asking for anything more than tonight. No strings." She could not believe what had come out of her mouth and she hoped she had not come across as hopelessly desperate and cheap.

"That's just it Ellen. If I was lucky enough to be with a girl like you, I know it would be for the long term, and I just can't do that yet."

Now Ellen could care less how desperate she sounded. "Well, when do you think..."

Bobby cut her off. "I don't know, but I just know that it's not right for me now." Bobby looked at her tear swelled eyes and smiled. "Cheer up. One day I'll probably be begging you to come upstairs with me, but by that time you will already have found your Mr. Right."

Bobby chuckled, and Ellen disingenuously followed him with a laugh. As far as she was concerned, the search was over. She had already found her Mr. Right.

For the fourth and final time of the evening, Bobby said his line.

"See you tomorrow partner."

During the drive to Massapequa, Ellen dissected and analyzed every second of the ten minutes they were parked at the curb on Havemeyer Street. She concluded that she had humiliated herself by throwing herself at this man, only to be unceremoniously rejected. She should be enraged, but anger was not the emotion pouring out of her. After the scene in her car, she wanted him more than ever. As she pulled into her driveway, Ellen Tomlinson ached for Bobby Moylan.

A week later Ellen sat in the muster room in full uniform forty-five minutes before the start of the day tour. Ever since that stressful sprint down Flatbush Avenue on her first day on the job, Ellen hated the prospect of being late for work. She always arrived at District 4 early, but today she was even earlier than usual. The day tour cops would begin drifting in shortly, but for the moment, Ellen enjoyed the unusual quiet of the muster room, with music on MTV providing background atmosphere.

Bobby Moylan was the first day shift cop to arrive.

"Good morning partner," he said as he walked through the muster room on his way to the locker room.

Just before disappearing into the male locker room, he stopped and turned toward Ellen.

"Oh, get out of the bag," he said using the jargon for working plainclothes. "There's been a spike in sex crimes and the captain wants us to catch a pervert."

Fifteen minutes later Ellen was again sitting in the muster room, this time in street clothes. Bobby Moylan slid onto the bench next to Ellen and began reading the morning newspaper.

Ellen interrupted his reading. "Where are we going to get this pervert?"

Bobby flipped pages to the sports section. "Grand Central is pervert central."

"Really?" Ellen realized the subway was a breeding ground for deviants. But she didn't think the situation was that bad.

Bobby closed the newspaper and removed a folded piece of paper from his shirt pocket.
"The captain gave me this. Citywide over a five-year period there have been over three thousand reports of bumping, grinding, groping, flashing, and outright sex assaults. Grand Central is the apparent epicenter of subway sleaze with 369 reported incidents."

Bobby folded the paper and returned it to his pocket.
"Remember - since sex crimes have historically been drastically underreported, that's just the tip of the iceberg."

"Why the subway?" Ellen asked, displaying her novice status of subway knowledge.
"The trains are too crowded, and some mopes take advantage. But it's not just Grand Central. Most of District 4 has a problem because nearly half of the forcible touching incidents occurred on the Lexington Avenue line between Brooklyn Bridge and 125th Street – just about all of the district"

Ellen continued to exhibit her ignorance. "Why the Lex. Line – why us?"

Bobby continued his explanation. "Gropers seek crowded places like subway cars or platforms that provide them with plenty of targets and the ability to shield their movements. And the Lexington Ave. line — one of the busiest in the nation, is ideal hunting ground for a pervert." Bobby continued, "That's why we're getting out here on the day tour. The peak hours for forcible touching are during the morning rush. Sometimes, women get victimized by touchy riders, but are unable to identify the perpetrator because of the sardine-like conditions on the train."

Forty minutes later, Bobby and Ellen stood together on the uptown Lexington Avenue line platform at Grand Central with thousands of other rush hour straphangers. Bobby surveyed the surroundings, then leaned into Ellen so she would be able to hear his continuing education.

"Gropers often operate like pickpockets. Looking for potential victims, they like to step out of a subway car when it arrives at a station and then reenter it after a new wave of riders has entered from the platform. Sometimes, they practice "looping" — riding line segments back and forth."

"What about flashing?" Ellen interjected. "That's not strictly a rush hour offense, is it?"

"You're right," Bobby responded. "Unlike groping, flashing incidents are spread throughout the day – so there's no predicting when a flasher is most likely to strike. It could be on an empty train, where they sit down right across from you and just whip it out, or it could be a crowded train when they take it out thinking no one is paying attention."

"Yuck. Why do creeps have to do that?" Ellen asked rhetorically.

She wasn't really looking for an explanation, but Bobby provided one anyway.

"I went to a training class a few years ago where a psychologist said that a flasher is a psychologically immature person who has difficulty with relationships."

Ellen laughed. "Gimme a break."

"Obviously, you're not very open to modern psychology Ms. Tomlinson," Bobby stated sarcastically. "So, what they do is they become turned on or excited by the idea of contacting someone else by shocking and surprising them and startling them. In some ways, it's a very primitive and infantile behavior. It's also very aggressive."

Bobby was finished with the psychology lesson.

"Ultimately, it's just the act of a sick creep." Bobby's eyebrows rose indicating that he had forgotten something important. "Your lesson in subway deviance would not be complete without mention of the friendly frotteur."

"Fruit – what?" Ellen asked.

"Frotteur," Bobby corrected. "A pervert who rubs up against unsuspecting and unknowing individuals and doesn't want anyone to know what he is doing — not even the victim. The frotteur is fearful of being caught, and when they get arrested they are terribly ashamed of themselves," he said. "They flip out."

Ellen laughed again. "Oh my God. What the hell is going on down here?" Her tone turned serious. "What about rapes down here?"

"Thankfully, there are not many, but most of subway rapes occur when the system is sparsely populated – between 10 PM and 6 AM." Bobby studied the throng on the platform waiting to push into the arriving uptown 4 train.

"Let's ride some trains between here and 59th Street and see what develops."

Bobby and Ellen pushed their way through different doors. They were only fifteen feet apart, but in the packed train, the distance might as well have been fifteen miles. Ellen began to panic when she could not reach a vertical or horizontal handrail to grasp, but her fears were quickly dashed when the train jerked forward, and she realized that she was packed so tightly in the car that it would be impossible to fall.

Secure that she wasn't going to fall, Ellen now focused on an unpleasant reality. How in God's name was she ever going to see a pervert operate when she could not see beyond the back of the tall gentleman she was pressed up against? She mused that if she moved her hands too quickly this man might be able to accuse her of fondling him. Oh well, when they got off the train at 59th Street she would ask Bobby what the best strategy was while riding the packed train. The train jerked to the right causing the person behind her to bump her. No big deal in a packed train, but she did note that most of the "bump" seemed to be on her butt. She was probably being overly sensitive. Again, the train jerked right and again the bump from the rear seemed to focus on her rear. The train was no longer jerking to the right, but the butt bumping continued with piston-like frequency. Ellen was not afraid – just frustrated. Someone behind her was having a good old time with her butt and she couldn't even turn around to see who it was. There was no sense in calling out to Bobby. He would not be able to get through the crowd. She was just going to have to let the creep grind into her butt until the train pulled into 59th Street.

Crowd behavior can be a fascinating subject, and there are some unique dynamics present in the crowd of a packed subway train. One such dynamic is the "pre-exit drift." No matter how tightly packed in, passengers exiting at the next stop will begin to drift toward the nearest door – even if the drift is only an inch. With fifty or more sardines all drifting an inch or two, breathing space can develop. In Ellen's case, as the train pulled into 59th Street, the pre-exit drift created enough space for her to make a quick 180-degree turn. She was now face to face with her butt bumper. The train was just about stopped as she made a quick assessment of the man she assumed was a pervert. He was White, of medium height and build, clean shaven with very well groomed short salt and pepper hair, and stylish eyeglasses. She could see a white shirt and tie underneath a black overcoat, and he was holding a briefcase in his right hand. Ellen was starting to question herself. This apparent businessman had even given the proper social response when she abruptly turned on him. Ellen stared right in his eyes, but as most people in crowded social settings will do, the male looked over Ellen's shoulder and would not make eye contact. Ellen was beginning to accept the fact that she could have been wrong. The doors would open momentarily, as she looked down, noting that this gentleman completed the profile of legitimate business man by virtue of his expensive looking brown leather shoes. Those were really nice shoes she thought. Wait a minute, what was that peeking out from the overcoat, partially obscuring her view of the shoes. It was an erect penis.

The doors opened, and Ellen was carried by the exiting crowd out the door and onto the platform. The pervert was able to remain on the train. Ellen fought against the flow of exiting humanity until she reached the door.

Pressing up against the door so it could not close, she took a deep breath and shouted, "Bobby – I got one."

Once the prisoner was secure and Bobby confirmed that Ellen was OK, they had a good laugh about the incident. As a matter of fact, one of Ellen's standard lines when using innuendo to remind Bobby of her availability was "Anytime you want to bump my butt – just let me know."

Throughout their partnership, along with turning Ellen into a savvy patrol cop, Bobby had one constant theme – study for the sergeant's exam. Bobby was constantly telling Ellen that there were no limits to how far a smart girl like her could progress on the job – if she was willing to put the work in.

Bobby Moylan was the proudest person inside One Police Plaza when the police commissioner handed Ellen Tomlinson her gold sergeant's shield. The police merger had put the Transit Police Department out of business, making Police Officer Moylan and new Sergeant Tomlinson part of the New York City Police Department. Ellen was assigned to District 20, the command within the Transit Bureau covering most of Queens. Instinctively, Ellen felt good about the comfort level of staying in the transit environment, but she regretted not having the opportunity to supervise in a precinct, and to learn the intricacies of policing on the street.

Like a river, Bobby Moylan just flowed on with life on patrol at District 4. Every month, Bobby and Ellen had a standing date for lunch or dinner, depending on their schedules. Their meetings were the highlight of Ellen's month, and she never cancelled, no matter how busy she was. A whole new avenue of conversation opened between them, with Ellen commenting, laughing, and complaining about life as a sergeant. Bobby Moylan had one constant theme during their dates. Ellen should not stop at sergeant, and should continue studying until she reached the rank of captain.

  At one dinner in an Irish pub on Greenpoint Avenue in Queens, Ellen lost the conversation and simply stared at Bobby as he worked on his burger and sipped his Coors Light. She loved this man. As much as it tormented her, she respected Bobby's feelings expressed during that night on Havemeyer Street, and she never formally broached the subject again. But she was human, and in love, so at almost every meeting her body language and humorous innuendos made it clear that as far as Bobby Moylan was concerned, Ellen Tomlinson was open for business. At least she hoped her message of complete availability was coming through.

  The monthly meals continued without a break, even after Ellen met Steve Patterson. Steve was an assistant district attorney in Queens who was handling the prosecution of a suspect in a string of Queens subway robberies, and Sgt. Ellen Tomlinson was assigned as the District 20 liaison for the case. Steve was not shy, and at the conclusion of their first case consultation he asked Ellen out to dinner. Ellen found Steve to be personable, engaging, and a lot of fun to be with. Steve had brown hair with an elegant face. He had the most amazing smile with very gentle features. He was well built and stood 6'2". He wore expensive button up shirts, with the shape of his biceps, triceps, and deltoids easily visible through his shirts. Unlike the quiet, brooding nature of Bobby Moylan, Steve Patterson was charming, and everyone seemed to enjoy being around him. Ellen could sum him up by simply saying that Steve was extremely handsome. In retrospect, maybe he was a bit too handsome.

  Steve maintained his charming full court press and six months later they were engaged. A year after the engagement Ellen and Steve lounged on a beach in Acapulco, enjoying their honeymoon. It was during the honeymoon that the unplanned conception of Patrick occurred. As joyous an event as Patrick's birth was, Ellen also noted the birth as the day her marriage quickly went south. She realized that someone as handsome and personable as

Steve had been a player before they met, but she had completely bought into his stated desire to settle down with his soulmate and raise a family. Her faith in him began to fade, however, very quickly. Maybe it was the time he spent on the computer. Maybe it was all the excuses he made to be out of the house while Ellen tended to the needs of their baby. She could not put her finger on it, but something wasn't right.

Her suspicions, as well as her marriage culminated on a beautiful summer evening. Steve arrived home around 8:30 PM looking extremely tired. Who wouldn't be after being in trial all day and then having to begin prepping a new homicide case before going home. Ellen had just put Patrick down to sleep. She gave Steve a hug and kiss and told him to relax on the sofa while she heated up his supper. The kitchen in their ranch style home was closest to the front door, so it was Ellen who heard the knocking on the door.

"Can I help you?" Ellen did not recognize the fortyish looking man standing on her doorstep.

The male very politely stated, "Excuse ma'am, my name is Jack Evans."

The name meant nothing to Ellen. "Do I know you?"

The male looked down. "No ma'am you don't know me. I just thought you should know that thirty minutes ago your husband was having sex with my wife at the Rainy Night motel."

Ellen Tomlinson and Jack Evans stared at each other. Neither had anything to say. It seemed that Jack Evans had been having his suspicions about all the time his wife Laura was spending on the computer. Finally, on this evening, he followed her for what she described to be a night out with the girls. The girls turned out to be Steve Patterson, and after a quick dinner at a fancy Italian restaurant, Steve and Laura were off for a four-hour romp at the Rainy Night motel. Jack had followed Steve home, and here he was, face to face with Ellen breaking the bad news. Ellen realized right then and there that someone like Steve was never going to be satisfied as a family man tied down to one woman for the rest of his life. Steve tried to be humble and contrite, but the die was cast. They were divorced ten months later.

All during the courtship, marriage and divorce, Ellen never missed a monthly date with Bobby Moylan. Her feelings towards Bobby had never changed, and she felt ashamed when she admitted to herself that her open for business sign regarding Bobby had never been taken down, even during her marriage. It was hard to resolve that she divorced her husband over his cheating, but that if Bobby Moylan had made a play for her, she would have jumped into his arms.

Ellen never forgot Bobby's advice, and she never stopped studying. Through hard work and good timing, she was promoted to Lieutenant and Captain with just over twelve years on the job. Captain is the last NYPD rank covered by a civil service test, but Ellen fared even better in the executive ranks appointed by the police commissioner. Three years after making captain, Ellen was promoted to Deputy Inspector, and two years later she was made a full inspector. Inspector Ellen Tomlinson, Commanding Officer, Transit Borough Manhattan, had been in her current position for a little over a year.

CHAPTER 8: THE LAST DAY – THE END

From behind the counter, Waheed Mosaab could see the headlights of the truck approaching. The speed of the approach meant only one thing. The New York Post truck was behind schedule and would be flinging a bundle of newspapers somewhere in the vicinity of the sidewalk without stopping. The sound of the truck's engine faded in the distance as Waheed exited the store to retrieve his newspapers. He grabbed the bundle by its tied string and lifted. After one short step, however, he froze, with the bundle landing on the sidewalk with a thud. Looking down at the stack of newspapers, Waheed prayed that he was experiencing a hallucination. But no, the back page of the sports section was crystal clear. It was a full-page photo of Ahmed Al-Fadhill, complete with FBI baseball cap, fighting Yankee shortstop Didi Gregorious for a foul ball.

Jimmy Boy put the finishing touches on a report he hoped would make sense to Lt. Galeno. In reality, no matter how favorably his report was viewed, it still may not satisfy the lieutenant because it was painfully lacking in solid facts. The theme of his eight type-written pages was that the Mosaab brothers may or may not be up to something, but he had no idea what their plans actually were. Jimmy Boy was just beginning to get dressed for his journey into Manhattan when the text arrived

STOP BY STORE – VERY IMPORTANT. The message was from Waheed Mosaab.

Jimmy Boy pondered his next move. He had to pass by the Mosaab brothers store on the way to the subway, so he decided to see Waheed before going to his meeting at the JTTF. He also decided not to alert Lt. Galeno of this impromptu meeting. Jimmy Boy viewed this non-notification as a strategic move because if the lieutenant was unhappy with his written report, he may still salvage the day with some verbal information gleaned from the meeting with Waheed Mosaab.

The sidewalk on 103rd Street was filled with its usual high volume as Jimmy Boy weaved his way through the human traffic. The bell rang announcing Jimmy Boy's entrance into the variety store. Rahsid Mosaab was waiting on a customer and paid Jimmy Boy no attention. At the far end of the main aisle he could see Waheed Mosaab standing in the doorway to the back room. Waheed motioned for Jimmy Boy to come to him before disappearing into the back room. Jimmy Boy had never been inside the store's back room, and he was immediately taken by its small, cramped dimensions. Adding to the cramped feeling was the fact that Jimmy Boy was now the fourth person inside these small quarters, as he joined Waheed, his creepy cousin Marwan, and an Arab male he had never seen before inside the tiny room. Jimmy Boy was a bit apprehensive entering the back room, and Waheed's greeting only served to make him more anxious.

"Welcome brother. This is a great day. It is the day of our great operation."

Jimmy Boy joined the other occupants of the room in several choruses of "God is great" Waheed continued his speech. "Today, our brother Marwan becomes a hero of the jihad."

Jimmy boy was trying to digest what was going on. His instincts told him nothing good was happening, especially when he took a close look at creepy cousin Marwan. His unkempt beard was gone. This was an unsettling red flag for Jimmy Boy. Traditionally, Muslims purify corpses by washing the skin and nails and sometimes by shaving the pubic hair. But suicide attackers are deprived of a proper burial, since there are usually no remains. To compensate, the attackers shear themselves ahead of time, both to guarantee some level of cleanliness at the time of instant incineration and to prove extreme devotion to personal purity. Jimmy Boy gulped as he noted how clean Marwan looked for a potential appointment in heaven. Any doubts about Marwan's intent were dashed as Jimmy Boy further studied the clean-shaven creep. The vest Marwan was wearing made Jimmy Boy's eyes widen. .

"That's a bomb vest," he thought.

The situation went from bad to worse when Waheed wheeled forward the green backpack/duffel bag he kept secreted in the back room since his journey from Guatemala.

What's in the backpack," Jimmy boy queried."

"A grand gift from God," Waheed happily responded.

Jimmy boy was stumped. If cousin creepy was already wearing the bomb, what great gift could God have put in the backpack? The answer was supplied in Waheed's next sentence, and its content hit Jimmy boy like a ton of bricks.

"Our courageous brother Marwan will be carrying a small nuclear device in the bag."

Jimmy Boy was frozen- not in fear, but in disbelief at what he had just heard.

Waheed continued. "Marwan will ride the subway into Manhattan. Once at Times Square he will detonate the bomb in his vest and God willing, that explosion will trigger the nuke." Waheed raised his hands in praise. "With God's grace, every infidel in Manhattan will be sacrificed."

As surreal as his situation was, a bizarre thought crossed Jimmy boy's mind. This better be enough solid information to satisfy Lt. Galeno.

Jimmy Boy quickly switched gears from worrying about his job to worrying about the City of New York. His plan of action was obvious. As soon as he turned the corner outside the store, he would be onto 911, and within minutes ESU and the precinct would be swooping down on Waheed and his crew. Jimmy Boy inched his way into the doorway of the backroom.

"Good luck brothers. May God grant you success."

Waheed's smile was gone. "Where are you going, brother?"

Jimmy Boy had not prepared for this exigency and was now fishing for a good answer. "I have an important appointment, and I can't be late."

Immediately, Jimmy Boy gritted his teeth in disgust with the bland nature of his response. The specifics of his appointment were not an issue as Waheed pressed him no further. To Waheed Mosaab, it was irrelevant what Jimmy Boy had planned because this would be his last day.

"There is nothing more important than the operation, brother." Waheed slid past Jimmy Boy and reassuringly placed his right hand on his left shoulder. He was also strategically placing himself between Jimmy Boy and the exit to the store. "Why do you think I called you here? You are an important part of the operation."

Jimmy Boy took a deep breath, telling himself repeatedly to remain calm. After all, at some point he would surely have the opportunity to separate himself from the crew to call for assistance.

Rashid Mosaab had locked the door and placed a CLOSED sign on the front door. At least the conditions were no longer cramped as Jimmy Boy and the crew emerged onto the selling floor.

Waheed addressed the group. "Our operation is now active and as per our protocols there will be no more outside communications until the operation is executed."

Jimmy Boy didn't really care what this communication protocol involved. He was too busy trying to formulate a plan to get alone, even for a moment, so that he could call for help. Waheed pointed to his brother, who was holding a large plastic bag.

"Everyone place your cell phones inside the bag. They will be returned after the operation."

"Holy shit," Jimmy boy screamed in his mind. What was he going to do now? Desperately, he was trying to formulate some kind of plan as the phones of Waheed, Rashid, creepy cousin Marwan, and the stranger dropped into the bag. Jimmy Boy had come up with absolutely nothing as Rashid held the open bag in front of him, and he obediently dropped his lifeline inside.

With the communications blackout in place, Waheed went over the tactical details of the operation. The simplest part of the operation was the route and destination. Marwan would be taken to the Willets Point elevated subway station where he would board a 7-train and ride into Times Square. If no problems developed he would carry his backpack up to the street, detonate his vest, and hopefully wipe out a large portion of Manhattan. If at any time during the train ride he sensed a problem, Marwan was to detonate his bomb immediately. The most difficult part of the tactics involved getting Marwan familiar with the trigger to his bomb vest. Waheed explained that it was a pressure trigger.

Marwan would hold the trigger in his hand and squeeze it. Once the trigger was armed, the moment Marwan released the pressure on the trigger, the bomb would detonate. It was actually a very simple trigger, but Jimmy Boy could sense Waheed's apprehension. Obviously, Jimmy Boy was not alone in his opinion that creepy cousin Marwan was also stupid cousin Marwan. The whole reason Waheed had brought cousin Marwan to America was because he did not want the honor and glory of martyrdom. Now, with the moment of truth at hand, Waheed was questioning whether his cousin could fully understand the concept of a pressure trigger.

For a good fifteen minutes Waheed made Marwan hold a hand grip exerciser. He would instruct Marwan to squeeze the grip and hold it tight. At some point he would tell Marwan to release his grip. At the moment Marwan released the grip, Waheed would shout "BOOM". Finally, Waheed was confident that even a simpleton like Marwan understood the pressure trigger. Jimmy Boy was becoming frantic. During Marwan's fifteen minutes of pressure trigger training, the pressure on Jimmy Boy continued to mount. He still had no idea what to do to summon help. He was not armed, and he had to assume that the Mosaab brothers and the stranger were carrying firearms.

Waheed nodded and the stranger left the store. Five minutes later Jimmy Boy heard three short blasts of a car horn emanating from outside the store. The horn stirred Waheed to action.

"Let's go," he said while grabbing the handle for the backpack.

Rashid stayed very close to Jimmy Boy as they exited the store and piled into the beat-up Toyota Camry parked in front. A million thoughts were racing through Jimmy Boy's brain as Waheed deposited the backpack in the trunk. Should he scream? Should he make a run for it? His potential options became a moot point as he remained frozen and eventually found himself stuffed between the Mosaab brothers in the back seat of the Toyota. The stranger pulled the Toyota to a stop on Roosevelt Avenue, adjacent to the stairway of the Willets Point elevated subway station. Jimmy Boy noted the same stupid look on Marwan's face as he took his backpack from the trunk and headed towards the station stairs with the stranger providing an escort.

"God is great." Waheed and Rashid yelled out the window to him as he disappeared up the stairs. Jimmy Boy was starting to panic. At some point he was going to have to do something, even if it meant doing battle with two armed men in the cramped quarters of the back seat of a Toyota. The stranger returned to the driver's seat.

"The device is armed and he's on his way." the stranger said without turning around.

"Good," Waheed responded. "Go to the next stop."

The Toyota pulled away from the curb with Jimmy Boy trying to figure out what the next stop was, and what he was going to do.

Where are we going now?" Jimmy Boy asked.

He did not like the cold emotionless manner in which Waheed responded

"Patience, brother. You'll know soon enough."

Within two minutes Jimmy Boy was staring at what could be best described as a post-apocalyptic landscape. What made the environment more surreal was that fact that Citi Field, the home of the New York Mets, was plainly visible to the west. The street being traversed by the Toyota was unpaved and full of holes.

Besides being an elevated subway station, Willets Point was also a section of Queens known locally as the Iron Triangle, due to its concentration of auto repair shops, scrapyards, waste processing sites, and similar small industrial businesses. There were no sidewalks or sewers and due to the area's geography and the lack of paved roads, flooding was common during heavy rains. Jimmy Boy bounced continually in the back seat, and on two occasions the bump was so severe that he struck his head on the roof of the car.

The scenery of dilapidated junk yards and auto body shops began to thin. Jimmy Boy's fear level was off the charts when the Toyota came to a stop. They were on a street completely devoid of people, vehicles, and buildings. Both sides of the unpaved dirt road were lined by weeds that were at least four feet high. Jimmy Boy gulped as he scanned the surrounding landscape. It did not take a genius to realize this was the perfect location to dump a body. Jimmy Boy could feel the perspiration building on his forehead. Waheed removed a piece of paper folded several times and handed it to Jimmy Boy.

"Here brother – I have something I want you to see."

Jimmy Boy began unfolding the paper. It was a picture of some kind, and the first thing he recognized was the figure of a baseball player. A terrorist was about the blow up most of Manhattan, and he was being given a picture of a baseball player.

"I don't understand." Jimmy Boy voiced in an annoyed tone, his frustration boiling over.

"Keep unfolding brother, and everything will become clear to you."

Jimmy Boy opened the last fold and his mouth dropped open. He was staring at himself in an FBI baseball cap fighting Didi Gregorious for a foul ball.

His recognition of himself lasted only a split second when it was disrupted by a sharp pain to his right temple. Jimmy Boy tried to fend of the blows, but Waheed pinned his hands down in his lap while Rashid continued to land blows to his head with his 9mm semi-automatic pistol. Jimmy Boy was straining to remain conscious as he heard Waheed direct his brother to stop the attack. He also felt his hands being bound together in front of him. It happened so quickly, Jimmy Boy realized that Waheed must have used a flexible handcuff known as a flexi-cuff. He felt another sharp blow to his face as he was roughly pushed forward, slamming his face into the rear of the front seat.

"Frisk him." Waheed directed his brother.

When Rashid had finished his rear search, he threw Jimmy Boy back into his original position and completed the frisk in his front. Waheed Mosaab then forecast the future of New York City and of Jimmy Boy Craig.

"Today, brother, many thousands of infidels will die, and you, Mr. FBI will be the first to perish."

Maybe the blows to the head had knocked the fear and panic out of him, but at that moment, seconds away from his own demise, Jimmy Boy Craig had never been more clear- headed. He was wondering if they were going to shoot him in the back seat or march him into the weeds before executing him. Before even thinking about some last-ditch plan to save himself, it came to him like a bolt of lightning. The belt – he was wearing the belt. That belt had become such a standard part of his attire he hardly remembered that there was a gun secreted inside of it.

Waheed had just slightly cracked open the driver's side rear door. Either they were going to take him out to the weeds or Waheed was simply going to get himself out of Rashid's line of fire. A quick scan revealed that Rashid possessed the only visible firearm, making Jimmy Boy's path clear. He took one deep breath and savored the complete calmness that had come over him.

The entire scene seemed to be playing in slow motion as Jimmy Boy, even with his hands cuffed together reached for his belt buckle. His movement never stopped as he withdrew the hidden pistol with his well-practiced quick draw technique and turned toward Rashid. For reasons unknown, his thoughts returned to Herb Stromeyer as he screamed at the top of his lungs,

"Fuck accuracy daddy-o."

His cuffed hands recoiled but he didn't perceive the sound of a gunshot. The blood and brains splattering throughout the car's interior provided Jimmy Boy with evidence of his gun's functionality. The recoil worked to his advantage as Jimmy Boy's hands were already moving in the direction of the next target. The stranger behind the wheel had not moved a muscle as he stared at Jimmy Boy with wide eyes. This time, Jimmy Boy let out a generic scream as the sound of the shot resonated throughout the car, along with more blood and brains. To Jimmy Boy, this was all one fluid movement as his pistol continued moving left. Waheed Mosaab had one foot out of the car, and his right hand was grabbing at his waistband. Jimmy Boy could see the butt of a gun in Waheed's grip, but it did not matter. With one more squeeze of his trigger, Jimmy Boy completed the trio of reluctant martyrs.

It was over. Jimmy Boy sat in the middle of the back seat with the deceased Mosaab brothers on either side. He could not see the stranger in the front seat, but when he saw his head explode, Jimmy Boy knew the stranger was no longer a threat. The calm, serene feeling he enjoyed during his moment of crisis was now abandoning him. Jimmy Boy began to uncontrollably shake as tears cascaded down his cheeks.

Despite his diminished physical condition, Jimmy knew his job was only beginning. By this time, creepy cousin Marwan was several stops into his trip to Manhattan. Waheed Mosaab was lying with his upper torso inside the Toyota and his legs out of the open back door. Jimmy Boy pushed the lifeless body out of the car and followed it onto the dirt road. His hands were still cuffed in front of him, and he suddenly realized that he was still carrying his belt-gun. Jimmy Boy could not think of anything better to do, so he tossed the pistol into the back seat and began to run.

With only weeds and unpaved dirt road around him, Jimmy Boy sprinted toward his only visible landmark – Citi Field. He was breathing heavily as he emerged from the weeds and onto 126th street. He tried flagging down a few passing vehicles, but no sane person was going to stop for the blood covered, handcuffed man running in the middle of the street.

The wrought iron gates at the prominently marked BULLPEN GATE were closed and locked. What really caught Jimmy Boy's eye, however, was the silhouette of a figure inside the gates. The security guard must have been scared out of his wits at the site of the handcuffed male with blood all over his face, sprinting towards the gates. The guard had backed away from the gates and was on his portable radio screaming for help as Jimmy Boy stood outside the gates pleading for his phone. Maybe it was fear, maybe it was hearing Jimmy Boy scream FBI…FBI – maybe it was just wanting to make the bloody lunatic outside his gates go away. Whatever the reason, the seventy-year-old security guard cautiously walked forward and eased his iPhone though the space between the iron rails of the gates. Although challenging, Jimmy boy could hold and dial the phone with his hands still bound by the flexi-cuff. 911 would do no good at this point. It would take too long to get the message understood and to get the troops responding. Jimmy Boy knew exactly who he had to call.

"Lt. Galeno, may I help you."

Joey Galeno was already ticked off that Jimmy Boy had failed to appear at their scheduled meeting, and now he was becoming infuriated with the stammering, stuttering voice on the phone.

"Listen up, Craig, this is the end. I'm ordering you to......".

Jimmy Boy cut him off with a shout. "WILL YOU JUST SHUT UP AND LISTEN."

Joey was stunned and just silently held the phone to his ear. Joey was equally stunned when he absorbed Jimmy Boy's message that a terrorist was enroute on the 7-train to Times Square with a nuclear device. Joey had to instantly process his options and solutions. According to Jimmy Boy's timeline, the terrorist was still likely in Queens, but in about ten minutes his train would pull into Grand Central- then Fifth Avenue- and then Times Square.

Joey was in full flight down the stairs to the parking garage while considering the lack of viable options. His tires screeched as he exited the garage. While he impatiently waited for the security guard to lower the Delta Barrier he ran through options in his mind that would not work. He couldn't just call 911. In fact, he couldn't have any visible police response. If Jimmy Boy's information regarding the pressure trigger was accurate, the moment the terrorist perceived police descending on him it would be game, set and match. Joey hit his siren as he accelerated onto the northbound FDR Drive. What was he going to do? Just wait at Times Square to blow up like most of Manhattan? There had to be a strategy that at least had a chance to work. Joey weaved in and out of traffic approaching East Houston Street. The train was probably just entering the east river tunnel, and within five minutes would be pulling into Grand Central.

"Grand Central." He shouted out load while grabbing his phone.

Ellen directed her driver to pull to the curb at the corner of 42nd Street and Lexington Avenue. After descending the stairs into the subway, she was relieved to see that no lengthy search would be required, as Bobby Moylan was plainly in view standing near booth R-241.

"Good afternoon inspector," Bobby respectfully stated while saluting the approaching brass.

Ellen returned the salute and directed her attention towards Bobby's partner, Steve Bryant.

"Go upstairs officer and return to District 4 with my driver. I have the post for the rest of the tour."

Steve was gone instantly leaving Bobby with a new partner.

Bobby sighed and half chuckled, "I hope there's no big thing waiting for me at the command."

Ellen cut him off in her best superior officer tone. "Shut up Moylan and patrol your post. We still have an hour before you go EOT."

Ellen had used the abbreviation for end of tour, and Bobby good naturedly corrected her. "Yes ma'am, but didn't you mean EOC – end of career." Ellen rolled her eyes at the corny joke as they began strolling to the passageway that connected the 4, 5, and 6 lines with the 7 line.

They stopped in front of the door to the police room and continued with the usual small talk that Ellen had wanted to get beyond for years. Bobby took a break from the banter, and took a deep breath as he took in the full scene of the passing ridership. Reality was finally setting in.

"I can't believe that this is it," he stated in his steady, even tone.

Ellen remained silent, but turned her head to look at him as he continued.

Bobby shook his head slightly and bit his lip as he spoke softly, in a voice slightly louder than a whisper.

"I can't believe it's over - 42-years and now it's over."

Ellen turned to face a side of Bobby Moylan she had never seen before. Were those tears welling up in the eyes of this strong, stoic man?

"What am I supposed to do tomorrow? Where should...?" The cracking of his voice prevented any further articulation. Bobby looked to the ground and shook his head. There were no more words.

Ellen could sense what was happening. 42-years of repressed emotions were about to explode out of Bobby Moylan, and she wanted to protect him from making it a public display.

She could detect a tear rolling down his left cheek as she barked an order, "Give me your 400-key Moylan."

The 400-key opened most of the doors in the subway system, and Bobby kept staring at the ground as he detached the key ring from his gun belt and handed them to Ellen. A moment later they were inside the police room, free from public view. The change of venue came not a moment too soon as tears rolling down Bobby's cheeks quickly were joined by audible weeping.

Bobby wiped his eyes with his right hand,
"I'm so sorry Ellen. I shouldn't be doing this."

"Oh, shut up Moylan," she admonished while putting her arms around him in a warm embrace.

The dam of emotion finally broke, and Bobby Moylan openly cried as he buried his head in Ellen's left shoulder.

Bobby's cap had fallen to the floor, and Ellen whispered, "It's alright Bobby, let it out." as she gently stroked the back of his head.

After about 30-seconds Bobby was able to reach a semi-composed state and remove his head from Ellen's shoulder. His watery eyes locked on hers. "Do you want to come over tonight?"

Now it was Ellen's turn to break through an emotional barrier as she heard the words she had given up hope of ever hearing.

"Of course I want to come over darling," she sang out as she pulled Bobby toward her and held him as tightly as she was capable of.

The emotional hug left them cheek to cheek, and ever so slowly both their heads began to turn. In a few seconds, cheek to cheek had become mouth to mouth and they were locked in a deep, passionate kiss. Ellen was amazed at how totally unprepared she was for this moment. She had spent years clinging to the casual relationship that Bobby would allow, longing for the moment when his icy self-protective layer would thaw. That moment was now at hand and although this fantasy had been played out countless times in her mind, she never imagined how warm and fulfilling his lips felt pressed up against her own.

As far as Ellen was concerned, time could have frozen at that moment and she would have been completely satisfied going through life with her lips locked to Bobby Moylan's. The vibrating tone from Bobby's cell phone ended that delightful fantasy, as he pulled back from the kiss and reached for the phone holder on his belt.

"Use a bookmark to keep the place Moylan, and we'll pick this up again tonight." Ellen punctuated her comment with a seductive wink and a seemingly freshly composed Bobby Moylan responded, "Yes ma'am." in a playfully officious manner as he freed the phone from its holder. With a quick glace of his smartphone's screen, Bobby pressed the connect button as he put the phone to his ear. "What's up, Joey?"

At once, Bobby detected the air of urgency in Joey's voice. The accompanying background siren was an additional indicator that this was not a call of congratulatory well wishes.

"You still at Grand central Bobby?"

"Yeah, what's up?"

Joey's mind was racing faster than his Caprice, and he consciously tried to slow himself down. He knew his next message to Bobby Moylan needed to be crystal clear.

"Bobby, I can't get into a lot of details, but there's a Manhattan bound 7-train that should be pulling into Grand Central in a few minutes."

"Yeah, and..." Bobby said apprehensively.

"Not the lead car, but one of the first few cars, there's a big problem."

"What type of problem Joey?"

"There's a suicide bomber with an active device on board."

Bobby had obviously displayed enough emotion for one day, as his response to Joey was steady and measured. "Is this information reliable?"

Joey shot back with much more emotion in his voice,

"I got it direct from the FBI undercover who saw him board the train in Queens. The UC says that the target is Times Square."

"Gimme a script and any info. on the device." Bobby's free hand opened the door of the police room and then beckoned Ellen to follow. Bobby led a bewildered Ellen in the direction of the stairway to the 7-train platform while continuing to receive information from Joey.

"Middle Eastern male, 20-25 years old, short, small frame, short hair, clean shaven, wearing a HEAVY coat." Joey accentuated the word heavy because in the late summer heat of the NYC subway system, a rider with a coat would surely stand out.

"Anything else Joey?"

"Yeah Bobby, there is" Joey hesitated before delivering the bad news. "The device has a pressure trigger."

At once Bobby realized that the situation had just changed from bad to worse.

"A pressure trigger - that's great," Bobby responded sarcastically.

"I'm not done yet, Bobby." Joey's voice had a somber tone Bobby had never heard before. "The bomb with the pressure trigger is being used as a trigger for a device the bomber is carrying in a backpack – it's a nuke."

Bobby stood silently with the phone too his ear, trying to comprehend the ramifications of the situation he was being thrust into.

Joey continued, "I'm calling ESU direct. I really don't know what to do at this point, but I don't want to call a 10-13 and have cops running toward that train from all directions."

Joey's voice turned calm as he drove onto the exit ramp at 42nd Street.

"I wish I had some great advice for you."

"Got it Joey. See you later."

Bobby hung up and moved his phone back into its holder with the same emotion as if he had just taken a lunch order from Joey. Bobby completed briefing Ellen on the situation as they arrived on the platform.

The 7 was an island style platform with the tracks on the north side of the platform housing trains emerging from the river tunnel from Queens, while the south tracks were for trains beginning the trip under the East River and into Queens. For trains just arriving from Queens, Grand Central was the first stop in

Manhattan. Fifth Avenue followed and then Times Square. Times Square used to be the terminal point in Manhattan, but a new station on the west side near the Javitz Convention Center had recently opened extending the 7-line.

Bobby and Ellen stood at the very front end of the rapidly crowding platform and peered down the length of the tracks and into the darkness of the river tunnel. Ellen was now aware of the situation, but she had no idea what Bobby planned to do.

"What do have in mind?" she asked while attempting to mask her nervous tone.

"I'll let you know when I know sweetie." They both slightly chuckled and Ellen realized that it was completely preposterous that in this tense situation she was still conscious of the fact that he had called her sweetie.

Slowly, the blackness of the tunnel began to transform. First there was just a hint of illumination followed by an explosion of light as the first car of the train became visible in the tunnel. The train roared into the station with its speed rapidly decelerating. The first car of the train came to a complete stop with the motorman's cab positioned directly next to where Bobby and Ellen were standing.

"Don't move this train again until I specifically tell you to, OK?"

"You got it chief." was the train operator's response.

Bobby and Ellen entered the train through the front doors of the first car and began a deliberate walk toward the rear of the car. Grand Central was a major detraining point for riders coming to Manhattan from Queens, so what once had been a packed train was now much less populated. Bobby led the way through the door of the first car and reemerged in the second car. All the seats were filled with riders casually reading newspapers or listening to headphones. A few people stood in the areas near the doors. No one caught Bobby's eye, so he continued through the doors to the third car. When he emerged into car number three he immediately performed a visual scan. His scan quickly stopped and locked on someone seated about midpoint in the car. A young, Middle Eastern male was sitting in the seat staring straight ahead. The male looked to be in his early twenties and was clean shaven. The heavy coat he was wearing was not the factor that made Bobby gulp deeply. What caused a chill to run up Bobby's spine was the tight fist the male's right hand was balled into.

This was the moment of truth and Bobby knew it. There was no time to huddle with Ellen to devise a plan or wait for Joey and the cavalry. He knew he had to do something, and he had to do it right now. Seated to the left of the bomber was a Black male in a business suit. The male was about 35 years of age and sported glasses as he read the Wall Street Journal. Bobby directed all his attention to the Black male as he stood directly in front of him and stated in a very loud, officious voice,

"Gimme some ID, now"

The male seemed stunned and responded in a confused manner "Is there something wrong officer?"

Bobby continued in his obnoxious tone "Yeah, there's plenty wrong, now gimme some ID."

The male continued to sport a puzzled look "Did I do something, officer?"

"Yeah, you pissed me off" was Bobby's terse response as he leaned in and grabbed the male by his shirt collar and lifted him off his seat.

"What the hell are you doing?" the male shouted in disbelief.

Most of the other passengers in the car became engaged with shouts of "hey", "stop", "leave him alone" and "he didn't do anything."

One male, however, did not acknowledge the confrontation. The male directly to the right of Bobby's victim kept staring straight ahead and maintained his right clenched fist, with his backpack secured between his legs.

In one motion Bobby shoved the Black male towards the open door, but then quickly wheeled around and dove at the seated male. More specifically, Bobby dove at his clenched fist. Bobby's full weight landed on top of the male, pinning him to his seat. Bobby immediately tightened his hands around the clenched fist and squeezed for all he was worth. With the trigger momentarily secured, Bobby screamed for Ellen

"Take the backpack." He must have sensed that she had not moved as he screamed again in a more desperate tone "For God's sake Ellen – take the bag off the station. Ellen...Please...do it now...I don't know how long I can maintain this grip."

Inspector Ellen Tomlinson knew what she had to do. She quickly yanked the backpack from between the entangled combatants and exited the car. She yelled for everyone to clear the train and platform, including the completely frazzled male who had just been in Bobby Moylan's grip. As Ellen barked her warning from the platform, she tried to think of some action she could take to help Bobby. She wanted to lead a rush of cop humanity into the car to completely overpower the bomber, but she knew what would that likely result would be. As much as she hated it, she realized that her responsibility was to evacuate Grand Central as quickly as possible, and she deployed any responding cops to assist in the evacuation.

As the 7-train platform became eerily silent Bobby Moylan and Marwan remained locked in a silent deaths struggle. Marwan had not uttered a sound, and Bobby was focused only on keeping his grip tightly around Marwan right fist. The evacuation was continuing at a record pace when Lt. Joey Galeno arrived and identified himself to Inspector Ellen Tomlinson. They had never met before, but there was an immediate kindred spirt in being connected through Bobby Moylan. Joey did not have to be told what was in the backpack. He called over four nearby Emergency

Services Unit cops and explained the situation. The ESU cops disappeared up the stairs, backpack in tow. With the station seemingly secure, Ellen and Joey raced down to the 7-platform. Bobby had been maintaining his grip on Marwan's fist for a full ten minutes, and his breaths were deep in near exhaustion.

Joey yelled from outside the car, "Bobby, you alright?"

Bobby's gasping alerted Joey to the dire situation "Get out of here Joey, now."

Ellen wanted to say a lot of things, but all that came out was her shriek of "Bobby"

Joey made a motion towards the Glock 17 sitting on his right hip. "I'm gonna put one right in his head Bobby".

Bobby summoned up his remaining energy to vocalize his feelings.
"Get out of here NOW Joey, and take her with you. Carry her if you have to. I'm losing it fast here." Bobby didn't wait for a response and shouted one last plea "GO, NOW."

Joey sensed the finality of Bobby's plea and pulled Ellen behind a steel pillar on the platform. Inside the car, Bobby Moylan was facing the inevitable reality. Even if his rapidly depleting strength held out, perspiration would be his ultimate undoing. The sweat on both his and Marwan's hands was making it impossible to maintain his tight grip. Very slowly his hands were beginning to slide. He could not break contact to get a new grip. All he could do was watch his hands slide ever so slowly off Marwan's fist. It was almost over. In a few more seconds Marwan's fist would be free enough to release the pressure on the trigger.

Suddenly, all the fear and stress were gone from Bobby Moylan. He was totally at peace. Just before the brilliant flash of light engulfed him, he heard the happy voices of two children shouting, "Hi daddy."

CHAPTER 9: THE AFTERMATH

It was less than twenty-four hours since Bobby Moylan sacrificed himself. Due to Bobby's heroic actions, as well as the quick work of Joey, Ellen and several Emergency Services Unit cops, Bobby and Marwan were the only casualties of the explosion. Now, this unlikely shell-shocked group sat around the large table in the police commissioner's conference room, clueless as to the nature of the assembly.

Lt. Joey Galeno recognized everyone around the table. Inspector Ellen Tomlinson was on his left and Jimmy Boy Craig was seated to his right. Across the table from him were four ESU cops. He did not know these cops, but he recognized them as the officers he had turned over the nuclear backpack to on the previous day.

The conference room door opened, and the entourage entered, led by the Police Commissioner. Joey recognized the Chief of Department, but he did not recognize the other two gentlemen. The PC welcomed everyone and provided the introductions. Present along with the Chief of Department were Frank Sanders, Deputy Director of the FBI, and Ken Collins, from Washington. Joey found it very odd that Collins was not identified by his agency.

The PC started the presentation.

"You all went through a traumatic experience yesterday, so we won't keep you long."

He placed both his palms on the table and leaned forward.
"I just want all of you to know that your actions yesterday were in the finest tradition of the New York City Police Department."

The PC seemed to be about to relinquish the floor, but suddenly caught himself.
"And I'm sure Deputy Director Sanders would agree that Agent Craig's actions made the Bureau proud."

Frank Sanders nodded as the PC resumed introducing the next speaker.

"Ken Collins has a few words for you."

The man from the unidentified agency replaced the PC at the head of the table. Even though he didn't know the agency, Joey thought Collins looked like a Fed, with the short sandy hair and conservative dark business suit. Collins stood with his hands in his pants pockets as he got right to the point.

"You seven hold a secret that must stay a secret."

Only silence filled the room as he continued.

"You are the only people who know that there was a nuclear bomb in that subway car yesterday – and the secret is going to stay with you."

The lack of eye contact and pace of his voice made it painfully obvious to Joey that Collins was not looking for any debate on the topic.

"The commissioner has confidentiality agreements that each of you will sign. Deputy Director Sanders has a similar agreement for you, Agent Craig."

Collins continued, "Let me be very clear ladies and gentlemen, failure to abide by these confidentiality agreements is a federal offense and you will be prosecuted to the fullest extent of the law."

Ellen Tomlinson could stay silent no longer. "Why….."

Collins cut her off before she could get started. "Let's just say, Inspector, that it has been decided at the highest levels that it is in the best interests of the United States of America that the citizenry does not find out that there was a nuclear bomb in the New York City Subway." Without allowing any opportunity for a response, Ken Collins was out of the door of the conference room.

The following afternoon the light on the phone blinked on the secure line in an office at Langley. The voice on the other end of the line spoke with a distinctive Israeli accent.

"You were right my friend. The Qataris plan on doing nothing. Do not worry – the situation is handled."

Ken Collins said, "Thank you," and hung up the phone.

Dr. Khaled Fadel had followed the story over various news feeds. What had him most irate was learning that Waheed Mosaab had double crossed him and used a replacement martyr. He was perplexed about the disposition of the nuke, but he wasn't worried. Without the assistance of the Qatari government, the device would never be traced back to him. True, he had lost his American cell, but there would be others he could send as replacements, and he could send Dr. Abadi back to Guatemala to work on another bomb.

The jihad could wait until another day. Dr. Fadel had more pressing business at hand. This was his last night in Paris on company business and he desperately needed some female companionship before he returned home. The Fontainebleau Escort Service was the doctor's favorite and most trusted avenue for female entertainment. Fifty minutes after he made the call, a knock on the door of his luxury suite indicated his wait was over.

She had a sculpted figure with gorgeous flowing dark hair. Her waist was tapered, and she had an impeccable olive toned complexion. A sculptor could not have fashioned her seraph's ears and pixie's nose any better. When she broke into a smile, her beguiling, oyster-white teeth lit up the room. It jolted Fadel like an electric current. Filed to perfection, her Venus-red fingernails reached out and ran through his curly black hair. Her nebulous, Eden-green eyes sparkled with the 'joie de vivre'. They were like two beryl-green jewels melted onto snow. She pulled his head forward for a sweet introductory kiss. Her calamine-pink lips tasted like rose petals. She whispered to the doctor in a dulcet voice as sweet as any songbird.

"I'm famished darling, can we get room service?"

"Of course, my dear. Make yourself comfortable."

Dr. Fadel ordered two surf and turf dinners. While placing the order he contemplated the voice of his sexy companion. It wasn't the English of a French girl. He couldn't quite place the exotic accent, but God – was it sexy.

Dr. Fadel was overjoyed to discover that her beauty was matched by her sexual prowess. The knock on the door thirty minutes later provided a welcome break in the festivities, as well as an opportunity for him to catch his breath.

A smiling waiter rolled the finely decorated cart into the room.

"It looks wonderful" she stated timidly.

Dr. Fadel walked toward the fully stocked bar.

"Would you like a drink, my dear?"

"Rye and ginger please."

Dr. Fadel stood with his back to his beautiful companion, manipulating glasses, bottles, and ice.

"I must say, my dear, you are the most beautiful girl I have ever seen."

She wasn't listening. She was lifting the elegant table cloth and searching for something under the room service cart. Cubes of ice landed in each glass with a clang.

"And your accent – so sexy and exotic. It's not French – what is it?"

There was no answer. The only sound in the room was the muffled blast of the silencer equipped 9mm pistol.

Five minutes later the beauty was through the lobby revolving doors and into a waiting cab. In the suite, her voguish clothes still kept captive an aroma redolent of cinnamon and meadow-fresh mint. It lingered in the room long after she had gone, mixing with the smell of gun powder.

As the cab sped into the night the girl politely said, "Airport please.".

The driver responded in a distinctive Israeli accent,

"Is there anything else you need to do before going to the airport?"

The girl meekly smiled while opening a paperback book.

"No, I've completed all my business in Paris."

EPILOGUE

The moment was surreal. It was 11 AM on a weekday morning in the City of New York – a time when the decibel level in the streets is permanently set to "high". In a one square mile section of Jackson Heights, however, the only sounds were provided by three flags flapping freely in the sporadic breeze. The NYPD color guard bearing the flags of the United States, New York City, and the NYPD served as the focal point in a sea of blue. Local residents and officers from as far as California and Louisiana converged on Our Lady of Fatima Roman Catholic Church on 79th street on this warm late summer day for a final salute to Police Officer Bobby Moylan.

Tens of thousands of uniformed officers stood in formation outside the church and in the surrounding blocks while hundreds of people attended the funeral at the close of a week which saw flags at city and state government buildings flown at half-staff and other tributes in Moylan's memory.

Shortly after 11 AM, eight pallbearers gently lifted Moylan's flag draped casket into the hearse as bagpipes played "Amazing Grace." The Emerald Society pipes and drums led the way in a solemn escort for Bobby Moylan's final ride. Among the dignitaries paying respect to the passing hearse were the governor, mayor, police commissioner, and all the NYPD deputy commissioners. For Dr. John Hickey, this was his first police funeral as Deputy Commissioner for Counterterrorism, and he prayed it would be his last. Kristin Bermudez-McGinn, civilian director of the Counterterrorism Bureau stood at solemn attention. Her eyes turned skyward at the final ceremonial tribute – three NYPD helicopters flying overhead in the "Missing Man" formation.

The funeral procession was more than a mile long. Like a giant snake it slowly weaved through the Queens neighborhoods of Jackson Heights, Sunnyside, and Woodside before entering through the gates of Calvary Cemetery. The plain marble stone was now complete with the name Robert Moylan added to Mary, Kristin, and Patrick.

Bobby Moylan had been the only child of two only children, resulting in no next of kin. Ellen Tomlinson was shocked when Austin Brown came forward as the executor of Bobby's will. Austin explained to Ellen that Bobby hoped she would assume the role of next of kin at his funeral.

Ellen obediently sat graveside, playing the role of grieving widow as the ceremony progressed. A lone piper on a distant hill wailed "Coming Home". The priest from Our Lady of Fatima prayed over the casket while two members of the NYPD ceremonial unit removed the flag from the coffin and folded it with military precision. The commanding officer of the Ceremonial Unit took possession of the flag and approached Ellen. He leaned down towards her while extending the triangular folded flag. Two NYPD buglers blared taps while Bobby Moylan was lowered to his final resting place.

Forty-five minutes after the ceremony, the scene was completely different. Aside from a couple of cemetery workers performing maintenance in an area nearby, only four mourners remained with Bobby Moylan. The four individuals had been silent for a long time, each reflecting on the moment in their own way.

Ellen Tomlinson broke the silence. "You realize he would have hated all this pomp."
Laughter broke out from her audience.

"You got that right," Joey Galeno chimed in. "I was half expecting him to open the coffin and tell everyone to go home."

More laughter.

"I wonder if this city will ever know what he did for them?" The question was framed in the fashion typical of a non-New Yorker. Jimmy Boy Craig came to the funeral with Joey Galeno. He had never met Bobby Moylan, and perhaps this lack of personal attachment put him in a better position to fully appreciate what this police officer had done for his city. The tone of Jimmy Boy's question touched on the fact that city, state and federal authorities had quickly decided not to inform the public about the presence of a nuclear bomb. As far as the public was concerned, hero cop Bobby Moylan saved hundreds of people at Grand Central by hanging onto that pressure trigger until the immediate area was completely evacuated. They had no idea how many more people in the city Bobby saved that day.

Joey shrugged. "Who knows? We have short memories. Tomorrow, life goes on."

"He's not going to be forgotten."

Austin Brown sighed deeply and continued.

"Every day I am able to open my store will be because of Bobby Moylan. Lord knows how many other people were able to continue their lives because of him."

Austin looked toward the grave and nodded. "He'll be remembered."

"Amen brother," said Joey.

Jimmy Boy weighed in,
"It's a shame he never got a chance to enjoy retirement."

Any of Jimmy Boy's audience could have answered his comment, but Austin was first to jump in.

"Over the years I must have talked about a thousand different topics with Bobby. About a year ago we were talking about World War II, and the subject of General George Patton came up. Bobby explained that his favorite quote was one of Patton's –*'There's only one proper way for a professional soldier to die: the last bullet of the last battle of the last war'*."

Austin looked at the others.

"Bobby Moylan went out the way he wanted – in the last few minutes of his career."

Ellen could no longer count how many times tears had appeared in her eyes. She wiped them clear again and looked toward the four names on the stone.

"He's home."

It was shortly past noon when Gene Cassidy strolled through the shopping center on 77th Street – two blocks west of the church. Three hours earlier almost every inch of the area was filled with uniformed personnel, so this was his first opportunity to fully assess the old neighborhood. Gene was twelve years old when his family broke up the Fatima Schoolyard Crew by moving to Maine, and he had not been back since. The Cassidy family move took place well before the age of social media and instant communication, and even though the FSC swore to remain friends forever, they quickly lost touch with Gene.

The shopping center opened two years before he moved away, and it became the anchor of the neighborhood. As far as Gene could remember, the post office, laundromat and liquor store were the only stores remaining from its opening.

Gene departed the shopping center and strolled north on 77th Street, eying the two-story attached single-family homes that had not really changed much. Gene had been tortured for years by the fact that he had not reached out to Bobby after Mary and the kids died. He had been vacationing in Europe when it happened, and it wasn't until after he was home for two weeks that his father mentioned in passing how terrible it was what had happened to some people from the old neighborhood. By that time a month had passed, and Gene didn't know what to say if he contacted Bobby after so much time had passed. Instead, he began thinking of an appropriate time and circumstance to contact Bobby. Twenty-four years later, Gene was still trying to formulate a strategy for contact when he saw the headline on his laptop computer. Suddenly, the appropriate time and circumstance was at hand. He gave no thought to the nature of his upcoming schedule as he jumped in his car and headed south to New York City.

Gene paused at the corner of 77th Street and 25th Avenue. The N&R Delicatessen occupied the northwest corner. Gene flashed back to the time the location housed Nick's Superette. He stared disgustingly at the commercially produced professional awning that lacked the character of the amateurish "Nick's Superette" sign which appeared to be a homemade version of a movie theatre marquee. Nick's would always have a special place in his heart as the store where a can of Krasdale soda could be purchased for a dime. Even during the 60s and 70s, ten cents was a bargain for a soda, even if that soda was affectionately known as "Crapsdale".

Gene emerged from the deli with an open can of Budweiser camouflaged by a brown paper bag. The orange brick buildings a block to the east drew him like a magnet. The entire block bordered by 78th and 79th streets to the east and west, and 30th and 25th avenues to the north and south was occupied by four buildings with similar orange brick construction. Our Lady of Fatima rectory, church, school, and convent looked pretty much the same as when he had departed after the seventh grade. Gene approached the schoolyard from 78th Street, and as he drew closer he began to notice significant changes. The concrete throne where the FSC had held court was gone, replaced by an extension to the school as well as the installation of two modular classrooms.

Gene walked slowly through the schoolyard, periodically sipping from his paper bag. He was so focused on taking in all three stories of the school, that he hadn't noticed the two figures lounging on the steps of one of the modular classrooms. Gene had finally identified the location of his seventh-grade classroom when his concentration was broken.

"My God – is that you, huge head?"

Gene's response had a similarly disbelieving tone. "Hose?"

Both men took ten quick steps forward ending their advances in Gene's warm embrace of Jimmy "the Hose" Dooley. Gene's eyes had filled up with tears.

"God, it's good to see you."

"How about me? Are you glad to see me too?

The feminine voice came from the steps as Amy Giordano rose and joined the embrace. The Fatima Schoolyard crew was holding court once more. The trio settled back on the steps.

Jimmy pointed at Gene's paper bag. "Whatcha got?"

"Bud" Gene responded.

"Totally inappropriate today," Jimmy stated while reaching into a large paper bag sitting on the bottom step.

Jimmy reached into the bag and handed something to Amy. He then revisited the bag and flipped something to Gene. Gene caught the object in midflight and smiled. He was holding an ice cold can of Coors beer. There were three popping sounds as the cans were opened.

Jimmy raised his Coors. "Here's to Bobby."

Made in the USA
Lexington, KY
09 August 2018